# Dark Corners

## Gayle Rogers

SOJOURNER
PUBLISHERS, INC.

Sojourner Publishers Inc.
23119 19th Drive N.E., Arlington, WA 98223
360-435-4622 • www.sojournerpub.com

ISBN: 0-9723078-1-8
Library of Congress Control Number: 2002111955

Cover art by Dorothy Bowles

Sojourner Publishing softcover edition.

Printed in the United States of America.

To my husband Jack,
my sons, Kendall and Kevin
and to my cousin Dorothy, the artist.

# One

Mary thought that Aaron was death as soon as she saw him. And she thought his house was a castle of death, too. Children can just *know* things. She was sure the only way you could escape Aaron was if you were more cunning than he. *We should never have come here!*

"Uncle Aaron," she said, "you smile all of the time, but your smile never reaches your eyes."

"That is a strange thing for a little girl to say. I am happy to see my sister and my niece, and that is why I smile."

*You smile because you are death.* The chill from the winter sea below crept up through the floor and went from her shoes to the top of her head. Her mother should not have rushed them here, right after Daddy's death on Aaron's awful road, or below it. Why would her father drive off the cliff into the ocean in broad daylight? *Aaron is death because he caused Daddy to die.*

"This is a magic castle," Aaron was saying. "All of my land, Mary, could be your own magic kingdom. Think on it. When the tide turns below, you can dance on the beach - hike to castle rock, as your mother and I used to do. Have a picnic there - lie in the warm sun and smell all the wonderful sea smells - watch the gulls whirling away with sea foam on their wings. I am very wealthy. If you and your mother stay here, you will be wealthy, too, a real princess with gold and pearls and every jewel ever made - the money to make every wish come true!"

"We have our own home."

"But not like this one!"

*He keeps smiling, and I see his face with all of its flesh gone - only the bones, and the teeth left - death always has the last smile!*

"Get your mother to stay home, Mary."

Grief, agony for her father swept over her, but the fear of Aaron was stronger, as if fear served to masque grief. Her father was security, safety - and now the only sun left in her life was her mother.

"Mildred and I loved to play down on the sand - we knew to time the tide - and we would run all of the way down the beach to rule the world from the magic of *our* castle rock."

"But when the tide goes out, it must come back in," said Mildred, entering the room and putting down their suitcase.

"Well, of course," said Aaron impatiently, but he still kept the smile.

"I think you wanted me to drown that day," said Mildred. "I could not climb the sea stairs as fast as you could, and, remember, you did *not* help me."

"A little girl's frenzied imagination! Never did I do anything but act as a much older *loving* brother who raised you from an infant when our parents died."

"A loving brother?"

"A *loving* brother." He affectionately patted Mary on the head.

*He reaches out his hand to kill me as he killed Daddy. Vampires just go for your blood; death takes all of you – only your eyes left for the wiggling of the worms -*

"Mildred, I am offering you all of my wealth, and it is considerable, if you and Mary stay with me here until I die. I do not want to die alone - without my family -"

"No. No. *No!*" Mildred's face was suddenly frightened, and her voice trembled.

*She sees him as I do!*

"I am old, and sick - the child can be home tutored as you were - and when I die, you will be owner of this estate, my stocks, my bonds - you will be wealthy!"

*How can death die? Aaron, are you scheming to transfer your death to us?*

"Mary can be taught here right through a college education, as you were, Mildred - and you went right into graduate school, remember? I want my only family with me. And I have another reason - I feel you should know it -"

Mary looked from her mother to her uncle, and there was a terrible tension between them. "Aaron, I did not come to stay. I came to find out if you knew why on earth Ray drove out here."

"Why would I know that? I never saw him."

"The police said he was driving *away* from here when he -" Mildred's eyes filled with a rushing of tears, and she wiped them away with her handkerchief and blew her nose. "We came for this very short visit, for you have no telephone, and you do not write. My husband died on your road, or at the bottom of it. I cannot imagine why he was on your road - you certainly did not like each other. I cannot reason out any way for him to die on *your* private road -"

"Now that you are home, stay here."

"*Home?*" Mildred visibly shuddered. "This is not home. It never was home - you have to know how I hate this old house. Why do you stay in it? I think the ocean cliff is moving toward it all the time."

"That is sheer nonsense. This house has lasted a hundred years and will last another hundred years."

"I won't stay here another night to find out."

"If you leave this house, you will bitterly regret it," said Aaron.

"*Bitterly* regret it?"

"You will. That is a promise."

Mildred stiffened and angrily looked at her brother. "I am not a child now, am I? You cannot terrorize me, as you did when I was a child! Those ghastly midnight nursery rhymes you used to sing - song outside of my *locked* bedroom door! How could you have done such a wicked and cruel thing?"

"I never did that! You and your vivid imagination! As if I would even think of such a thing!"

Mary shivered, looking up from one to the other. She saw such rage between them. But they were so quiet and calm about it. She thought of the quiet eye of a hurricane, centered in chaos.

"You would think I was not there, Aaron! When the great monster clock in the hall struck midnight - you were always there, outside of my door, saying those damned *ghastly* death rhymes!"

"I never did that. You had such an imagination - it was almost pathological. Stay and find out how wrong you are to even *think* those dreadful things about me."

"No. Never," said Mildred. "I should never have come here at all. Not ever - for any visit - ever again! Even the road here is like a path to suicide. No wonder it killed Ray. It is half off the cliff like this cursed old house."

"This is an estate, not a house. And it is not cursed."

"Why don't you enter the twenty-first century, get a telephone, electric lights, redo the ghastly horse and buggy road here?"

"I will, if you and Mary stay."

Mildred studied her brother, and as she did, pity slowly replaced the anger upon her face, and even in her voice. "I am so sorry, Aaron. I really am. You are, with Mary, my only blood relative. Maybe I did imagine all of those childhood horrors - maybe I was so lonely - I would rather have felt fright than feel so *alone* -"

"Of course that was it. Now stay here at home and be left a very wealthy woman."

"Aaron, I can't. I just can't. This house - I escaped it, got my doctorate - had a wonderful marriage – and I always feared if I came back here, I would never escape again."

"*Escape* this fine home? All of its servants - all of the luxuries, and we do have deliveries here all of the time, and the road doesn't send their cars off the cliff - Mildred, we are sister and brother!"

Mildred moved toward Aaron as if to embrace him, and shuddering, she stopped.

"Mildred," he said gently. "There is another reason you must stay. I have cancer. Terminal cancer. I have a horror of being buried alive when I do pass on. I have had endless nightmares about this. If you were here, you could see that this would not happen. I don't want my blood drained from me when I am alive, or I cannot bear to think of being buried - alive. I want you to be sure before embalming or burial - that I am *dead*."

Mildred wiped at her eyes again. "You make your own arrangements for that, Aaron. I am so sorry that you are ill - but I cannot stay here."

"Think of Mary," said Aaron. "Think of her, if you do not care for me or my money. Think what a fortune would mean in her life."

"Believe me, Aaron, I *am* thinking of Mary. Our home does not have the - the -" She looked around them. "There is such a feeling of *menace* here."

"It is too late for you two to leave the point," Aaron sighed. "It is winter. You know how the fog can come in from nowhere and hide the road. You know how the fog outside *can hide your hands!* It's too dangerous for you to leave now. Mildred - wait until morning -"

"It is clear and sunny without a cloud in the sky. Good by, Aaron. If you ever get a phone, you can call my number, and as you know my address, you might even send a letter on to me - with one of your deliverymen -" She picked up their suitcase again. "Come on Mary, say goodbye to your uncle."

"Mary, I am so sorry you lost your father," Aaron said.

He still smiled. Tears welled in Mary's eyes and ran down her face. "So are we."

"How *could* Ray have driven right off my road?" asked Aaron.

"How could he have been here in the first place?" asked Mildred, her voice breaking. She ran her fingers through her hair, which she always did when she was in deep distress.

They were in what Aaron called *his* room, the great library, with windows from floor to ceiling facing the ocean on the west, and his long tree lined drive to the east. "Look at all the books here for the child. I know how tiny your house in the city is. "

"It is fine for us," said Mildred, picking up her purse and taking the car keys from it. "Mary, will you please gather up your things? We have to go - *now!*"

"You are taking a fortune away from your only child," said Aaron. "If the fog comes in, you may be taking away both of your lives."

Gulls flew by the ocean windows, the sun glistening on their sleekness. The sky was summer blue.

Mildred said nothing, but Mary could see that her hand holding the car keys was shaking.

"Mildred, I fear you will bitterly regret leaving."

This is a threat. Will you keep us here - Mr. Death?

"I will never regret leaving here, Aaron. I didn't once, and I won't again!" Mildred sighed. "I am sorry - really sorry, Aaron that you are ill, but - I never should have come back here."

They went into the great entrance hall, and near them the grandfather clock began a musical introduction to a slow and deliberate chiming. Mildred touched its dark shiny wood. "How I hated this clock," she said.

"You even hated a *clock?*" asked Aaron incredulously.

"Yes," Mildred replied.

"Oh yes, it chimed the midnight *murder* rhymes," said Aaron.

Mildred was leading Mary to the double entrance doors. She paused at them, and looked back at her brother, who had walked behind them without making a sound. "Goodbye. Cancer does not have to be a death sentence, Aaron. With your money -"

"People with money die, too."

Mildred looked right into his eyes. "You will never know how much I wanted to accept you, Aaron, even love you."

"Mildred, you should *not* leave now. I sense terrible danger to you and the child!"

Mary looked up at Aaron, and shook with terror. *He will not let us leave.*

Mildred was opening the door. *Somehow, the doors will get stuck, and we will stay here.*

But Mildred easily opened the doors to the clear bright day outside.

"You won't see me here again," said Mildred.

"I know I won't," Aaron said, and did not close the doors after them.

*He will stop us on the brick stairs.*

He did not. He just looked after them, smiling.

They reached the car. *He will keep the car from starting.*

He did not. The car started on the first turn and purred like a kitten. "Thank God!" said Mildred, but her key hand was still shaking. "Mary, we are away from here!"

Mary looked back at the house. Aaron stood at the doors watching them. "He has such a baby sweet face."

"I never understood him," said Mildred. Their car was leaving the long driveway a little too fast, but as she approached the narrow sea cliff road, Mildred slowed it down. "I should never have come back here," she said. "I understand no more why Ray was on this ghastly road than if I had not come at all. Why on earth would Ray drive out here to see *Aaron*?"

"Maybe he has the power to *will* people here," said Mary, looking fearfully at the narrow road ahead. The ocean to their left sparkled little suns and was capping under a rising west wind.

"Thank God, we are not on this road at night," said Mildred. "No one goes on it at night. I would not even *walk* on it at night!"

With the ocean and the day so beautiful, Mary sorrowed that her father was not there to share it with them. "Tell me again," she said. "Tell me again that Daddy did not die with his body."

"He didn't. He never accepted that we are a mere body, and neither do I."

"Then where is he? If he is not dead, why doesn't he let us know it? When he left his body, did he leave behind his love for us?"

"Of course not. Your daddy would never stop loving us. Death can do no more than absorb itself."

"But death did *not* absorb itself. It absorbed him instead."

"His body. Not his soul. What did he always say about our immortal soul?"

"When we die God gathers our souls back to him, as the wind carries away the scent of the flowers."

"Daddy was a rare and a wonderful man." A catch came to Mildred's voice, and tears ran down her cheeks. "Understand, Mary, that I am grieving for myself. I have that right. *We* have that right." Her voice became huskier. "But I miss him. We miss him so, and we have a right to do that."

Mary looked fearfully back at Aaron's house. All she could see of it was the second floor mullioned windows, and they reflected no light of the day.

"I *was* afraid of him," said Mildred. "I cannot believe that I made him your legal guardian if something should happen to Daddy and me."

"You did *that*?"

"He is your only living relative - I don't know who could take my place - but - but -"

"But *anyone* would be better than Aaron!"

"I will change that when we get back to the city," said Mildred.

"That is the *first* thing I will do."

No sooner were her words spoken, than out of nowhere, they were shrouded in a blinding fog. The sun had just gone. The day had just gone.

As if they were not where they were.

*We are in a graveyard and vapors here have risen from the ground as the dead ooze silently out into the night.* Mary moved away from the car door and huddled near her mother. She would not look out her window. Aaron would be there, looking in at them, *smiling.* She could not bear to see him again!

Mildred slammed on the car brakes. "Now where did that fog come from?" she gasped. "I have never seen a fog come from nowhere!"

"It is Aaron. I knew he would keep us here."

"Aaron?" asked Mildred. "Aaron - fog?"

"It's his energy – his evil energy."

"It is night! Suddenly - we are in *night* fog! Or - have we lost track of time? What made us lose track of time?" Mildred shivered, and rubbed her cold arms, peering at the moving fog in disbelief. "Aaron would not be out in a night like this."

"Mother, Aaron *is* a night like this."

"We have to be rational. It is not night. This darkness is thick fog, thicker than I have ever seen before -"

"Aaron has come for us as he did Daddy."

"Mary - listen to me," said Mildred, looking for a blanket for them and not finding one. "Aaron has no supernatural power. Do not give him any. The only way he can have any power over you is if you allow it!"

"He is death."

"Mary, that is because Daddy died on this road, and you are in such grief - you have transferred its pain to this fear of Aaron -"

"We will die here."

"No. I will not move this car until this fog clears."

They sat still, as afraid to move themselves as they were afraid to move the car.

"You fear him yourself," whispered Mary, as if Aaron was outside and might hear.

"Maybe I imagined the horror there -"

"And maybe you didn't."

They sat long in silence, and the night was still, if it was night, and the only thing that moved in it was the fog, and the fog moved as if it could contain human malice.

"I have never seen anything so *strange*," said Mildred, and she was whispering, too.

"You think he is out there."

"Of course not!"

"This is his energy!"

"Mary, say Aaron *is* death to you. He is a mere mortal man and he is not death. But say he is – say this *is* his energy. Fog? Fog is a stealthy stealer of light – here all is illusion, for now there is no sun in the sky. But it is not night. Afternoon cannot turn into night in seconds."

They grew colder, and it was as if their own life was draining into the fog.

"I am so *cold*," shivered Mary.

"I am not moving this car if we turn into ice cream cones," said Mildred, but her teeth were chattering, and she rubbed her arms more vigorously.

"Tell me again what Daddy said about our return to God. I have to hear something good that makes sorrow so I can stand it -"

"He is in that magic tide of all return," said Mildred. "And in it he will create beautiful and good things for us, just as he did here on earth."

"Tell me of your favorite poet."

"John Keats. Shakespeare -"

"John Keats. Why is he a favorite poet?"

"He reached beyond the dark corners of the mind."

"What are they?"

"The belief that the mind is all, and that when it dies, so do we. It is the denial of all things that are eternal - love, the truth of beauty - the denial of the soul's master, God, the light that transcends time and place and the deaths confined within them."

"Is God within the soul of an *evil* man?"

"Of course. The evil man denies his own sanctity."

9

"Daddy talked like that."

"The soul creates many mansions, and the soul will create a mansion wrought in love - or it will not."

"Why cannot I see my soul?"

"Can the tongue taste itself?"

"We can never *see* our soul?"

"You can see what it bears. Like a diamond of all light and all energy, the jewel of the source of all love – in some hushed time beyond time, in some glory beyond glory – some rapture in the unfolding of the soul to its heart – it will be manifest and you will be forevermore sustained."

"God?"

"What you reflect and increase in love - in music, art, poetry - the creation of anything that is good for your fellow traveler – a sojourner of light to return to light to bring any comfort to the night of a fellow traveler – we can do no better."

"What did Keats believe about this? Why are we here - mortal in body but immortal in soul?"

"To become individualized - to become individuals. He believed we are light from light's primal source, and we find that light on earth through the magic casements into our soul."

"Did John Keats find the magic casements?"

"He certainly did."

"How?"

"Through the creation of such - beauty."

"He fell in love?"

"Yes, but he died before his love could be consummated. That was so bitter - so bitter to him, he turned from himself and all he had *experienced* as truth - as he drowned in his own blood."

"How horrible!"

"He did have a horrible death, and the worst of it was that he had to leave the woman whom he termed the star of his soul - so young - so young." Mildred's voice was sad, and she wiped tears away for her own loss and the loss of John Keats.

Mary shivered. "I am cold and I am scared. Aaron is out there, and he is waiting to kill us!"

"Aaron is not here, and I will not move this car until it is safe for us to go on."

"Tell me a tale of magic. Tell me a tale of a magic princess and her magic prince. Tell me how he comes to save her life and bring her a love as you and daddy had - tell me how love banishes death and the dark corners of the mind that accept it! I need to know I am safe."

Mildred rubbed her arms again. "Well - here we are, right in this magic fog, for it came from nowhere, didn't it? You are the magic princess Mary, decreed so by this magic fog! Who will be your prince?"

"John Keats!"

"Why?"

"Because I am in love with him."

"His poetry."

"Him!"

"I didn't know that."

"You do now. I want to be the reincarnation of Frances Brawne."

"Then you are."

"All right." The fog was moving with more energy, and there was not the slightest breeze to make it move. Mary felt charmed and she felt powerful, and she silently spoke to John Keats. *Dear love, find me again! Beyond the most distant sun, beyond all spent tides, come to me again!*"

She sighed, cold, so cold, but warmth came over her, just as if the fog had gone and the sun shone above them again in full splendor. "I did it," she said shyly. "I willed John Keats to love me again."

Mildred gently touched her face. "Good. When will he find you, rescue you into a new life?"

"On my eighteenth birthday. I will be beautiful then - for him - I will be *so beautiful* -"

"Have you willed a marriage this time?"

"Oh, yes!"

"Good," Mildred said again, and she smiled for the first time since her husband's death. "It will happen," she said. "I believe this fog *is* one of enchantment. Look at the lights ahead of us! Magic lights from no where - to lead us home, Mary!"

Mary saw red taillights of a car parked in front of them. "Where did they come from?" she asked. "How did that car get here?"

"We must have reached the doctor's house! We went almost to the freeway and did not even know it. Mary, we are all but off of Aaron's land!"

The car ahead of them began to move slowly forward. "Thank God for the doctor going out tonight," said Mildred happily.

"And his car," added Mary.

"And the tires on it," laughed Mildred. She started the coupe, and they followed the red lights ahead from a very safe distance. "And do you know something else that is *marvelous?*" Mildred asked.

"What?"

"Daddy is here with us. He is here to guide me home. I feel it. I *know* it."

Suddenly, Mary was afraid of her father *as a ghost.*

"Maybe Daddy got the doctor out on this road to lead us from it," said Mildred, her voice clear and happy with relief.

The car slowly and cautiously led them forward.

"Is Daddy still here?" Mary asked nervously.

"Oh, yes," said Mildred, her voice trembling with joy. "He is so *close* to me - so very close!"

"He should not have killed himself," Mary said angrily. She was feeling more and more fear, and anger helped drive the fear away. "He should not have died."

"That is the only thing we could ever fault him for, isn't it?" said Mildred.

*There is something about those lights that is wrong.* "I will read every poem of John Keats before my eighteenth birthday."

"Good - that driver is picking up speed. We must be about to enter the freeway."

"We are going to lose the lights!"

"No. I'll keep up." The coupe picked up speed as if there were no blinding fog around them at all.

"Daddy had a riddle, and I wish you could explain it. It goes, *'When does the shore become the sea, and when does the flower become the bee?'*" Mary suddenly had to have her mother explain something, *anything!* "Mother, what does that mean?"

"They *already* are."

"What?"

"One. It all is really one. There is no when. The all – is the all."

"Mother - *mother* -something is *wrong!*"

"Mary, you sound as if you are coming down with a cold. Get into the glove compartment and get some vitamin C."

The lights of the car ahead veered sharply to their left.

Mildred followed them.

"Those lights aren't *real!*" Mary screamed.

She was too late. The lights vanished, but not before Mildred had followed them off the cliff. The coupe left the road and hit a great gnarled old oak head-on, shattering its windshield, and then the coupe was held impaled in the silent fog, its wheels spinning around and around until they stopped moving at all.

When Mary awakened, the first thing she saw was the fog streaming into the car through its broken windshield. She looked down and could see the ocean foaming against the rocks below. Her face and upper body were covered with blood. Her head was shattered.

She looked over at her mother. The fog was caressing her face with wraith-like tenderness, and her eyes were as beautiful as ever, and very dead.

# Two

It was the eve of Mary's eighteenth birthday. The eve, as just before midnight, and now the clock below in the great hall was striking the midnight hour, its musical chimes reaching up the stairs, just like the sweet smile of Aaron, and as full of menace. The midnight hour always called him, a horror manifested, just when the day was done, the next one unborn. Here he would come, as he did every single night, this grotesque. She heard him leave his room, the creaking of the floor leading him to her. A lamp always burned in the upstairs hall, and he now cast his shadow against it as he stopped outside of the locked bedroom door of her mother's old room.

Another rhyme from his demented mind; in a sing -song voice it came.

> Five years it's been,
> Since the loss of kin,
> Daddy stone dead,
> And Mummy, too,
> What's a little girl to do?

She said nothing. Let the mad beast think she slept through his midnights, his sickened poetry.

The floor creaked again as he pressed himself against her door.

> Mary, Mary, quite contrary,
> How do your nightmares grow?
> Dying bird trills,
> Decaying daffodils,
> All in a tombstone row.

She got noiselessly out of bed, and went to the sea windows that allowed the light of a large moon. Moonlight was always so special to them. And *their* evening star still shone, even as the sky brightened all around it. *I love him and I always will. Comets may skim the sky, stars may come and they may go, but I love him, and I call him again to rescue me from Aaron on my eighteenth birthday. He will come to me, and I will look into his eyes and know him, and we will love and we will marry, and Aaron can have his putrefied poems all to himself!*

She looked at the evening star and remembered that he said his love for her was as constant, as eternal, and she thrilled to the magic of that memory, and she saw him now, John Keats, lover and poet, and she saw his tender lips, the light in his beautiful eyes when he first saw her. *Thy love has balanced away Aaron and his house of horrors, and when I say the lines from the light of your being - the night is absorbed and Aaron is powerless within it. Today has begun. I am safe even in this castle of death, for you will take me from it, as you saved Madeline in your great love poem to me.*

"Aaron," she said, replying at last. "Listen to what you can never touch!" She said lines that made magic the night.

> Bright star, would I were as steadfast as thou art -
> Not in lone splendor hung aloft the night
> And watching, with eternal lids apart,
> Like nature's patient sleepless Eremite,
> The moving waters at their priest like task
> Of pure ablution round earth's human shores,
> Or gazing on the new soft-fallen mask
> Of snow upon the mountains and the moors-

Aaron's mocking voice broke in.

> Ring a ding -ding,
> Another Keats' thing!
> Hang on to your bed,
> But John Keats is dead!

The magic of the night vanished. The lines from *his* soul fled, and the travesty of death masked the beauty of the sky and its luminous reflection of a tranquil sea. She shook with rage. She shook with grief. She bitterly wept for her parents, and she saw herself all alone while they had abandoned her to be together in a golden tide of God rapture.

"Now, Aaron, you sick malignancy, here is a little poem for *you!*" she snarled. "Aaron, you ass, your life will pass in what a bull does with many a blade of grass!"

He replied instantly, "Into your room I can whirl, to drink the blood of a little girl, and when death does come for me, to your mind I keep the key!"

"You bloody bastard! You are not going to kill me like you murdered my parents!" she shouted. She wrenched open her door to scratch at his hateful face, and looked instead into the startled and frightened faces of Molly and Meg.

"Child, child!" said Molly, her voice trembling with fright. "What has happened to you?"

"*Mary?*" asked Meg, as if she was not sure who was standing before them.

"Where did that damned devil go?" asked Mary looking around her. There was no sign of Aaron. "He was just here!"

"Who?" asked Molly, looking around, too.

"Aaron!"

"Your sweet uncle?" asked Molly, shock on her face and in her voice.

"The monster - he was here saying his perverted nursery rhymes, as he does every night when the clock below chimes midnight!"

"You never told me that," said Meg somewhat reproachfully.

"Why are you two looking at me like this?" asked Mary. "I never told you this because you adore that - *monster!*"

"Your uncle - who dotes on you, Mary, a monster?" asked Molly.

"You never told me you hate him," said Meg, very reproachfully.

"Mary, dear child," said Molly. "Were you having another nightmare spell?"

"What do you mean?"

"Your uncle says you have terrible spells when you scream so he wakes up and worries about you." Molly now looked worried and still frightened.

"In the five years since you have been here - you have not learned *at all* - what Aaron is?"

"Is - what?" asked Molly.

"Is evil! Mad! That behind that mask of a smile - he is - is -" She could not say death, even if she knew Aaron did have the power to murder.

Meg looked in shock at her mother, as if neither had met Mary before.

"Is what, child - is what?"

"Aaron is not what you think he is," said Mary lamely.

"We brought warm milk as he rang for us," said Meg. "Mary, we are like sisters, and you never told me you hate Aaron." She might as well have said that Mary hated Jesus.

"I thought you should find him out for yourselves."

"Mary, child - did you say that he *murdered* your parents?"

"He did."

"They were killed in auto accidents."

"Molly, he caused them."

Molly's face, even in the lamplight, was suddenly filled with sadness beyond compassion. "Mary, that was such a horrible thing you went through - such an injury - and that lasts for years -"

"Molly, I am not crazy. Aaron has the power - to murder."

Mother and daughter looked at each other as if Mary had just admitted she was crazy.

"Your uncle is such a sweet man," said Molly.

"He is no sweeter than murder."

"Mary, reasonably - reasonably - how could your uncle have killed your father who was driving on his *road*?"

"Because it *is* his road."

"What do you mean to say?"

"He has a supernatural power here - in this house and on his land - all of it - right up to the freeway."

"Supernatural power?"

"How?" asked Meg.

"I learned."

"What did you learn?" asked Molly.

"He has the power to create - create - *illusion*."

"Illusion?"

"Yes. Illusion can kill. The red tail- lights were never there, and my mother followed them right off the cliff. Only that tree stopped the car from going into the ocean."

"Your uncle killed both of your parents with - a power to make you see something that is not there?" Molly said slowly, as if she were reciting the alphabet in kindergarten.

"And the fog - *blindness* -"

"He creates - fog?" Molly had tears in her eyes.

"I wonder if the fog was really there."

"There is ocean fog here all the time - about *every* morning - fog and oceans go together, Mary."

Mary looked at mother and daughter, very dear to her and very dear people. "You must listen to me. Aaron will never let you leave this point."

"I wouldn't leave your dear uncle! Meg and I are very happy here, and cooking and keeping this house is a pleasure for us both!"

"The lawyer is coming today to take you away to the University - Mary, do you think your uncle will try to stop this, when he sent for his lawyer - will pay for your graduate degree - or degrees - Mary he loves you! You are his only blood relative, and he says he is leaving you all of his fortune!"

"He *has* to let me leave when I am eighteen. It is in my mother's will, and he cannot stop me from leaving - for it is - I *will* escape - be free from here. Never mind how I know it."

"Why do you believe he killed your parents, Mary?" asked Molly.

"He did not want my mother to leave."

"Why would he kill your father?"

"To bring my mother here." Mary suddenly knew this to be true.

"Then - will he let you leave? With all of this - *supernatural* power - won't he kill you, too?" asked Molly, with more sadness on her face and more tears in her eyes.

"He cannot kill me. He cannot stop me from leaving him."

"Why not - if he had the power to murder your parents?"

"Because it is ordained - solemnly and magically *ordained* -"

"What is ordained - solemnly and magically?"

"That *he* will rescue me from this castle of death."

"Your uncle's lawyer who is coming this afternoon? He is sixty if he is a day! Is he the magic and ordained - *he?*"

*"John Keats?"* asked Meg and her face glowed at the thought, for she was deep into the romantic side of Mary's nature. She had not before seen the side of Mary she was seeing tonight. "John Keats is now a *lawyer?"*

"What are you two talking about?" asked Molly crossly.

"It is a secret," smiled Meg.

"You have no secrets from your mother!" said Molly.

"I have plenty of them," said Meg.

When Molly and Meg were in their room downstairs, Molly was still angry with her daughter. "Why would you have plenty of secrets from me?"

"They are with Mary."

"What are they?"

"If I told you, they would no longer be secrets."

Molly sighed and began to unloosen the braids of her bright red hair. "I am so shocked at Mary - swearing - calling that sweet dear man a -*bastard!* How could she do such a terrible thing?"

"I know she has always wanted to get away from here. She calls this a castle of death."

"Humph! This glorious mansion is a castle - but a castle of *death?* Where does she get such an idea?"

"From *The Eve of St. Agnes.*"

"Written by John Keats. I know that poem. What does this have to do with Mary - here and now?"

"Everything."

"How?"

"That is the secret."

In her mother's bedroom, which she never felt as her own, Mary went to the windows and looked out on the moonlit sea. The night was clear, the sea whispering calm, smooth and unruffled by the slightest breeze. Even the combers vanished without sound into the shadow of the cliff below. *We loved moonlight. I know we first met when the moon was full, and we walked a moonlit path, and the*

*Evening Star followed us all the way.*

She went back to bed, but the enchantment of the night shone so brightly into the room it kept her awake.

*I will be with him again tomorrow! It will be a summer day as golden as the wine shared by lovers, wine cooled a long age in the deep delved earth, tasting of flora, country green, dance, Provencal song and sun burnt mirth* - and with these lines of his, from her favorite poem, she drifted into sleep and a beautiful dream that they rested, as light as air, upon the tops of trees, and all those trees about them suddenly burst into bloom.

In bed, Molly could not get Mary from her mind. "She is such a beautiful girl and so brilliant. But now we know what that accident - that terrible brain injury did to her. Now we know its awful and terrible extent."

"What is it?"

"The poor girl in her own way - is quite mad."

# Three

When Mary entered the kitchen, Molly and Meg were not happy with each other, or even with the glorious summer day. "Happy birthday to me!" Mary said, her own mood as bright as the sky.

"I made you a chocolate pie," said Molly with no particular enthusiasm about it.

"And I made us some honey candy to take with us," said Meg. "Although my mother here acts as if we should both have arsenic."

Molly had finished with her pinto beans, and she was peeling garlic. Anything that was not dessert was cooked with all the garlic she had the time to gather from her vegetable garden. "Have you seen your dear uncle this morning?" she asked. "I am sure he would want to wish you a happy birthday."

"Oh, he smiles that to me every day," said Mary, smelling the cooking beans.

"He is getting so much better. I wonder if he ever had any cancer at all," said Molly, adding onions and peppers, and then more garlic to the beans. After them went her homegrown mushrooms. And wine. That was as important as the homemade salsa.

"Molly, he never had cancer. He does not have cancer. That is just an anchor thing to keep you here."

"No problem. I love it here," said Molly. "I will stay as long as Mr. Aaronsby lives."

Mary helped pack the lunch and at the sink looked down at the ocean. Sea and sky were a placid blue. "Those are magic lights sparkling out there," she said. "Those are sun diamonds from heaven."

"Mary, Mary," said Molly, her face filled with affection. "How your fancy roams all around mine!"

"Oh, we all have to have fancy," Mary said. "It stretches us out, and through fancy we find ourselves."

"Child, child," Molly laughed, but she allowed Mary this, for it did not seem to be an attack on Aaron or even the Bible.

"Today is your last day here," said Meg, wistfully, and a little sadly, although she was smiling while she talked. "You *will* leave tomorrow with the trust lawyer?"

"You didn't tell Aaron that?" asked Mary anxiously.

"No. I told him what you told me to tell him, that you have changed your mind and will not leave."

"What is the matter with you two?" asked Molly, getting some of her ill humor back. "You would think that Mr. Aaronsby would not let you leave, Mary."

"He has to."

"I don't think you two should walk to castle rock," said Molly.

"Why not?" asked Meg.

"We love the view - it is *charmed!*" said Mary.

"You two might forget the change of the tide and drown your silly heads."

"Never," smiled Meg, wanting to leave for the beach.

"It's my birthday!" said Mary. "I get to do what I want to."

"We won't be too far away from the sea stairs," said Meg.

"I would never even go down those cursed things," said Molly. "You never know about the tide changing -"

"I do," said Mary. "And I am wearing a watch, to be sure that I *do* know."

Meg and Mary took their picnic lunches and started for the kitchen door.

"Remember how the tide rushes in and covers up the sea stairs," said Molly, worry stronger on her face.

"We know, we know," said Meg impatiently.

"As if we don't see it every day," said Mary.

Molly watched after them as they rushed down the stairs. "You never know what foolish young people are going to do nowadays," she grumbled, sitting down to peel more garlic for her beans. "And you never can have *too much* garlic," she agreed to herself agreeably.

Like children Mary and Meg skipped along the shore. They had taken off their shoes to leave by the stairs, and now each squealed in joy as they made little toe holes in the sand and watched them fill up with sea foam. They dug sea pools, and walked into them right up to their knees. They gathered rock treasures and then discarded them for new ones. "It is my day," said Mary, letting the sea withdraw through her toes. She loved the pull of the tide. The water was not too cold; the day was warm with the sky stretching right up into heaven. From her toes to her head, she was clothed in joy. "I am a sea princess!" she laughed. "I reign in the sand strewn caverns *cool and deep, where the winds are all asleep* - Coleridge, so there were other poets besides my Keats!"

"And he will come and carry you away!" Meg tenderly examined a shell. "Today?"

"Of course."

"Aaron's lawyer?"

"How silly, Meg. He is in his sixties, at least."

"Well - then - who? How? None of the deliverymen are young - no one else comes here since the tutors, who were old men, anyway. Where on earth is John Keats going to come from?" asked Meg.

Mary looked out at the sparkling ocean, breathed in its energy, its salty smell. "From there," she pointed. "From the tide."

"Like a whale?" asked Meg.

Mary laughed, and Meg laughed with her. "Well?" Meg asked again.

"Wherever from, he will come to me. *Today.*" She sat down near one of the ocean pools they had created. Her beautiful face glowed. Meg thought she had never seen a more beautiful girl than Mary, but now her beauty was breathtaking, as if she had taken this perfect day and made it a part of herself. "Meg, we live in a magic tide of the *all,* back to the *all,* in our own will, and God's sweet grace."

"The tide which today is going to bring in John Keats," Meg laughed. As they walked on, Mary twirled on the sand, in a kind of a slow dance of exultation. "I feel a part of - *everything!*"

Meg was as joyous. "I feel it, too!"

"Each gull, each comber marching in like white horses -"

"Mary!" said Meg, suddenly dumbfounded. "We walked to Castle Rock!"

"Wonderful! Let's climb it and be the sovereigns of time!"

"We had better rule *shortly*," said Meg, climbing the rock after Mary. "Don't forget the tide."

Mary looked at her watch. "We have eons and eons to rule from our castle," she said, and they ate their lunch. The rock was softened by grass, and they lay down on it, and looked up at the sky. Salt air ruffled their blouses, their skirts, and their hair. "We are extensions of something - that loves us *so much* - "

"Is that what you were dancing to?"

"Was I dancing?"

"Yes, a beautiful slow dance of - joy."

Mary sighed. Her long lashes were closed, and a smile was on her lips. No sorrow, no loss, could live within this *now*. It had been dispatched within life's wonder, as when a bridegroom lifts the marriage veil away from his bride for the first kiss of marriage.

"Listen to the sea that -" Mary said softly,

"Keeps eternal whispering around,
Desolate shores, and with its mighty swell
Gluts twice ten thousand Caverns,
'till the spell
Of Hecate leaves them their old shadowy sound."

"Are those *his* lines?" asked Meg.

"Yes." Their view from Castle Rock remained a jeweled union of sea and sun. "You and your mother think my head injury left me mad, and Aaron is as sweet as his baby smile - the ever constant smile -"

"I cannot imagine Aaron saying those terrible things to you at midnight," said Meg, but suddenly, and ominously, she could.

"He has done that every night since I moved into his house," said Mary. "He might have driven me mad if I had not been so sure that I was Frances Brawne, and that John Keats and I would complete our love affair in this life -"

"You didn't last time?"

"No. Nothing more than kissing."

"How do you know that? I mean - you don't remember *that*, do you?"

Mary laughed. "Meg, that is common knowledge. He said that himself in a letter."

"Say that tribute to physical and spiritual love he wrote for you. The rescue of his Madeline from the castle of death -"

Mary began, caressing the lines.

> "St. Agnes' Eve - Ah bitter chill it was.
> The owl for all of his feathers was a -cold;
> The hare limped trembling through the frozen grass,
> And silent was the flock in wooly fold..."

She finished and was enraptured again with the poem. With the sun so comforting, their meal so sustaining, without meaning to at all, both girls drifted off to sleep.

Far out on the horizon a wisp of fog gathered and drifted slowly to shore.

Molly heard the ringing of the old-fashioned door- bell right away and rushed to meet Aaron's lawyer, who didn't look like he had too much time left a year ago. She could not imagine his survival into this year. She reasoned *he only drives the awful road because he is dying anyway.*

But the most glorious young man she had ever seen in all of her life stood there. "Who are *you?*" she asked in shock.

He smiled a dazzling smile that would have melted a stone angel. "Hello," he said. "My name is Michael Covington. I am the new lawyer for the firm that represents Mr. Aronsby. I have come to see him about taking his - niece - I believe - to the University?"

"But Mr. Aronsby's lawyer -" began Molly, confused by all of this brilliance in one male.

"Is unfortunately suddenly deceased," said the young man.

Molly still stared and did not move to invite the new lawyer in, for she was never eager to embrace change.

"I am at the correct house?" he asked. "I mean - being as there is no other house around here - don't I *have* to be at the correct house?"

"You are," she said, ushering the new lawyer into the hall and right up the stairs into Aaron's bedroom. When Aaron saw him, he leaped out of his bed as if it had started to bite him. "Who are *you*?" he asked, not liking changes either.

"I am the new lawyer for your sister's trust."

"That is Mr. Creighton!"

"I'm afraid not, sir. Mr. Creighton has unfortunately passed away."

Aaron looked very angry with this. "I *knew* Mr. Creighton," he began ominously.

"Well, I regret that I never did," the young man replied easily, and introduced himself in full.

Molly was still staring at him. Aaron was glowering at him, but never had lost his smile from his first glance of distaste. I think I am in a very strange house, thought Michael Covington. I wonder if the niece is as strange.

"You know my Keats had a very dark side to his nature," said Mary to Meg, awakening her.

"What do you mean?"

"He was very, *very* jealous. Finally, he could not stand it if I even talked to another man. It was because his disease kept blood from his brain. He wrote to me, and he said - *do not withhold one atom from me or I die.*"

"Well, we know how he loved you."

"He wrote terrible lines written to haunt me after his death. It was a *terrible* thing to do. They were ghastly lines. They killed me to read them; they hurt me even now."

"How can a poem do this?"

"How could he have done this?" Mary asked, and there was actually a catch of emotion in her voice.

"Did you ever forgive him?" asked Meg, totally committed to Mary being Frances Brawne.

"No," Mary said bitterly. "Would you?"

"I never heard that poem. You never recited that one."

"It is too horrible to say even now," said Mary, and Meg could not believe the tears in her eyes.

"How can I know if you still should be angry - if I do not hear the lines?"

"All right. All right! Now think of a *dying* man writing this to his *love!*"

> "This living hand, now warm and capable
> Of earnest grasping, would if it were cold
> And in the icy silence of the tomb,
> So haunt thy days and chill thy dreaming nights,
> That thou wouldest wish thine own heart dry of blood
> So in my veins red life might stream again,
> And thou be conscience calmed - see, here it is,
> I hold it toward you."

Meg shuddered. "I can even understand that! If he is dying, he begrudges you your very life! *You* are to replace *him* in death to free you of guilt that he died? Did he do this - outside of this poem?"

"No. He did not. This rose from some *dark* side of his mind."

"I would hate a man who left me with those awful lines."

"My dearest one. He hated his death, because he saw it as the loss of me. If he had let me go to Italy where he went to die. If I could have held him in my arms when he was dying." Mary wiped her eyes. "But, of course, he spared me that, so I guess the ghastly bitterness of these lines was nothing to see him struggling for each breath of life. But Meg - I never withheld one atom of myself from him. Ever - since I first looked into those beautiful eyes and fell *right* in love with him."

"I am sure he knew that," said Meg, touching Mary's hand.

"I want to be told that he *did* know that," said Mary, and then she suddenly saw what was sweeping in at them from the horizon. "My God," she said. "Did you see that fog coming in?"

"No," said Meg, and they did not stop to gather a thing, but climbed off the rock as fast as they could.

"These fogs are so blinding," said Mary, leading them on a fast run back toward the sea stairs of Aaron's house. "Run as fast as you can!"

And they both did, and the sea was still touching the shore with hardly a sound.

"*The tide!*" gasped Mary. "My watch stopped. What time is it?" She searched for the sun through the slowly enfolding fog. "It is certainly way past noon."

The fog shrouded the shore and wrapped softly around them, and Mary thought of it caressing her mother's face, her beautiful eyes. "It's that damned murderer," she said, pushing herself and Meg down the beach, jumping over rocks, not daring to fall.

"Aaron is not fog," panted Meg. "Even *your* imagination cannot think Aaron fog!"

"How could we have forgotten the time?"

"Mary, I see a kitten trapped there - over there! We can't let it drown!"

Meg had stopped running, and was even turning back. Mary rushed to her, and pulled her forward. "There is no kitten. I know it. He is creating another illusion - like those tail lights."

They both were running again, but the fog grew so blinding they had to slow to a walk and feel their way forward by following the foot of the cliff.

"*The rail.* I feel the rail of the stairs!" said Mary, feeling it again to be sure that this was no illusion like the kitten, or the tail lights that her mother followed right to her death.

Then in a mighty roar, or in total silence, the tide rushed in and they were in water, with combers breaking over them.

With all of her strength, Mary turned and pushed Meg up the sea stairs before her. When the first breakers roared out, she screamed at her friend. "Meg, go up the stairs, even if the water covers us. Hold on and *go up the stairs!*"

Then another great comber came crashing in to break and sweep them out to sea. The tide began to eat up the stairs, their feet, and their waist –

"Keep going Meg!" Mary choked.

The tide was to Mary's shoulders. *I will not drown. The tide will not take me away - it will bring him to me!* The waters rushed in and they rushed out. The sea stairs were being covered up to the top rung. Meg turned back to her, and her eyes were filled with terror. "Mary," she called, and then the waters rushed in again, and covered her words, her face, and Mary gave a mighty push and sent Meg above the waters, and herself down deep into them.

*I know how he died now. There was not another breath left in the world for him, and now - not for me.*

"I really don't know why I felt such a compulsion to come here," Michael admitted. "Someone else was supposed to come - it is really strange, Mr. Aaronsby, but out of nowhere something *compelled* me to come here."

Aaron said nothing. He did not like this young man. He did not like any young man.

"Maybe, Mr. Aronsby, it is because I knew you had a house on the ocean, and I knew that tonight was going to be full moon. Full moon on the ocean -"

Aaron said nothing. He still smiled, but that had been on his face for so long it was like a frozen muscle.

"I have always been enchanted by the full moon on water," the young man said.

Molly came rushing into the room. "Something *terrible* has happened!" she gasped. Her face was deathly white.

Mary still clung to the rail, but she had no strength for another step. She seemed to move away from her body and its drowning. She was drifting into total peace, a quiet rapture of light and love, and it was as if she were witnessing a miracle and still growing within it. *I am the sacred between the thought and the act of creation.*

She released herself from the rail, the stairs, from life.

A powerful hand clasped her own and pulled her up and up the stairs and into the air above them. Then someone carried her, for her legs were useless. She choked up water and felt herself covered with a warm blanket. Or her body was being put back on her, and her body felt so strange and so *confining.*

From a distant and a strange place someone asked, "Is she all right now?" Meg. It was Meg.

"She is all right now," said a strong masculine voice.

"You two had no business doing this to me!" raged Molly. "It is a terrible thing how you young people today show no consideration! You have no right to be so *frightening!*" Molly's face was as red as her hair.

Mary looked up at the man who had saved her life. His face was a shadow to the sun, but she could see he was a large man, and when he moved, she saw he was a handsome man. "You *are* all right?" he asked.

"Yes, of course," she said, but she was still partly in the tide that was not of the sea, and the energy that was not of the sea, or anything she had ever known. She looked up into the stranger's eyes, and then he was a stranger no more. *His* eyes! This man had *his* eyes! She would know them anywhere, their vivid energy - *life!* She stared and she stared, right up into his face, and after a while, a long while, he revealed annoyance at the rudeness of her staring. *An uncle with a tic smile, two girls trying to drown themselves, a hysterical and rude maid - what made me come here?*

"You," she said. "*You.*"

"You? You?" shouted the other half drowned one. "Mary, is it the YOU? Mary - is HE - the YOU?"

Michael helped the Mary to her feet. Her face was blue and her teeth were chattering. He wondered what she would like when she really came back to life. She just stared at him and said, "You, you, you," and then she began to cry about it.

"The YOU! YOU! YOU!" the other wet girl screamed in joy, while the first one cried about it some more, whatever it was.

"Meg it *is!*" said the Mary, and the Meg then did a weird little jumping on her shoeless feet, and the red headed maid glowered at him, just as Mr. Aronsby had, and *continued* to glower at him as if *he* had created this mess.

"Meg, shut up," said the red headed woman who was probably the girl's mother, but that did not have to be necessary, either, for he had not been overwhelmed with courtesy since his arrival. Then, to his complete horror, the near drowned mouse he had pulled up the stairs and had given first aid to, walked right up to him for a closer look, as if she needed one, planting her shoeless feet right on top of his to give herself the height, and then proceeded to passionately kiss his lips, and never in all of his life, in marriage and outside of it, had he had a kiss with the passion of this one- the passion of *these.*

"My love," she said, "Thank God you heard -

*My love? I heard? They are ALL crazy here!*

The red headed maid recoiled in shock and horror and yelled,

"Mary - what are you *doing?*"

"Mother - it is all right! It is perfect! It is - *decreed*," said the wet Meg. "He is the he - the *he!*"

Meanwhile the passionate kissing of his lips continued and, to his own amazement, he felt real possibilities arise. The girl standing on his shoes drew away, so she could breathe again he guessed, having had so much trouble over that under the ocean, and her eyes ran with tears again. She tenderly touched his face. "I am *thy* eremite," she said.

*Eremite? Did she rise from the bottom of the ocean thinking she is a monk?* Whatever she was, she had the warmest softest lips in the world. He looked at her, during their mutual breathing spell. "What on earth is this *he, he* thing?" he asked.

"A miracle," the girl still on his feet sighed. She was losing her blue shade, and with the energy of her kissing his lips she had managed to stop the chattering of her teeth. She had beautiful lips. She had beautiful eyes. *Shit, she is just plain beautiful!*

"Miracles come every day," she said, "but love found again, is God's greatest miracle."

He swallowed and he wondered which one of them had been at the bottom of the ocean. *Love found again? Love - FOUND - again? AGAIN?*

"Don't you remember me?"

"Well, we were not introduced," he said. He swallowed again, and found there was nothing left to swallow. "Remember?" he slightly choked.

"You *will!*" she smiled radiantly, and then she left her perch on his shoes, and the two wet girls ran away giggling about this he, he.

"Thank you for saving Mary's life," the red headed maid and mother of the Meg grumbled, looking at him in fear as if he had dropped by after ravishing a nunnery.

"I think I have found a very strange house," Michael said, for he always told exactly what he felt, and even being a lawyer had not eliminated this habit.

Molly shook her head in emphatic agreement. They had found something in common. "There is more," she said.

"It gets more weird?"

"I think you will find out it does," she said, and went into the kitchen, leaving Michael to look below thinking, I had better jump down into the fog now - where everything around here will become perfectly clear.

# Four

Mary had just stepped out of her shower after washing her hair and body free of the sea water, when Meg, who had done the same downstairs, was in her room to hear all about the arrival of the reincarnation of John Keats. "Is the gorgeous one *really* he?" she asked.

"Yes. Of course."

"How can you be sure - aside from the fact he arrived on your birthday?" She lay on Mary's four- poster bed, and watched her friend as she brushed her long curly hair dry. Molly might be wrong, Meg thought. Mary is really so perfect *outside,* maybe her fancy and her imagination are not dangerous to her, and maybe - this handsome young man *is* John Keats - brought back to life with the power of love seeking reunion. "But John Keats was five foot two, and this man is well over six foot four," she said.

"That is only natural," replied Mary, always having an answer for everything. "He did not like being so short, so now he *would* be very tall."

Into Mary's room the setting sun cast such a luminous light it seemed to Meg as if Mary was an enchanted princess in some medieval castle, just as she had been in Keats' great love poem to her. The whole afternoon had turned so eerie, their loss in time and tide, blinding fog menacing in *seconds,* and now this strange brilliance of a fading sun." Mary, I believe you. At last - I really believe you!"

"I know you do."

"Not just about Keats - about your uncle, too."

"He created the fog to blind and to kill us."

"But - how?"

"I do not think that you can *reason* out the power of death."

"Aaron is death?"

"I keep saying that."

"How can a man - be death?"

"Well - he has the power to murder through - creating illusion."

"Then he *symbolizes* death to you -"

"Yes."

"Because your parents were killed on his road. But you tell me no one has power over you that you do not allow."

"Yes. That is why I have willed myself away from here and away from him."

"By willing back the love of John Keats."

"Yes. We will defeat death and have a long and happy life this time."

"This is all so strange." The light of the day lingered in such a mystical way that Meg felt captive within a time forever lost, as if the sunset was reaching back into a time now termed the long, long ago. "It is so *strange*," she repeated softly, as if they were both charmed and the spell must not be broken.

"There are *many* things beyond the mind's grasping, Meg. We use such a small part of our mind, and the mind is such a small part of our totality."

*Oh, what would Molly say to that!*

Mary was studying herself in the mirror, and Meg realized, with a start, that she had never seen Mary study herself in the mirror before. "I looked like a drowned rat when he saw me," she was saying. "I must have looked just *awful*."

"Mary, you just cannot look awful. You must know that you have a gorgeous figure and face."

"I was a wet *rat*. And my breasts are too full. Brassieres hurt them. They cut me right in two."

"You are so - *female*, more than any girl I have ever seen," said Meg affectionately. "I am sure he found that out when you kissed him."

"I kissed him? I thought - I just *thought* of that."

"Oh, yes, Mary - you kissed him. And how you kissed him!"

"Really? Why don't I remember it?"

"You *were* totally - totally *there*, Mary."

Mary went on brushing her hair and studying her face while she did it. "I guess it was because I am so anxious for us to consummate our love in this life. Instinct - I guess. I am not going to sit around *this* time and wait for it to happen - when it never did."

"What?"

"Sex."

"We don't know about sex. We have not even seen a man here under sixty since we don't remember a man alive under sixty."

"Well, sex must be wondrous."

"Probably."

Mary sighed and looked at herself in the mirror again. "I promised during my decree for this meeting - I promised to be *perfect* for him."

"Well, you kept *your* promise."

"Did I?"

The light on Mary's golden hair increased its color and Meg thought that on Mary's forehead there should be a wreath of pearls, and her robe should be gossamer from the jeweled wings of butterflies. Then she could stand at a castle window and those in her kingdom could cheer themselves hoarse for having such a beautiful queen.

"We all should be our totality," Mary was saying.

"How do we do that?"

"Well - it is in the acceptance of ourselves through love."

"Totality sounds wondrous."

"Oh, my, it is better than that!"

"How can it be better than wondrous?"

"Love and the sex that must go with it."

"How do you know?"

"Well - it is in his poetry, the rapture of spiritual and physical love. He wanted both. He wrote about wanting both. Now he shall have both!"

"Mary - now think on this, and very, very carefully, as Molly would say."

"Think on what?" Mary began to get dressed, and she discarded more than one dress, and chose one finally that clung the most to her perfect figure. "I think this one will seduce him," she said. "Meg, what do you think?"

"You can do that no matter what you wear."

"*What* do I have to think on?"

"What if -"

"He *is* John Keats!"

"Mary - what if *he* does not know it?"

"I'll make him remember who he is."

"What if you can't?"

"Meg, don't be silly!"

"What if he is married?"

"Meg - of course he is not married! Why would he have replied to the love decree? He was here to save my life! He is here to rescue me from this castle of death, just as if it was the Eve of St. Agnes!"

"But that was in January."

Mary shrugged. "Oh, *time*," she said, as if it did not exist at all.

"It does exist, Mary -"

"Only, if you are mind - trapped."

"But most of us here are."

"That is why we are here to learn, the physical life absorbing the truth of the soul -" said Mary, beginning to put on make up. She had never done that before, either. "This is my mother's make up," she said, and her mother's make up made her look more stunning. The rose lipstick was just the right shade, and her eyes looked more beautiful, if possible. "I *must* arouse him, Meg, to ravish me right way."

"Sex? You think you are going to learn that - *tonight?*"

"Of course. I so wanted him to make love to me! I know how he suffered when he could not give me one more kiss - even in goodbye -" Her voice caught. "I never got that last kiss, that last sweet kiss -"

"Mary - what if - what if -"

"When true loves meet, Meg, there are no *what - ifs.*"

"He is dark - his eyes and hair are dark. He does not have that gorgeous auburn hair you always talk about. Did he hate the color of his hair, too?"

"No. He did not. He only hated being so short, for his brothers were tall -"

"Weren't you as short?"

"Shorter. I was five foot."

"You were not blonde then."

"No. I had dark brown hair. Sometimes I almost see me then - in the mirror - just a quick glance - and then it is gone. I had a pink bow in my hair - maybe two bows - I must have loved pink -"

"You never told me before that you have *seen* yourself as this Frances Brawne."

"I have not told you a lot of things, Meg. We do have to have privacy - about - what is private."

"Why don't I see *my* past life?" Maybe it is because I did not have my head split open, Meg thought, but not too unkindly.

"He still has those beautiful tender lips - and the eyes - their light - their *incredible* light - still the same. And my Keats had very broad shoulders - he was so athletic and so strong. He beat up a man much larger."

"Why would a sweet gentle poet do that?"

"Meg! About the man torturing a kitten - remember?"

"Well - yes, but Mary, there are so *many* things to remember."

Mary smiled at Meg lovingly. "I should realize you could not remember *everything* I told you. I am the one who is in love with him."

"I have to see if Molly needs help," Meg sighed. She left and Mary hardly knew it. She went to her windows and opened them as far as they would go. The evening star shone to absorb the vanishing day, and its silvered rays spoke to her – *here survives forever my enchantment for young lovers.* A full moon was rising in such a poignant sweetness Mary could have embraced the whole night, the whole world, every life lived and yet to come. *Tender is the night, and the Queen moon is on her throne -*

Meg was quickly back. "Mary," she began.

"Hush," said Mary. "Breathe in the night, for it is magic, and we are charmed and made magic within it! Tonight - he will make love to me and all sorrow will be gone from my life as the moonlight on that sea will vanish in tomorrow's dawn!"

"Mary -"

The sound of combers crashing against the shore below drifted up to them, the smell of the sea, the energy of the tide moving in, retreating to return and return. "I never stopped wearing his ring, Meg, though I did marry, years after he was gone. But I loved him, *passionately* loved him - until the day I died."

"I forgot when you did that last time," Meg said meekly.

"1865. This time, Meg, I will *not* lose him. This time we *will* have the child we wanted so much."

"Oh, he is some kind of a *strange* liberal now. Mary, Molly heard him talking to Aaron about the poisoning of the earth, the wasting away of democracy, all the poor abused, and everyone else, except the moneyed top percent of the *world's* population. He called them gnomes of greed. Do you understand any of that?"

"No. But as Keats he did admire the ideals of the American Revolution. He loved our Declaration of Independence. He opposed *all forms* of colonialism he said."

"You even remember his *politics?*" marveled Meg.

"He was more interested in that than I."

"This isn't from reading all of those books about him in Aaron's library, or your parents' books in their library?"

"Of course not." Mary turned from the window and went over to her vanity for perfume. "Where do you put this?" she asked, and then she remembered Mildred putting this same perfume behind her ears and at the base of her throat. "I *must* get pregnant right away," she said. "We wanted a child so much - but he was so desperately poor - are lawyers poor?"

"I don't think so. Aren't they rich like doctors? And, anyway, aren't you to have Aaron's fortune?"

"Yes. That is good. Then my darling will not be poor again!"

Mary looked at herself in the glass. "Is this dress - ravishing enough?"

"Mary, the man does not have a prayer."

"Where is he now?"

"In Aaron's room."

"Tell me *everything* Molly found out about him - with the gnomes of greed stuff."

"Well, I found out from Molly who found out from Aaron that

he has been married, is recently divorced and will never get married again. He said he would die before he fell in love again, as that makes a man mad so he gets married and is then miserable. He likes women now only from a distance, and Aaron says that this is smart for such a young man."

Mary recoiled in shock, and then had to sit down. "Marriage makes a man *miserable*? He believes that - now? How could he!"

"He said it was not for him and should never have been, and if a man makes the same mistake twice he is a fool, and he is no fool. Molly said Aaron is bonding to him even if he is way too young for an Aaron lawyer."

"He told all of this to Aaron?"

"As if Aaron were a beloved uncle - or even a father - maybe. Molly heard everything as she was getting supper ready for them in Aaron's room."

"I am to eat with them?"

"That is the plan, and the table setting. Aaron does not want to go down to the dining room tonight. He is even giving - this man - some of his best brandy. This man - Michael - Keats - what *do* we call him?"

"He is now Michael -" Mary said, frowning and losing any glowing from the beauty of the night or the beauty of love. "He *hates* women? What will he do with his life?"

"He is going to devote it to helping the poor from those gnomes - whatever they are, or wherever they are."

Mary was so desolate within the crashing of her dreams, it was as if the evening star, *their* star, had fallen right out of the sky to drown itself in the ocean. "He can't be like this - he can't be! He loved women! He loved his mother and his sister and me - so *tenderly!*" Mary began to worry about her brain injury herself. "Meg - I don't know what to say!" Suddenly, all magic had fled the world - there were no magic tide of love beyond time, no golden tide of God's grace for her parents and no magic tide that had formed the reincarnation of John Keats to bring him to her. "Well," she said. "Well," she repeated glumly, pacing the room. "I have a brain injury, don't I? My head was cracked open, wasn't it?"

"Yes, and that was terrible!" said Meg.

"And my great romance with John Keats, all of my once being another person - is probably its ghastly result."

Meg was stunned. "Mary - *Mary!*"

Mary sat down on her bed and looked out at sea and sky. The sea was as stilled as the moon. "Meg, maybe I *am* crazy."

"Mary, I don't think so, though Molly does -"

Again Mary saw the broken windshield and the fog coming through it to caress her mother's dead face. She saw Aaron's smile and heard his voice - *mummy dead and daddy, too -*

"Maybe, Meg, I made myself up *then* to deal with the *now* of Aaron! Maybe I have made up this the castle of the Eve of St. Agnes and my magic rescue *to be* from it - Meg - *it was to give myself a safe haven from Aaron!*"

"He did say the midnight death stuff?"

"Oh, yes. That is true. But what else is? Is what sustained me for so long, the beauty and the magic of his poetry - no more than in a *book?*"

"We all have dreams of romance and love - you were so sure, Mary, that yours was not a dream!"

Mary began to weep, and she wept as she had never wept before for her parents, and she wept for a thirteen year old girl, scarred and bereft, who looked up at the evening star for sustenance and said - *you are as constant as human love.*

Meg took her within her arms, and they both wept together.

"Meg! What is the power of fancy when it is not fancy? Is it madness?"

"Mary, I don't know. You always teach this stuff to me."

"He is not John Keats. John Keats is dead. I never knew John Keats!"

Meg recoiled. "Don't say that! We have to believe that death is not a finality - that love cannot be absorbed by death - that death can only absorb itself - all you have told me for so long!"

"It is all a mockery!" Mary said bitterly, wiping her eyes and blowing her nose."

"That dark corners of the mind that accept death and deny the light of the soul - the mind's master - *Mary!*"

"Stupidity!"

"The dark corners of the mind that deny the light of God - within us - within all living things -"

"Stupidity," Mary repeated. A big fat moon had even absorbed the evening star. Or it had reeled away with all the dreams of young lovers.

"He saved your life in a changing tide. Instead of the tide bringing him *in* to you Mary, he stopped you from being swept *away* in it. He came to you, just as you had decreed, Mary, on your birthday!"

"How can Aaron be death? He can't be - yet - I know his power! I know it! He has the power here - *on his land* - to create illusion - or - am I simply - mad?"

"Mary!" Meg moved away and looked as forlorn and lost as Mary did. "Your belief in the magic power of love - being here - right here, Mary, made my life brighter. It was so true to you, and so true to me - don't forsake our acceptance of it, Mary!"

"Of what?"

"Magic."

"Magic," Mary repeated dully.

"The magic that decrees time illusion and allows the soul to mock all the fleeing hours."

Mary looked at Meg and then looked away, out into the night that no longer held any charm. "Meg, you sound just like me," she said sadly.

"Go into Aaron's room where they are waiting for you, I am sure."

"Did I really kiss him? I don't believe I did that."

"You did. You stood on his shoes and you kissed him. And kissed him. And kissed him."

"*Wildly*, you said."

"*Wildly*, you did."

"I still think I just thought of doing that."

"You did it. Now brush your hair, put on some more perfume - and go down the hall into Aaron's room."

"I don't want to."

"It would be very rude of you if you did not. That young man is driving you to the city tomorrow."

Outside of Aaron's bedroom door they heard Michael talking.

"He has the same musical voice," whispered Meg.

"I can't go in there."

"You *have* to go in there. When did he die last time? I forgot when he died."

"John Keats died February 23, 1821."

"Well," smiled Meg. "It *has* been a long time, hasn't it? Now go in there right now, and make all your dreams of love come true."

# *Five*

When Michael returned to Aaron's bedroom sitting room, the old man had taken a Victorian chair by the grate, and brandy was on a marble top table before the fire, a large decanter of it, and when offered, Michael poured himself a generous glass. *Maybe if I get good and drunk, this place will appear* normal. He found that his hands were shaking. He felt danger in this crazy house, and he felt the passion of the weird wet girl's kisses. He was torn between the absurd and something sweetly opening within, and he thought of a beautiful flower, long closed, opening its heart to the sun.

"What happened downstairs?" asked Aaron. "Did the girls forget the tide, so you had to drag them up the sea stairs?"

"I just dragged one up," said Michael. "One called Mary."

"My niece," Aaron sighed. "Did you notice her - *really* notice her?"

"Notice her? She was drowning on the sea stairs. Of course I noticed her."

"I am so grateful you were there," said Aaron, smiling. *How do you know when he is really smiling, for he does that all the time? But his smile never reaches his eyes. They are so - dead.*

Michael's face flushed with the brandy and the memory of the wet girl's kisses. Never had a woman opened so totally to him with a kiss - by two kisses - four - they had just had melted into each other beyond his ability to remember how many there were.

"Michael, did she say she was to go back to the city with you? It is *very* important that I know if she intends to leave this house."

Michael put down his glass and shook his head a little. Hadn't this old man sent for him to take his niece to the city and enroll her at the University? Hopefully, graduate school? Well, why mention that. They were all crazy here, from the wet kissing girl, to the other wet one, that kept yelling the *him, him,* or the *he, he* thing, to the hostile red headed cook, and now this uncle - of the weird smile grimace.

"Well? Well?" asked the old man impatiently. "Is she leaving with you?"

"We really did not speak," Michael said. "I just pulled her out of the water, got her to breathing again, and then she - she - she left," Michael concluded, leaving out the long passionate kisses.

"Meg said she has decided to stay with me until I pass away. I have terminal cancer, you know."

You sure do not look terminal to me, Michael thought. "I was sorry to hear that," Michael said.

"It would only be the right thing for her to do. And if she does not go away, I am leaving her all of my money."

Michael well knew how much money that was. More than he dreamed one man could gather together - or a generation after him.

"I was sure Meg heard her right," said Aaron looking relieved. "They might well have drowned. You know that along an ocean fogs come in so fast and seemingly from nowhere," said Aaron. "I told them about the fog, and I told them to remember the time of the tide."

If Michael did not know better, it would seem the old man was talking about a different kind of tide. As for the road to this place, it was just a prelude for the people living here, *scary.*

"How did you find my niece?" The old man was studying him closely.

Under the ocean, he wanted to say. "Pardon?"

"What did she *look* like to you?"

"Oh. She looked wet. Very wet."

"I hope you are more clear in your briefs and before a judge."

Suddenly, Michael did feel as if he were before a judge, and not one the least interested in justice. "What do you mean?" he asked.

"Did you feel - as if you have *known* her before?"

"How on earth could I feel that?"

"Did you feel a sudden - *attraction* to her?"

Michael felt her lips on his again, the soft pushing against him of her breasts, and he flushed, became warm from the brandy. "Why on earth would I feel that? I don't know her. I just pulled her out of the ocean that would surely have carried her away to drown." *What in the hell did I get myself into?* The lifeless eyes of the uncle were sending real chills up and down his spine. It was the expressionless eyes - in such contrast to the smile, or a smile/grimace.

"I must tell you, even if you are not taking her to the city. I hate to tell you, but I must. Mary - is not just a *little* awry. She is - not balanced in her mind. She had her head cracked open and really had a death experience, they say, in the accident that killed her mother."

"How terrible, and to lose both of her parents. They were so popular among students -"

"Did you have them for professors?"

"No. I was into government and law. I do not like poetry or philosophy."

"Mary is quietly, *very* quietly, Michael - *mad.*"

"Oh." Michael could say nothing else.

"She - dreams things up and thinks they are real, and if you do not agree, she says *you* are the one who is mad, and you do terrible things to her."

Molly came into the room and began setting the supper table and continued to bring in food for it.

"That is very sad," Michael said. "The poor girl - knowing such tragedy *so young.*" Suddenly, he felt as if he were speaking of himself, and his only tragedy was succumbing *once* and *once only,* to love.

"Are you married?"

Michael actually shuddered at the word. "No. I am divorced, and marriage taught me - marriage is not for me. Women - well - love for one makes you lose all reason, and I did that once, and if I ever do it again, I am a bigger fool, an idiot, and not so *quietly* mad."

"I never married, either. It was not for me."

"There are people who should marry, and people who should not, and there is no disgrace or condemnations attached."

"Absolutely," agreed Aaron. Aaron almost liked this man even if he was still a young one.

"Now my life is full and *perfect.* I spend my money and the time

I have for it on my cause. My life is for my cause of helping the poor against the gnomes of greed. I fight for democracy. I fight for democracy, the rule of the people by the people in the tradition of Abraham Lincoln. And that gives me more joy than marriage ever did. Or any marriage ever could!"

"Hmmmm," said Aaron, still studying him like a judge, and as if he did not know whether to suspend the death sentence.

"My life is centered, perfect. I am the captain of my own ship. My ship is trim, balanced and *on course.*"

"I hope so," mused Aaron, the smile not abating, nor the cold judging in his eyes. "You see, Mary has believed ever since she came here, that *today,* on her *eighteenth* birthday, John Keats is going to arrive and take her from our home, which she says is a *castle of death.*"

Michael's head reeled, and it was not from more brandy. "John Keats?" he asked. "That poverty- stricken English poet- the failed *dead* English poet? How can a poet who is long dead, or just *dead* - save her?"

Aaron shrugged, and sipped more brandy himself. "His death does not bother Mary. His poetry lives on in her heart, and so he does."

Michael suddenly felt himself sinking into panic, and he was the one beneath the ocean, and there was no strong hand to pull *him* away from it. "John Keats, the dead poet - is to come to her on her eighteenth birthday? Why - does she have a reason for - *why?*"

"Of course. Mary has a reason for all of her madness. He will save her from me and my castle of death, and they, she is the reincarnation of Frances Brawne you know, can finish up their love affair that it seems death had so *gravely* interrupted, no pun intended."

"Who was Frances Brawne?"

"The woman John Keats loved. You do not like poetry?"

"I never read it. I find it usually - depressing." The memory came back of the wild kissing and he clawed at his collar. In this crazy house he still felt under the ocean. "Who has arrived today - on her *eighteenth* birthday? Who else?"

For once the smile/grimace was appropriate. "Only you."

46

"I am John Keats?"

"In the flesh."

"My God, the poor girl."

"And it gets worse. Molly tells me that she is going to marry you this time and have many, *many* babies."

"How sad to pin your life on a mirage - on *illusion*."

"It can be *deadly*," said Aaron, and there was a clear threat in his eyes. "See that she stays here, Michael, unless you *have* to have sex with her."

"*What?* What are you saying? What kind of a demented rapist would do that?" He shuddered and almost became ill. Maybe this damned house was a castle of death - certainly its horror. "The poor sad case of a girl - who would even think of touching her? Even a decent man *committed* to love and all of that - no decent man would take advantage of - this form of madness!"

"Speaking of which -" said Aaron, as Mary entered the room. He watched Michael when Michael looked up and saw her.

There was genuine shock on his face, and he looked plugged right into a socket of raw wires and Aaron expected the hair to rise on his head and waited for him to chatter off into a coma. "Michael Covington," Aaron said. "May I formally present my niece, Mary O'Brien?"

Michael rose and it was difficult as he had stopped breathing and had to *will* himself back into that helpful habit. *Here is every love poem and song to woman personified. Here is the goddess of the sea, and the goddess of the moon, the goddess of love, the goddess of beauty, the goddess of every male heart in the world,* and she shimmered toward him in a clinging gown that made her enchant above and beyond a mere goddess.

Aaron filled his glass again, but he never stopped looking at the way Michael was looking at Mary.

Michael formally took her offered hand, and he ached to hold it to his lips, and what more he ached to do he would never admit, and it was instantaneous, and totally out of his control. This woman, this girl, simply had risen from his own nether depths as if he were pulling her up from the depths of his soul. He felt as if he had been parched from life, lost for eons beyond memory to thirst, and here was its surcease, a surcease of any deprivation. "You looked so different wet," he burst out and could have killed himself, for he should have said, *I will place rose petals at thy feet, and bring the light down from the moon for thy dress, and your kisses four - forever more - will never be enough!* And he was insanely jealous of a girl he did not know - *if any man knew her but himself* –

The night radiated magic; the moon radiated enchantment and the glory of a perfect woman who outdid them all.

Aaron looked at his niece, for the look on Michael's face revealed Michael now as no ally. "Mary, dear child, you're staying here as you promised until I pass on?"

She went to her uncle and kissed the top of his head. "Yes, I am. I changed my mind about leaving, so you sent for this nice young man for nothing."

"I will pay you well, Michael, for that road of mine does need repair."

"It needs another *place*," said Michael.

Mary smiled down at her uncle. "I have always had such kindness here - nursery rhymes to get me through the night - your own sweet rhymes just for me." She sat down near Michael and he felt her kisses happening, felt the pressing of her breasts against him happening, but his thoughts had never regained decency since she had first entered the room. He was deeply shamed, and he hoped the indecency did not show. To be sure, he covered it with a napkin, probably to be used for the supper, but he needed it now. His ship shape ship was listing as its lower half was devouring its upper half, making the whole ship dead on the water, compass gone, its captain partaking of a banquet and sliding clear off the deck.

"Michael," scolded Aaron. "One *sips* brandy. You are gulping it."

Mary smiled at him and the ship was sunk, the captain adrift with not a thing to keep him afloat.

Her uncle studied him as closely as Mary was doing. "You *are* leaving tomorrow?" he asked, sudden fear in his voice.

"Who?"

"You, Michael," said Aaron. "You, the young man here, who is so enjoying my favorite brandy."

"What?"

"Are you leaving tomorrow?"

"Am I leaving tomorrow?"

"That is *my* question."

"Of course," said Michael, covering his pants more securely with the napkin. *Damn this thing - so unbidden - it never has happened before - not even on my wedding night!*

The smiling tick uncle began to cry, and Mary went to him and wiped away his tears with a napkin, and thank God that napkin is not this one, thought Michael, for his problem with the unbidden was not inclined to go away. "Uncle dear, how could I leave you?" said the sea goddess, moon goddess, love goddess, saint goddess.

The old man wept in joy. "You will be one of the richest women on the earth," he sobbed, and still managed the tick smile.

While uncle and niece devoted their attention to each other, Michael used all of his will to will away what was still below decks with the sunken ship. *I have morphed into the organ of fatherhood!*

"Michael," said Aaron. "Your face has lost all of its color."

Meg and Molly carried in soup. In the steam from its warmth, Michael smelled such tantalizing aromas he thought he might now concentrate on supper. "Mary tells Michael and me she is not going away with him," said Aaron happily, and for once his eyes agreed with his smile.

Meg just dropped her part of the hot soup, and so Molly had no real recourse but to do the same, and, unhappily for Michael, the food tray was over his lap and its problem. "My God!" he yelled. By prehistoric instinct he found his way to a bathroom.

Molly and Meg cleaned up the mess and left. They came back with more food, and Michael ate it, still in deep suffering from the supper's first course. Mollie and Meg apologized sincerely, and the sacred Mary sat by him and gave him tender and loving looks. "My dearest uncle and I so share our love for poetry," she was saying, and Meg, who was pouring steaming tea, teetered in shock, and, as she was teetering over Michael's lap, Michael leaped to safety by running to the window, and pressing against its coolness. "I will return to your side of the room when the tea is poured," he said.

Molly and Meg left, but as Michael returned to his chair near Mary, she left, too.

"My dear niece really made quite an impression on you," said Aaron.

"Really?" Michael said.

"*Really*," Aaron replied. "You are leaving tomorrow morning?"

"Of course," said Michael.

"How could you two almost kill him?" Mary asked mother and daughter in the kitchen.

"Meg dropped it first," said Molly, dishing up their own dinner.

"Mary, you are such a good actress. Anyone would think you were going to stay here until Aaron dies."

"She's not?" asked Molly.

"I'm not," replied Mary, sitting by the warmth of the wood stove.

"Well - why did you tell Mr. Aaronsby you were?" asked Molly.

"Because if he knew I was planning to leave, he would find some way of killing me as he killed my parents!"

Molly was sitting at the table, and she covered her face with her hands and groaned.

"Oh, Mary," mourned Meg. "You have changed about your uncle doing that."

"I was right, Meg. I changed back. I was right all the time!"

"What are you two talking about?" asked Molly. "Why do you talk in secret code around me? Mary, your father lost his way in the fog and went over the cliff into the ocean. Your mother was following a car in the fog, and when it stopped, she swerved and hit the tree. What has this to do with your dear uncle?"

"Everything," said Mary.

"Child, child," said Molly sadly. "You are a bright girl, learning so much and remembering it, too, but you must learn that the way you think about your uncle's so-called supernatural power is not *normal*. Red tail lights cannot just appear to guide your mother off the road!"

Mary's face revealed real fear. "You have not told Aaron that I am going to try to get away, have you? Meg, you didn't?"

"I didn't. I told him you were staying," said Meg.

Seeing Mary tremble, Molly had to reassure her. "We won't tell."

"Have you told Michael yet - that you are leaving with him?" asked Meg.

"I will tonight," said Mary, "after he gets into his own room." She looked at her two anxious and dear friends. "I love you both very much. I will miss you both terribly." Her eyes were filled with tears. "We are going to have to sneak away before daylight, so we will be gone from the point before Aaron wakes up."

Molly wiped her eyes. "Someday, dear child, you will know your uncle for what he really is."

"I already know, and I pray you never find out." Mary gave Molly a kiss on the top of her bright hair, and then she and Meg tearfully hugged each other. "You are like a sister to me," Mary said. "Write and send letters to me by the delivery men."

"We will. We both will," said Molly. "Now off with you, child. Remember, *all* of us here love you."

Mary shrugged, negating any love from her uncle. "Don't you two *think* of leaving while he is alive."

"We never would think of it," said both mother and daughter. They looked after Mary, the closed kitchen door. "Poor little thing," said Molly, not wiping away her tears now. "Poor little thing - so lost in all of that *fancy*."

Michael was told to take the guest room across from Mary's bedroom. This hall is larger then most people's front rooms, Michael thought as he walked down it to his room. A beautiful cut glass kerosene lamp burned in it, but full moonlight streaming in from the sea window in the hall made the lamp shine like a tiny lost star. There was no light under Mary's door. She probably was asleep by now, for he had talked for so long with Aaron, but the talk was mostly by Aaron and about his niece, and how she managed to hide her insanity with her charm and beauty.

Now, that he only had this night to get through and would leave first thing in the morning, Michael was no longer threatened by his nether mind or the nether part of his body. It had been a ghastly experience, this onslaught of *immediate* sexual desire. "Oh, my," he sighed, looking at the path the moonlight made on the hall floor. Moonlight spoke for her - *I will be normal again when I get out of this madhouse!*

His room was a beautiful old room. In this house you stepped back a hundred years in time, but in this room, you were five hundred years back in time. The arched windows with colored leaded glass looked medieval, and so did the great antique bed. He would expect the walls and the timbered ceiling to be an extension of a medieval castle high on a cliff off an English shore, or within the winds of an English moor.

He changed into his pajamas and carefully folded his clothes on the rack for them. He would have done nothing else, for Michael liked his surroundings as neat and orderly as he did life. He touched his jacket, but in his mind he was touching the shimmering dress she had worn, felt its smooth silken touch, and then his touch was upon her and the indecent became a full - fledged dragon, snorting hell fire.

"*Monster, back into your cave!*" He was actually talking to it as if it were alive, which it very much was. *I'll show you, you untamed beast. I will turn you into five hundred sleep sheep.*

But the sheep sleep did not come. The moon moved and spitefully shone right down into his face. Ordinarily, he would have liked that. A full moon beguiled him. He could not remember when a full moon had not beguiled him. But this one created a mourning and sadness that could not be assuaged. It was this crazy house! This *was* a castle of death. Ghosts here haunted him as if he had lived before in this house and a ghost was his own of a life long gone. He got out of bed and went to the window.

Before him shone a sea of pale enchantment, its breakers fanning out into white lace as they nudged the shadows of the rocks below. He was lonelier, more bereft, than he had ever been in all of his life. He felt as if he had lived for no reason. He felt as if he had even loved for no reason, which, indeed, had turned out to be the case.

The Mary - goddess of the sea, of the moonlight upon it, silvered waters clinging to white shoulders, full breasts, and there he stopped his thoughts, but the beast below had caught enough of them to roar back into life. *How can this sexual desire control me?*

Me?

It could. It did.

He saw her lying with him, heart- to -heart, breast- to- breast, and he possessed her. He could not have stopped in possessing and loving her in all tender ways any more than an angel could shed its wings, and the light that made an angel an angel. He was craven with passion. He was craven with tenderness, love that could have stilled the stars. *How can I be such an idiot?*

But there it was. His fancy, his dreams of making love to a strange girl he knew only for hours, and one said to be mad, to boot. It went on, this dream he would die to fulfill. He was kissing her beautiful lips, kissing her breasts – and the vision would not stop. He was cast into the rapture of union, the holiness of the moonlight upon the sea, the light of the Evening Star that shone above him not even dimmed by a full moon. Tears streaked his face. *Have I just been born? Shit – created?* Something opened within his soul. There was a lost melody so sweetly regained. From where was this now unsung song? And while he wondered he thought of a flower opening to the sun, and then he saw the flower and the sun, and love, as one.

Where is this nonsense coming from? Am I a ghost of myself? Do we haunt ourselves? Are all the graves empty and the soul bearing forever what was?

Sighing, he went back to bed. Where were the sweet sheep and sweet sleep? Nowhere. The moon seemed to have picked up the color of the stained glass window - he *saw* color reflected within the light on the floor, the ceiling, *but moonlight does not pick up color, does it? This is a crazy house, all rational thought gone from it, and its old timbers and plaster and brick facade speak for the dead, not the living, and who is smiling baby- faced Aaron -death always lurking behind a baby's smile?* He tossed and he turned, and there she always was, beautiful lips waiting to be kissed, and he could kiss her as wildly as she had kissed him.

He slept. He thought he did. The clock downstairs struck three times. He was walking into winter, and it was bitterly cold. He walked on iced stone floors and there was little light in which to see them. He had to be quiet, so quiet, or death would find him and he could not rescue her from this castle of death.

Dead knights in frozen armor looked sightlessly down upon him from their high arched pedestals. Stone angels entered his vision and let him stealthily pass, and he left them to hushed silence with their wings folded icily over their breasts. A dying beadsman was shivering, counting his beads with numbed fingers before the last coals of his spent fire.

Thou art my Heaven, and I thine eremite.

The words came into his dream, as if he was saying them, and then he thought - I must be silent! If they hear me, we both die!

"Thou art my Heaven, and I thine eremite," a woman's soft voice repeated.

He awakened from a dream of enchantment into a moment of a greater one. She was there, right next to his bed, and moonlight shone upon her robe, and upon her fair hair. He could imagine those tresses wreathed in pearls, and he could imagine a crown of diamonds upon her head, or a crown of the stars now lost to the moon.

Full on this casement shone the wintry moon.
*Upon the honey'd middle of the night...*

Mary slipped off her robe and was going on about some poem apparently with its own moon.

Of all its wreathed pearls her hair she frees,
Unclasps her warmed jewels one by one;
Loosens her fragrant bodice; by degrees
*Her rich attire creeps rustling to her knees...*

With this, she took off her nightgown. Her hair moved from her face in a sudden rippling of light, and she got into his bed. Instead of his being naked and on top of her, as the indecent one had thought of since her first night appearance, she was naked and on top of him. "Mary," he gasped with the greatest of difficulties, for he was out of breath, and she was covering his lips with the same passionate kisses of the wet one right up from the ocean bottom.

"Mary? Mary? *Mary!*" he choked incredulously.

"What?"

"What are you doing - lying on me - *naked!*"

"Lying on you naked."

"Why?"

She stopped kissing and caressing him, and looked annoyed that she had to. "Why? Why? To have sex of course!"

"What? *What?*" The sea beast shrank back to its cave and covered its eyes.

"Is this not how the sex thing begins?" she asked impatiently.

He gasped. "Do you do this to all of your overnight guests?"

She looked shocked and hurt and tears glistened in her eyes. "It is only you," she said. "Only *you.*"

He sat up and covered her with a blanket. "Mary, in today's world, or any world - a girl does not get into bed naked with a strange man. Or just get into bed - with a strange man. It is not proper. It is not wise. Mary, it is *indecent!*"

She recoiled and tears flooded her face. "How could you?" she wept. "How *could* you?"

"How could I - *what?*"

"Come back to me - *stupid!*"

He was angry, and so angry, the beast below went into fits of sobbing. "I just met you today. We are *strangers!*"

"Liar!"

"Now what are you saying? Oh, my God! *That!*"

"What is the - *that?*"

"Aaron told me that you love John Keats, called him back to life and I am supposed to be John Keats as I arrived here on your birthday! That is when you sent out the magic call - or when John Keats rises from the grave - it is so confusing!"

"Molly told Aaron this! How could she," and Mary wept so bitterly that Michael took her within his arms, the blanket, too, of course. Finally, she stopped weeping, and brushed her hair back from her face, the moon goddess again. "I want us to have a baby right away," she said, removing the blanket and Michael leaped out of bed with such energy, he and Mary both landed on the floor. He flung her nightgown right into her face, as if she could put it back on before she had taken it off. "I am not John Keats! I never was John Keats! I do not even believe in reincarnation and if I did, I would *never* be John Keats!"

"Why not?" she asked angrily.

"He had a horror of a life!"

She finally slid the gown over her body, but she did it right in front of him, and had not tried to hide any part of herself while she did it. "Put on the robe, too," he snarled, and had no idea why he was so enraged. *My God - the look of her, the touch of her - the satin over her now made glorious by her breasts.* "Do you take off your clothes and jump into the bed of any man who finds his way here at the end of this shitty road of your shitty uncle?" he asked furiously. The thought of sex with her - the returned *image* of it, drove him into unspeakable rage. He shook with it. The indecent did not feel the earthquake because it had given up the ghost.

"You *have* to know who you are! You *have* to!"

"I know who I am, if you do not know who *you* are!"

"I know who I am!"

"Well, so do I!"

They were yelling at each other. He sat down on the bed because he had no strength left to do anything else "Oh," he groaned.

She came to him for more kissing.

The indecent one went into instant reincarnation and was growing by the second or just instantaneously. "No you don't!" Michael said, leaping from the bed and making of it a fortress between them.

She began to pace. "You came back *stupid!*"

"I am risen from no damned grave, and I am not stupid. You wanted sex with a total *stranger!*"

"I wanted you to fall in love with me *again!*"

"You wanted sex."

"All right. Sure. That, too."

Michael shook his head. "I am in a mad house," he said. "You are ALL crazy here."

Even with just the light of the moon he saw her hurt, and how deeply it went. *How could I be so cruel?*

"I am not crazy," she said evenly. "And I am not a little awry, either, a little mad. I am filled with fancy, but I well know the dream from the reality."

"What is that?"

"Fancy *leads* to the reality."

"That I am John Keats because I arrived here to save you - on your birthday?"

"You saved my life, and it was on my birthday. Aaron again -"

"Yes. And I saved your life as Michael James Covington, and not John Keats." *She is any goddess of myth and magic, and no more perfect woman ever lived, or shall live, within a man's longing. For you, if I could be John Keats - I would be!*

"Did you hear me?" he asked.

"Yes."

"People do not rise from the dead."

"They do in every birth."

She was so desirable he could have bathed her feet with his tears.

She sensed her power and moved toward him, and he backed against the cold window, and compared to what was going on before him, falling out of it would be quite rational. "Now let's run over this together, *calmly, intelligently -*"

"All right." Again she came to him, and he pushed her away. "With you - *over there.*"

"Well, I am back over here. Now be calm and intelligent."

"I did just arrive here today, now yesterday - didn't I? That is agreed?"

"Yes."

"And we met for the first time on the sea stairs - we met, more or less, when I pulled you out of the ocean."

"Yes."

"And as soon as you apparently realized that you were not at its bottom, you stood on my shoes and began this weird kissing of my lips - "

"Weird? *Weird?*"

"Well, Mary, we were not introduced were we? I have never been kissed so wildly and so passionately by a woman I have never even *seen* before."

"You reincarnated backwards! You reincarnated into a *jackass!*"

'I did not, and I repeat, I did *not* reincarnate into anything!" *My God, such passion- she is as mad as a hatter! Her smiling tick uncle is right, she is mad!*

"Oh," he groaned in misery. The indecent had recovered in its

cave and was turning cartwheels in his pants. It was very painful.
"Mary -"

"Mary- what?"

He felt he had thirsted for eons and had found a spring in the desert and was struggling on past it.

"You look terrible. I thought men liked to see women naked."

"Oh, God - oh - *Mary!*" He hid his head within his hands, right there at the window with sea and sky made magic by the full moon.

"I willed you here. I willed you by a tide you *cannot* deny -"

"A tide?"

"The tide of God's grace -"

"What is that?"

"Eternal love between God and man, and man and woman."

"Man and a woman - *bound* for eternity."

"Man and woman *fulfilled* - for eternity." She paced again and thought on all of his shortcomings some more. "How could you *not* make love to me?" she finally asked, angrily. "How could you have done such a *wicked* thing?"

He slapped his forehead. *Now any minute a flying saucer is going to pass through this window and say to her - Oh, this is where you went!*

"You came to take me from Aaron. You came to save us both."

"From what?"

"Death!"

"Of course - why not?"

"I don't think that you reincarnated into a very bright man."

"I did *not* reincarnate. And you told your uncle you were going to stay with him. I heard you say that in between being scalded to death. I thought you were going to stay with your tick uncle until he died from the cancer that makes him look so damned healthy. I thought I heard you say that, and your uncle repeat it to Meg and Molly, just before they wanted to see my reaction to being parboiled."

"I had to lie to save our lives!"

"Save our lives."

"There you go - not understanding again! *Save - our - lives!* How can *you* be stupid *now?*"

They glared at each other. Finally he sighed, and ran his hands through his hair. "Mary, what do you have planned for the rest of the evening?"

"We have to get out of here and off the point before Aaron wakes up!"

"Before Aaron wakes up." He paused, swallowed. "Mary," he said cautiously, and a little fearfully, "Why?"

"Why - *what?*"

"Why do we have to leave before Aaron wakes up?"

"To escape his power. We must be gone before he knows we are going."

"What - power - Mary? Mary? *What power?*"

"Aaron causes death through the power of illusion," she said quietly, and on the surface, quite rationally, too. "And *don't* repeat me again!"

He wouldn't. He couldn't.

"We must leave right now!" she said. "We will get dressed and leave *right now!*"

"It is night. It is dark - too dark for that shitty road. I say we wait for daylight. I say - *no*. What will you do about that?"

"I will take off my gown and make you nervous again about what your pants are doing."

She paused at the door, and looked back at him. "*Were* doing," she amended. "By the way, what *were* they doing?"

He sighed. "I'll meet you at the car."

"And why do you keep sighing like that?"

"Mary, it has been a *long* day."

# Six

Michael threw his clothes, his shaving cream and his toothbrush into his suitcase as fast as he could. He dressed and had brushed his teeth and had shaved as fast as he could. He would take her to do graduate work at the University, and he was sure she would do well, and even better, if she imagined all of her professors to be John Keats. Well, out of this nut house. It was its road. He wanted to get off of it and home as soon as he could. He ran his hands through his thick dark hair, and did it again when he met her at his car. "Where on earth have you been?" she whispered, looking fearfully around as if Aaron might be walking in his sleep toward them.

She must have zoomed down the stairs on the incoming flying saucer, he thought.

"What took you *so long?*" she asked again waiting for him to unlock the car door.

"I thought I moved very rapidly," he said stiffly, unlocking her door and then his own. He gave inner thanks that she had changed from the nightgown that shimmered, and had put on a tailored suit with some kind of a high collared white blouse. He never wanted to see that nightgown again, especially after she had stepped out of it.

"Stop!" she exclaimed suddenly, and in terror.

"What have I started?" he asked in real bewilderment.

"The car!"

"Mary, I know you live way out here, in the past century, or five before that, but modern vehicles have to be started before they can go anywhere."

She jumped out, and began to push her side of the car as if she could. "Get out and help me!" she commanded fearfully.

"Push - push the car?" He looked at her in disbelief.

"Yes, yes!" she said, as if he were a reincarnated jackass.

He shrugged, and got out of the car and pushed it along with her. "Why are we doing this?" he asked as they were making some progress pushing his car down Aaron's long brick drive.

She was too engrossed in pushing to even hear him. "Mary," he said, trying to be very kind. "Since the car was invented it has been recognized it is better to drive one than to push one. You do not even have to push a *horse*."

She looked up at Aaron's bedroom window. "Keep still and push harder, he *must* not hear the motor start."

"Mary, that old bastar - bast - boy - cannot hear my car start if it were right under his window which it is not. And I think he has this smiling thing because he is deaf. I don't think he knows what is going on around him."

"Aaron *is* what is going around him!"

"What?"

"What? What?" she mocked angrily.

Molly had gone to the library east windows because she had been up and had heard the front doors close. Meg joined her. "What are you doing here?" Meg asked.

"Looking at Mary making Michael push his car down the driveway. Did I ever warn him or what?" said Molly.

"She doesn't want Aaron to know she is leaving!" Meg whispered.

"Did I ever warn him or what?" Molly repeated.

As they pushed, Mary looked at Michael. "Can't you sense the *evil* here? The malignancy? The power he has over us?"

"I am supposed to feel *that* old man's power?"

"I am not talking of anything physical - anything you can see - touch - understand -"

"Is there something else?"

"The *real*. And why are you letting me push this thing by myself?"

Michael did not like his beloved car to be called a thing. "My car is named Betsy, after Elizabeth Tudor the Great," he said, determined to give Mary some of her own medicine. "And she resents us doing her job - which is *Betsy* moving *us*."

"Don't mock me."

"Are we going to push Betsy on to the freeway? They have laws against that, you know."

"I said for you to stop mocking me."

"All right," he half apologized. What he was really doing was remembering what she looked like naked, felt like naked, and even with this pushing the car thing, the beast was cautiously opening its eyes way down in his sea cave – where it was supposed to stay for at least five minutes.

"I think we are far enough away so he won't hear us," she said, and got into her side of the car. He got into his side and fired Betsy up, and she purred without a sound as he guided her toward the sea cliff road.

"All right," Michael said, not even looking at her blouse. "I can believe Aaron is evil to you. Was mean to you. But he is *there* and we are *here*."

"If he is still asleep."

"If he is awake?"

"If he knows we are gone, we are in danger."

"Why? Why on earth - why?"

"We are still on his territory," she said logically as if she had any.

"He can do what - here – still on his territory?"

"Kill us."

"Mary, that is just impossible."

"No. He creates blindness - illusion - and within its malignancy you are *dead*."

"Here- on *all* of his land? He controls - has a magic power -"

"On *all* of his land."

*How could she have by-passed her mind when the rest of her is so wondrous?*

They had reached the ocean road, and the moon was already beginning to fade.

"Watch the road. Do NOT take your eyes from it for one second, and if I tell you to stop, you STOP, for I know that monster, and I know how to get away from him. We have to concentrate on *living with illusion not mastering us*. She was peering out at the ocean horizon with real terror. "Careful- careful -" she said softly. "Dear God, let him stay *asleep!*"

"I think this damned road is falling off into the ocean," Michael said grimly. "The state should condemn it."

"It was built for a horse and buggy."

"Well, it would be dangerous for them, too."

"You are doing fine. You will get us off of here, and when you do, I want you to stop at the freeway, and I want us to give a solemn promise to us that we will *never* come back to this road again."

He had glanced to the ocean brightening with the new day. A fog bank was a wisp on its horizon.

"My God!" said Mary, her face going white. "He is awake!"

"Quite ordinary," said Michael. "People do that every morning. And that fog is way out there - we'll be gone before it comes to land -"

"No. Keep going as fast as you safely can. We cannot be trapped in it - I cannot be trapped in it again!"

"Mary - it is way out there."

But it wasn't. It was all around them and it blinded them - totally.

"I told you Aaron is awake," she said very quietly.

Michael stopped the car.

"Don't do that! We passed the doctor's house. We are almost on the freeway!"

My God, thought Michael - what is illusion here and what is not?

"Go on. I know the road. He did not wake up in time to kill us."

Michael obeyed, and drove so slowly the car motor sputtered. Or he thought it did- if the car had a motor.

Or he had a car.

Or he was anywhere around.

The fog had energy that caressed the windshield, and Michael thought of her terrible accident, and all of her illness was as if it was his own. "I am so sorry," he said. He saw her so young, so bereft, and it was as if he sorrowed for her because she sorrowed so deeply for *him*. "Mary," he repeated, "I know how you suffered." The sentence was strange to him, but it was not to her. "I did not want my tears to reach you, or any of my pain," she said.

*What are we talking about?*

The fog seemed to veil its fall over violets he had wanted to pick for her as he always did when they were first in bloom.

Then the sky was clear and the fog was gone, only to linger

behind them on Aaron's road. "I had a strange vision from that damned stuff," he said.

"What was it?"

"Fog on violets. How is that for a bummer?"

"It is fog on violets in England. You always brought violets to me. You said they matched my eyes."

He shuddered. "Those tears - that pain - for John Keats."

"Yes. I know he knew of my suffering over his death - but I could not stop it!"

"Mary - one life at a time!"

"They meld. Every life is haunted by past ones."

He had felt the same thing himself back at the crazy house of tic uncle death. "We are ghosts of ourselves?"

"Yes."

"Why don't we remember?"

"Because one life is enough to bear."

"But not for you."

"I guess not." She looked back at the road still lost to fog. "I called you back to me. When there is the need, there is the reply."

"I am not what I am not," he said angrily. "No ghost of what *was* - ever."

"Maybe not," she said. "But it would be a shame."

"Why is that?"

"Because what is learned in one life can help another life - maybe even *save* that life!"

"How your fancy roams!"

"Molly always tells me that." She stretched, looking gorgeous. She looked at him and smiled, looking gorgeous. "Let's solemnly promise each other, in an oath even to God, that we will never go back to Aaron's."

"I told you I never would."

"Never let me. Promise."

"I will be your guardian?"

"More," she said.

They stopped and had breakfast, and it was marvelous for him to see her across a breakfast table, but it was more marvelous remembering her in her nightgown and without her nightgown.

The indecent one was alive and had had its breakfast on all the bars Michael had placed across his cave door.

In the car before they began the drive to the city, she gently traced his lips with her fingers. "They are still beautiful," she said. "You are still as handsome."

"Mary, you have to drop this fantasy that I am John Keats."

"You will remember," she said firmly.

"I will not," he replied as firmly.

"You don't remember," she smiled, "being of the sun, the moon and the stars? The very first light from the dark?"

"I don't remember that either," he smiled.

She continued to study his face, and gently caressed it with her fingers. "*This* time, we will marry," she said. "I will go to graduate school for awhile, but then we will marry."

"Mary, *slow down*. You do not know me at all."

"I know you better than you do."

"I have a horror of a marriage. Marriage is not for me, and I will never, *never* marry again."

"That shows how little you know about it."

"I am *not* your fancy - that love summoned becoming love returned."

"That shows how little you know about it," she repeated.

He kissed her because he could not stop himself. It became as necessary as breathing, and he wondered if he had the choice between a last kiss, and a last breath, which he would choose.

*You are the lover in your dream of an iced castle of death, corpses armored for nothing, stone angels forever tearless, the beadsman with frosted breath for the last counting of his beads as he and the fire before him die.*

*I am in love.* But he did not say it.

"You will remember," she said softly, after another kiss.

"Remember what? Kissing you as John Keats?"

"The magic casements. You will remember them."

Another kiss. "What are magic casements?"

She put his hand to her heart and its wild beating. "The casements into light."

He caressed her breast. "Like a window casement?"

"Yes."

"Where do they go?" He was kissing her throat, down onto the swelling of her breasts.

"Into the light of your soul."

He touched her face, caressed her soft hair, and he held her to his heart. She was so perfect, so fragile as all perfect things are. *I am as lost as that poor fool in my dream sneaking around in the ice palace.*

"Could I find those window casements?" he asked seriously.

"You created them for me," she said, as seriously.

"I am not John Keats. I would give you the world, but I have *never* created anything for you."

"I don't know if you *will* remember what you created for me."

"What happens if I should? I won't - but what if I should?"

"Then we are together again, and, for us, death did no more than absorb itself."

"You so positively know who *we* were."

"Yes."

"Well, I have enough trouble with who we are *now*."

"Why?"

He could not say. He did not know. The ship shape ship was sunk, and all of the safety and what was sure in life with it, and he was in an alien world, the captain without a ship to captain. He looked around them. People went into the restaurant and they came out of it. Cars passed them on the freeway, going north or going south, and it was as if they were not there at all. "How can I get through that window?" he asked.

"What window?"

"The magic casement window."

"When the need is there, the reply comes."

"What will I find aside from I was your lover?"

"The light that is love and the truth of beauty."

"Beauty has a truth?"

"Most certainly."

"He said that."

"Most certainly."

"I don't understand how truth can be beauty."

"You will," she said. "For us, you will do anything." She touched his face, and again, traced his lips, ever so gently with her fingers. "You had such beautiful lips - and eyes - We always wanted to make love - but couldn't."

"Now why would that be?"

"We couldn't get married."

"Too busy with his poetry?"

"His poetry was going to allow us the income for marriage."

"I can see why that did not work out."

She recoiled away from him. The time between them had been magic, ethereally magic, and it was as if he had taken the jewel of its center and smashed it to pieces. "How can you say such a cruel thing?" she whispered.

It was just a summer morning. People around them were just people around them, and the cars passing on the freeway made noise and smells.

She drew farther away from him, and not just physically. "John Keats was a great poet. Milton and Shakespeare did not equal him at the age in which he died."

It was as if he had never kissed her, caressed her breast, kissed her throat down to her beating heart - it was as if he had taken all of his tenderness to her, the pure enchantment of her being, her power to enthrall and enslave him, and left it all behind them to the fog of Aaron's road. "No marriage - no sex?"

"That was *your* idea. *You* - then."

"And *now*," he said, starting Betsy for the freeway.

"No marriage - no sex?"

"Yes."

"Are you poor?"

"Not rich. My causes and I just get by."

"Your reformation of capitalism? Your gnashing of the gnomes?"

He looked at her. "Were you listening to my conversations with your uncle when he was not conjuring up fog?"

"Molly hears everything, and she tells Meg, and Meg tells me. You do not find me attractive?"

"With or without clothes I think you must be the most beautiful woman on earth."

"Then let's go immediately to your place, wherever it is, and have the sex we could never have before!"

He shuddered and about disintegrated in two, his upper half and his bottom half having different goals. "That is a *terrible* thing to say! You are not some tramp! How can you denigrate yourself like this!"

"I am doing no such thing! I love you."

"You love John Keats, and John Keats is not here to do anything about it, is he?"

"He is - whether you know it or not. We fell in love at first sight last time, too," she added.

"Oh, God."

"It was at a dance - a ball for the veterans of Waterloo -"

"You read that."

"I *remember* that. And we cannot have sex until - when?"

"You don't know how lucky you are, Mary, that you found a *decent* man to tell this to."

"You were *always* a decent man," she said, as if this was one thing she remembered about John Keats she did not like.

In the city Michael found her a lovely and very expensive apartment, which she furnished from Aaron's money with lovely and expensive antiques. She was caught up in graduate school, and men in it saw her as enchanting as Michael could - had he chosen to be enchanted, which he now grew out of. *Will I let someone else control my life, all of my waking hours? No.*

Men began to cluster around her, like bees to their hive. He hated them. He hated hives and he hated bees, and he called them all damned drones and cursed them off the face of the planet where they could build their hives and make their honey on Mars.

He taught her how to drive and helped her pick out her car. When she had the time, in between the *bastardly buzzing* of the drones, they *companionably* dated, went dancing, to museums, hiked on the beaches and went on picnics in the redwoods. On one picnic they lay together and looked up at the wonder of light reaching down to them through the trees that were filtering sunlight when Jesus walked the earth. He looked at her and was weak with tenderness; she was looking at him so lovingly, it broke his heart. *Why can't I take this woman for my wife when I know I love her?*

Be controlled by someone else – this idiot passion?

*But she does not love ME, so how can I do that?*

"If you don't let John Keats die, I cannot live," he said suddenly.

"But all of our yesterdays are in all of our tomorrows," she replied.

"Why do you torture me - endlessly?" he asked in anguish.

The day was glimmering away, and then there was the evening star, and its rising made him sink into the deepest of despair.

"How am I torturing you?" she asked, doing it unbearably.

"You are shallow and fickle, and women don't love as deeply as men!" he said, and actually believed it. "If I gave you my heart, you would dig around the grave of John Keats and bury it with him!" *This is just lust - no I love and she loves bees and I want her so much and if Keats had this problem he was lucky to pass away from it!*

What do you do when someone has stolen your heart, your mind, and even your dreams at night? What do you do when her smile, the light in her eyes, her lashes, her lips, her perfection makes you ache to hold what can never be held? It was like trying to hold a shaft of sunlight, moonbeams on water, the Evening Star itself. It was like trying to make the magic in dreams face the dawn. He wanted every atom of her being, her soul, and he could not bear the pain of it. He felt so enflamed with love it was torture, and she was fickle and she was faithless and hid it all in a fancy for a dead poet.

"I am not going to see you anymore," he said to her one night as he took her to her door and refused to go into her apartment.

"Why won't you come in?"

"I said I am not going to see you any more."

"Why would you say such a silly thing?"

"I can't stand the pain of it."

"What pain?"

"Those bastardly damned drones that follow you like a wedding veil - that is the pain. Why do you allow it? Why don't you swat at them?"

"How can you possibly be jealous? I have told you I love you and want to marry you."

"You want sex with John Keats, and believe me, Mary, that is a real turn off. And all of those bastardly bees buzzing around you all of the time, so when I pick you up, I only see *them*. You are fickle and faithless and would not love as I love -*would* love - if I had the mind to."

"The *mind* to? The mind has no clue to love!" She looked dreamy. "It is almost December - and then it will be Christmas – glorious, glorious Christmas again!"

"What did you and John Keats do on Christmas?"

"We were engaged on Christmas Day, 1818," she said wistfully, searching his eyes to rush them both back there on that Christmas day of 1818.

She was so open, so innocent, so vulnerable, and he felt so entrapped within it all. "Talk about *long* engagements," he replied, and then he was horrified at what he had said.

She slapped his face. "You mock what saved me from Aaron. You mock the beauty of the deathless - you mock the treasure and the wonder of my soul - all I hold as sacred - you mock. You mock the possibility of the wonder of life itself!" She hid her face in her hands, and when she freed them, tears were in her eyes. "If you are not John Keats, I do not like you, and if you are John Keats I do not like you now, either."

"Mary, I should not have ridiculed what is so dear to you. I am sorry. So sorry."

"His poetry I still have. And Michael, you are more dead now than John Keats is."

And so they parted, and so all the mystical and the kind of fey magic that had come into his life with her - was gone with her.

# *Seven*

Women are all awful, all deadly, and *all* mad, Michael continued to say to Betsy who purred like a kitten, hardly ever demanded oil changes, new tires or even gasoline when he sometimes forgot to keep her in it. If that did happen, she saw them through and ran out of gasoline right in front of a pump. If he turned the key she started right up. If he turned her wheel left, she went that way. If she turned the wheel right, she went that way and it all was so simple, and if women could be as human it would be a wonderful gift for the earth and for every man on it.

So he was a fool. That was better than being a pollen patch. He had to have order, system, logic to build a case around, and he liked an intelligent, *reasoning* judge. He liked plans; he *had* to have plans, where he could make what was necessary in the future, start *now*.

His life was ordered again, just as it was before he went to Aaron's madhouse, or death house, or whatever. He must *not* have fallen in love with Mary, but if he had, love was an illusion, just as she said the fog was that was conjured up by her tic uncle.

His life was ordered again. Thank God.

He began to have nightmares, terrible, terrible nightmares, as if he was trapped in the fog that he and Mary had left behind them on Aaron's road. Within the nightmare, the life he was living within it, he knew the fog to be no more and no less than death. Shrouded to blindness within it, he was clinging to a wall, and *is this wall my life* he wondered as he clung to a precarious hold. He could hear sounds of an ocean below him. As he struggled to stay alive and on the wall, he knew he had to enter the casement of a window that dimly reflected a light. Then, so clearly, in almost a blinding revelation, he knew he had to reach that window, go through its casement or Mary would die. The ocean below became more menacing. One slip and he was in it and being swept away to his death. *Mary! Mary!* He was sobbing in despair. In all of his life he had never known the depths of such anguish. Inch by inch he groped his way to the dim light above him, barely visible above the fog. He was clinging to a wall of roughly grouted bricks. His hands were bleeding from their sharpness and he knew that he would find light if he remembered how to create it. He could not remember. There was magic even in the fog, but he did not know how to find it. He was lost because she was. *My dearest girl – my dearest girl, I have lost you.* He was saying this aloud and the words awakened him and there were tears upon his face.

He lay still, in a nether world between sleep and awakening, as if it was a world within the chiming of the midnight hour, the pause between the thought of creation, and the act of creation, between the ending of one day and the beginning of the next. "My dearest girl," he whispered.

"I keep having this nightmare," he told his secretary. "I mean it is a horror. It haunts all my days and all my dreaming nights."

"What is it?" she asked.

"I am clinging to a wall, and the only way I can keep from falling into the ocean to die is to find a window to get into a house." He did not say that Mary was in the house because he did not want to.

"What does the house stand for?" asked his secretary, loving to do dreams for all of her friends.

"A house is a house," he said, annoyed. "Maybe the wall is life," he ventured, wondering if he had thought that during the horror of the nightmare.

"Did you know that in your dream?"

"Maybe. Yes. I think so."

"So what would the *window* be?" she asked as if she were a teacher to a dull student.

"A window is a window, and a house is a house," he frowned.

"A window brings light to the house. The wall is life and the window is - entrance into what gives your life light."

"You sound like someone else I know."

"Do you find the window?"

"No."

"Why not?"

"I can't see it."

"Why not?"

"It is too foggy."

"What is the fog?"

"Fog!" said Michael impatiently. "A house is a house and a window is a window, and fog is fog!"

"What is the house?"

"I just said. It is a damned house!"

The secretary looked dreamy, or dream riddled, or spaced out. "The wall is life - the house - your mind?" She nodded, finding the right answer. "The window is to bring light *beyond* the mind -"

"Who wants to go there?" he shuddered.

"Michael, you fool, the window is a casement into your *soul!*"

"Then if I have a soul, why didn't I find the bloody thing?"

"Because, Michael, you said its casement was hidden by fog!"

"So what is the fog?" *It is your death,* a quiet thought spoke.

"The *acceptance* of death!" his secretary beamed.

Michael scowled. One Mary in his life was enough.

"You know, Michael, lately, you are really looking terrible. Whatever you have started doing, you had better stop."

"As if I could," he groaned. "As if I could!"

"Even your nightmare is telling you this."

"How?"

"You aren't finding what you are trying to find."

"Which is?" he growled.

"The light into your soul."

"What is in there?"

"The glory of yourself."

"Of *myself?*" he asked grimly. He was not looking for *himself* in the house. He was looking for Mary, and that, in a dream, he was not able to deny.

The nightmare was the same and it wasn't. He was always on the wall, scared of death, totally, totally afraid of death. He was always looking for a light to find the window, a window that he could enter so he could save Mary - and become alive.

"Where does this garbage in nightmares come from?" he asked his secretary the next week.

"From past lives," she said promptly, and he had thought her intelligent!

"It sticks around like the Evening Star," he said in sarcasm.

"How lovely!" his secretary beamed and he groaned and went on reading his brief of a case he hated, but generally, now he about hated everything.

As if it was not bad enough to be out of control in sleep, when he was not - what thought appeared and reappeared - like a sickening clown in a circus? *I should have made love to her when I had the chance!*

"Am I going mad?" he asked his secretary.

"Well, you are still looking good if you are."

"Looking good."

"That is a fine attribute, Michael. Don't knock it."

"I want sex with a girl so much - I cannot stand it!" Did he say this or think it?

His secretary was not shocked. "Well, if males did not feel this way about us, we might all be murdered," she said, having trouble with her husband.

"But I did not do it when she - she -"

His secretary was totally interested.

"Well - she thought it was a good idea."

"And you disagree?"

"I love her! How can I do that? How can I be so *crazy* in love?"

"Michael -"

"I feel - if I have lost her, I have lost myself!"

"Oh, Michael," said his secretary, getting tears in her eyes and blowing her nose about it. "That and your evening star image are so beautiful! I didn't know you had poetry in your soul!"

"Don't say that!" he yelled.

His life had lost its center. It was as if it had just fallen out of his life like his ship shape ship. His goal to alleviate suffering had lost all of its allure. *How could I love her?*

She is mad. She is gorgeous. But she trails bees.

*I will get over her. I will not make love to her, marry her, live with her or seek one more of those frenzied kisses. This is my sacred vow to myself, to God and every heavenly host that ever beamed up to heaven.*

And so he went out and bought them a house that they could live in together. He had seen her parents' lovely Victorian, and he searched for one just like it, or close to it, and he found it. Then he spent all of his deceased parents' savings and his savings down to the last penny to make it a dream house for Mary.

Being without his savings and not being able to watch them grow up sent him into a panic, so now that was added to his growing and *growing* sexual frustration, and *who* caused him all of this misery?

Not Betsy!

And so he called on Mary and drove her to see *their* house, but she did not know about the *their* yet. Greeting him, she was polite. She was distant, but she was polite. And God, she was even more gorgeous, and he had thought she had pushed gorgeous to the limit.

"Michael, what a house you bought for yourself!" she exclaimed as Betsy approached it. "Could it be half as lovely in the inside?"

"See for yourself," he said soberly, and drove Betsy into the garage that had been a great carriage house. "I could live here, right in this beautiful garage!" she said.

He said nothing. He should have said please live with me in the house so I can make love to you until I die.

The first room that sent her into rapture was the kitchen. She loved the brick around the stove, around the windows that looked out on a small but beautiful garden. "You should plant your vegetables there," she said. "There would be the sun for it."

He said nothing.

She seemed not to notice and went into the dining room off the pass pantry to it from the kitchen. "A fireplace!" she squealed. It had a bay window, too, as did the front room, and she loved the antique Victorian fireplace he had left intact. But it was his richly paneled library with the rock fireplace he had had added that made her breathless. "This is the most beautiful room in the world," she said, touching his law books, even some of the still empty shelves. "Do you know what my father said about books?" she said softly, her eyes wet.

"No," he replied.

"He said that with them we share in the fire of their creator."

Upstairs he had had the master bath done in her favorite color, lilac - lilac tile and with violets in the Victorian wallpaper. He saw them making love in the large shower. Or anywhere.

"This is enchanting," she said, her face glowing with appreciation. "Did you choose all of the decor?"

"Yes."

"It is all that I would have chosen - had I been asked."

He let that slide.

The master bedroom had a skylight right over his bed, and an extended sun room, all glass, to the left of where he had placed his/their bed, and the sun room looked out at the bay and up into the sky for all of the sunsets to come.

She sat on his bed. You are having other furniture in here?"

"Of course."

"You have marvelous taste, Michael. Isn't this a rather large house for a bachelor?"

"No." Now was the time to propose marriage. *My dearest girl, marry me and be my love, and we will all wonders of life and heaven prove -*

"In such a beautiful old house - *your* house - why do you look so glum?"

"I don't like to be *pushed* into anything."

"Here? You were *pushed* - here?"

"I don't like you dating. I think it is a terrible thing for you to do to me."

She got up, straightened up the bedspread. "That is no concern of yours, Michael. You said you had stopped calling on me. So why did you bring me here?"

"Swarms of them - *buzzing bastards, buzzing, buzzing* - I could not commit myself to a *shallow - flirty - fickle - woman!*"

"I don't think you could commit to a woman of any kind. I think you are wise not to marry again. Now drive me back to my apartment, and all I can say is, I hope you and your lovely home are very happy together."

And on the way to her apartment that was *all* she did say to him. She locked the door noisily behind her once she was inside.

He lay in his great bed that would love all of the sunsets making brilliant the sky and the bay. He tried to sleep. He had no luck. His eyes were sealed wide open. He went downstairs for wine, which he drank out of the bottle. She was supposed to be here with him now, and they would have that Agnes poem sex thing, but here he was alone, his antique Victorian clock hissing away downstairs - ass - ass - ass, bong, bong, bong, bong – ASS, ASS, ASS.

The indecency was out of its cave roaring hell fire again. "Why did I not propose?" he asked aloud, and the beast took such giant bites of its cave bars they set him to groaning.

He phoned her. She did not want to see him. "Ever?"

"Ever."

"Why?"

"I don't like you."

"But you kissed me so wildly - when you didn't even know me -"

"Now I know you."

"I can't be who I am not -"

"You can't be who you are," she said and hung up.

He went ahead with the same old nightmare in which he didn't find anything but fog over a threatening ocean, and his waking time was as bad.

I'll sell the damned thing, Michael thought of the house. He had bought it and restored it for HER dream house, not his. He phoned the realtor who had sold it to him in the first place. "I want to sell the damned thing," he said.

The realtor was young and pretty and recently divorced. "Things didn't work out between you and the lady?" she asked with real sympathy.

"I didn't talk of any lady," he said, remembering clearly he had not.

"Michael, you did not have to. It was in your eyes, all of the time you were planning the restoration of the house. I am so sorry it did not work out."

"It's for the best," he said, as if he were not dying.

"Maybe something could be worked out yet," said the realtor, and Michael knew the participants she was thinking of, herself with himself, but the beast below did not even open one of its multiple numberless eyes.

"I don't think so," he said, pretending he did not know what she said by not saying it, the way in which women always talked, because it was a part of their ovaries and that whole system.

Christmas was coming, that damned holy day of all enchantments for Mary and Co. of *December 25, 1818*. The realtor had a buyer for his house, and at a very, very good profit, for they were into many fireplaces and lilac baths, too, and the view - the one from the master bedroom that would meld fire shadows on the ceiling with a moonlit bay and sky.

He could *not* sell their union of fire shadows and moonlight, and phoned the realtor and told her so. He had not yet finalized the sales' agreement, and the realtor sounded happy he had backed out. "You do not mind losing your commission?" he asked in astonishment.

"You have a right to change your mind. I had left some details out of the contact. I am glad you are keeping that gorgeous house, but we need to go into some details -"

He was a lawyer. He knew the contract was not flawed, and told her so over dinner. They began to date, and she was intelligent, charming and fun to be with. He furnished the rest of his house with the large bonus he got for Christmas, and the large fee just earned concerning the poor who could not pay and the rich who could and did. Now he had little in the bank, nothing in savings and nothing out at interest. It did not matter in the least. He was in hell anyway.

He knew where Mary and one of the buzzers were going for Christmas dinner. He found that out very cleverly, for he wanted to take his new girlfriend there, too, and drive a stake through the heart of his constant yearning for the princess of tic castle.

He saw Mary and the drone buzzer enter, and began flirtation with his new girl that made her glow in delight and Mary stop dead in her tracks.

"Do you know that girl?" asked the realtor.

"I drove her here from her uncle's home. He is one of our clients."

"Oh. Well, you really made an impression on her."

"I think we should have sex," Michael said suddenly, and the realtor choked on her drink. She quickly recovered. "I was wondering when you would ask." She had been doing more than that. She had been praying and doing yoga and real meditation over it. "Why should we finish our dinner?" she asked eagerly.

But they did finish, and she was cooing over him, adoring him, and he was watching the effect on Mary.

She was not looking happy, even if the drone was buzzing into her ear and was heading right down her neck. Michael leaped from his table in fury. He grabbed the drone and slapped him off of her. "Your sick and oversexed behavior is really disgusting," he snarled. "It is disturbing the whole restaurant!"

The drone quivered free. "Who are *you*?"

"Have you had the poetry sex test yet?"

Glasses stopped tinkling; in fact, they froze in mid air as heads turned to Michael, who brushed himself off, as if he had spattered bee parts all over his best suit. "Good, you are breathing again. I hope I did not squash you too much," he half apologized.

"Why would you disturb me at all?"

"Impulse -" He turned to Mary. "I thought this was *our* holy and sacred night."

"What?" Mary was ashen, but no more so than the realtor. She was hastily gathering up her purse and what had suddenly fallen from it.

"Now here is what I am going to do," said Michael to Mary, and the little bee looked as if his buzzing days were over. "See that beautiful girl over at my table?"

"I saw her when I first came in."

"Well," he whispered in her ear, "we are going to make love tonight, just the *two* of us. And guess what? *John Keats will not be present!*"

And he and the realtor, either Susan, or Margaret or Jane - or whatever - left.

He drove her home and took her to the door. "I'm not coming in," he said.

"I thought we were going to have sex."

"I find - I can't."

"Why not?"

"I am not in love with you."

She embraced him. "Good sex can lead to love," she said. Gently he freed himself. "I am already in love with someone else."

Christmas lights were up on the houses he could see from his own. They looked terrible. It was cold, cold, and women were so shallow and so fickle they should not have the chance to crush a man's heart. If he heard one more Christmas carol he would yell. If another person told him to have a happy new year, he would kill him. He was curt to even his victims of corporate fascism. He had not driven a stake deep into the heart of the fancy and the glory of love.

Finally, to his relief, the damnable cheerful lights came down. It was a dark dismally wet January, and he suddenly knew how to win her back. She wanted John Keats, so he would find him for her! *He would be John Keats, fresh out of his grave!*

That night he rushed into the library, right up to the shadow librarians whom he had always regarded as more shadow than substance. "Where would I find the Department of English Literature?" he whispered, because he always saw everyone whispering in libraries; it was an unwritten law, like proper gentlemen keeping their indecents away from formal dining.

A young gum -chewing librarian looked him over, passed him with an A with honors, and said, "You are in the Department of English Literature, and all literature in general."

Michael was in such a rush to carry out his new love plan he wanted help without *further* delay. "Have you heard of a poet named John Keats?" he asked.

"Is he American?" she flirted. "It does ring a bell -"

A librarian with snow-white hair, and a really lovely face, turned to her young counterpart as if she had just done pee on the library floor. "Cathy-y!" she gasped, as if Cathy was doing it again.

"John Keats?" fumbled Cathy, grasping at some straw in her mind.

"*John Keats,*" hissed the snow maiden. "The greatest poet of the Romantic age. *The Romantic Age!* Ring one bell?"

Looking up into the earnest handsome face of Michael, Cathy

was hearing every bell ring since they first began to do it, long, long ago. "I can help you with the computer search," Cathy said.

"I can use the computer," Michael smiled and did so. The snow maiden apparently wanted to pull off Cathy's head. "No one *ever* equaled his poetry by age twenty-four," she snapped, and Michael heard the *Mary* rage and thought, *I have to find his poems. They seem to have a real effect on women, Praise the Lord!*

He found the Keats' life/poetry volume, and sat down with it in the middle of two old men. *Where do I look?* He went to the snow maiden. "There is a poem Keats wrote - but I do not know its name."

The snow maiden looked bitter. "You young people," she said in strong disapproval.

"The poem is about some girl who takes off her clothes and they rustle about her knees - and it is full moon -"

"*The Eve of St. Agnes.*" The snow maiden turned away as if he was not worth another word. Michael went back to his book between the two old men. They were reading ancient poetry or literature - one in Greek, and the other in Latin, so no purity perfection could be lost in mistranslation. So engrossed were they in their purity quest and the glory of spending their last days in it, they glared at Michael for the two second interruption he caused when they took their eyes away from their books to watch him sit down.

Michael went for *The Eve of St. Agnes* immediately. He looked ahead and groaned at the poem's length, and received more glares from his either side. He read. *And* read. "Why this is all fore play," he said, thinking he was just thinking it, and not saying it.

Both neighbors raised shocked white eyebrows. "We are *really* getting into the *sensual* here," Michael explained to them. "Ah, here at last. *Union.* Wow, *what sex!*"

The two old men lost interest in their reading. "Who is the poet?" asked one, a professor of dead languages.

"John Keats," said Michael, reading on after love's consummation to see what happened next. "Hmm, this man must have been *always* cold. Reading this could give you pneumonia and -"

"And?" said both old men, together, as if using one breath.

Michael glanced through the pages again. "Listen and freeze to death! 'Bitter chill - frozen grass, numb fingers, freezing statues, pale latticed chill, and silent as a tomb, full on the casement shone the wintry moon- soft and chilly nest - frost wind blows - sharp sleet pattering against the windows -' "

"The foreplay, man - the foreplay!"

"Why that's almost the whole damned poem!" whispered Michael. He moved to face both fascinated faces. "Listen to me. *This poem is magic!* I met this gorgeous girl who wants sex even if you mention the name of John Keats! And if you just *mention* this poem - *she demands it!*"

"A modern poet?" asked one.

"1795 - 1821."

"A modern poet. I am still fifty years before Christ," said the dead language scholar.

"Well, *I* have reached 50 AD," replied the other.

"Well, *I* am off to buy this volume, if I can!" said Michael, and he left on a half run, and the two men looked at his doing this with disapproval. "You must not run in a library," one whispered to the other.

They started to go home. Both looked at the Keats' volume of poetry that Michael had left on the table with their own books. "These young men nowadays," one said, shaking his head in disapproval. He grabbed for the Keats' volume.

"All they think of is *sex*," said the other, getting the volume in his hands and arms first. He pushed away with it to the check out desk as fast as his walker would carry him.

# Eight

Mary watched the sliver of the January moon grow, and her heart really hurt. How could he bitterly humiliate her and her sacred belief that love never dies and lovers will always seek and find each other on earth as they already had done in heaven? And he had mocked her in front of a beautiful woman who was his date, on *their engagement* anniversary. How would she remember in her soul and he forget in his? How could he so vehemently deny the glory he was, and the glory they had shared when they fell so deeply in love?

And how could he say he was going to make love to this woman? He wouldn't. He couldn't.

She sat down on her bed and watched the moon as if it could speak to her, or - as if there ever would be for them another full moon of St. Agnes Eve. Michael, Michael, her heart mourned. But deeper lay the question she had never before addressed. Michael, you scorn John Keats. Would you so scorn what you were? She was so mixed up. What if her fancy had led her nowhere but to Aaron's mockery of it?

She cried before her period. She cried during her period. And she continued to cry after it. She went into the bathroom and washed her tear swollen eyes. She looked at herself, the stranger within the mirror. *I was always so sure. I thought I had summoned him to me again. Did I really create John Keats as my lover to create a sanctuary for myself? Did I create his return to deny the death of my parents, my own death to come?*

*Are the dark corners of the mind - really - its ultimate reality?*

Lines whispered into her mind, his unfinished masterpiece - *The Eve of St. Mark.*

Upon a Sabbath day it fell;
Twice holy was the Sabbath-bell,
That call'd the folk to evening prayer . . .

No. *Cut it off.* The magic casements into the truth of beauty had died with John Keats. A tall handsome man had saved her life, a charming intelligent man who was fickle and shallow. He was not the John Keats she remembered. Perhaps, John Keats was not the John Keats she remembered. Yet, when she said his poetry, her favorite, his *Ode to a Nightingale,* why did it seem as if a window to the past had been quietly left open for her?

My God, she thought, drying her face. *Am I my own ghost? Are we haunted by our lives - long vanished to nothing but dreams?*

Oh, God, *Oh, Michael,* she moaned, and each night the moon grew and silvered more and more her part of the city. The beautiful woman he now dated could be in his bed, and he could be making love to her, when she had flung herself naked on him, and he had done no more but jump out of bed, and so fast, they both landed on the floor. This moon could be radiating light to him, his new love, from the bay view window, and from the ceiling of his sunroom, open to the sky.

Tender toward him, then bitter toward him, she suffered.

She wept tenderly for her Keats who remained so *stubbornly* dead.

A long letter had come from Meg, Aaron apparently paying a bonus to get mail out over his lethal road. "Dearest Mary," Meg had written. "I know you are having a wonderful time in graduate school, and I know how you love to learn, but don't you think you should marry John Keats right away? How many girls who love him get to marry him? To have your dream of TWO - TWO lifetimes come true?"

Mary put down the letter. *My dreams of one lifetime could not even come true.*

"Mother has Aaron on raw vegetables and fruits, home grown in season, as you know, and little meat, which we do not have here except for our chickens, anyway. Aaron - Aaron is asking about you through Michael (Keats) and he is very, very happy that you are doing so well in school. MARY WHY HAVEN'T YOU AND MICHAEL GOTTEN MARRIED? Anyway, Aaron understands how you fear the road to and from his house, and he just asks now that you do that one simple thing to get his fortune. He still has a horror of being embalmed alive, and wants you to look at his body after he is dead, to be sure that he IS dead. It does seem so little to ask. Mother and I both think so. He is so good to you - now - at least - and he is so kind to mother and me. Mary, dear sister I never had, how can he hurt you when he is dead? Mother sends her love, and of course Aaron does, too. Love always, Meg."

Mary took her mother's volume on John Keats and read.

> A thing of beauty is a joy forever:
> Its loveliness increases; it will never
> Pass into nothingness; but will keep
> A bower quiet for us, and a sleep
> Full of sweet dreams, and health, and quiet breathing.

Beauty- his truth of the timeless. All he wanted was to quietly breathe, to live, to love. My darling, my all, she wept, drenching the page, and generally ruining its shape.

When she could not sleep, due to the bright moonlight, she did not close the drapes, and she sought the moonlight as much as she sought her sorrow. She said *Ode on a Grecian Urn,* right up and through its last verse.

> Thou shalt remain, in midst of other woe
> Than ours, a friend to man, to whom thou say'st,
> 'Beauty is truth, truth beauty.' That is all
> Ye know on earth, and all ye need to know.

*He* brought her some degree of comfort - just some degree. *The Eve of St. Agnes* was just too painful for her memory run through, but *To Autumn* was calm, tranquil, short, and would allow grief to fade into the sweet serenity of that autumn he had immortalized.

Season of mists and mellow fruitfulness,
Close bossom-friend of the maturing sun;
Conspiring with him how to load and bless
With fruit the vines that round the thatch eaves run;
To bend with apples the mossed cottage trees,
And fill all fruit with ripeness to the core;

To swell the gourd, and plump the hazel shells
With a sweet kernel; to set budding more,
And still more, later flowers for the bees,
Until they think warm days will never cease,
For summer has o'er-brimmed their clammy cells...

Mary covered TO AUTUMN with her tears, and generally soddened it out, too. *My dearest, how could you have written that horror of an epitaph for yourself? Here lies a man whose name was writ in water -*

She touched the cold glass of her windows, latticed with the enchantment of wind and moon shadows. *How can he be what he is now?* How could such a tender man be born again to be so cruel? Flaunt another woman in her face, flirt with her while she cooed at him like a drooling turtledove - and to come over and call her date a *buzzing bastard* - and the humiliation of his poetry *sex test!* Sex? She saw him holding and loving that woman. She just could not stand it but the image remained, and she did not know all of it but what she did not know would be wondrous. She remembered his hand on her breast, as if it were tenderly caressing her very heart, and when he returned her kisses outside of that restaurant of the freeway - she felt something unleashed between them that left her craven for completion.

She could not sleep for night after night. The moon mocked by getting more full and perfect. Darkness came to be enveloped in silvered magic. The evening star shone first and it shone last, and its sweetness was unbearable. It seemed to follow them when they had first met in 1818, and so sure she was that it had followed them, she lost all doubt that she was Frances Brawne, and that Michael was John Keats. An unconscious John Keats. A John Keats still in his grave, or yet unborn into that very brief life. *I called you, did you not hear? When our love was so powerful - you would not even read my last letters to you? When you could not even hear my name, and wanted to know how I was in some kind of a secret code?*

I still see you, your eyes swimming with tears when I pleaded for a last kiss and you refused me.

Beloved of all my yesterdays and all my dreams past and yet to come - I will have that kiss!

*There is a tide of divinity, of the rapture of reunion - and comets may fall in the sky, and great suns vanish, but that tide is and always will be!*

She wept before her brief sleep, and from it, she wept again. He loved her. There was no doubt he did. It was always in his eyes, this life and their last one. The turtledove was cooing alone.

Surely.

He was still jealous, jealous over nothing as he always was. *Bees buzzing down my neck* - just as silly as his having a terror of her loving another man after that soldier ball of 1818 when they fell instantly in love.

*Tomorrow night the moon will be full. Tomorrow night is the Eve of St. Agnes. You gave us the rapture of union in that poem and that night casts a light upon us forever. Do you think you can really forget what your soul created?*

She went to her window and across the moonlit city she spoke to him. But she still saw the cooing turtledove, the beautiful older and sophisticated woman, and she shook with anger and with jealousy. "Tomorrow night is the Eve of St. Agnes," she said to him. "And in it the moon will be full, just as it is supposed to be. And tomorrow night I am going to your house and show you what love is all about.

You son of a bitch!"

# Nine


Since he had read *The Eve of St. Agnes*, Michael was on a joy roll. He had it all figured out. With so much fore play going on in her mind, she would come to him on St. Agnes Eve, without a doubt, and she would say those same lines from the poem just as she took off her clothes, and then she would do the exact same thing she had done in his bedroom at the smiling tick castle, but this time he would *not* do the same thing, that is dump her on the floor. He knew John Keats now like the back of his hand, the thing of violets between them, and he sent her a large bouquet of them, and in it he sent a card on which he had written, *hold not one atom of yourself from me*. It was close enough. He did not want to suddenly burst out with all of St. John's poetry, for even she might suspect something awry about that. Now with the violets sent and the full moon coming up on the Eve of St. Agnes, he had it made. The indecent below was singing and swallowing a whole sea cave continent with more and more relish. Michael could hardly sleep now and tried to take an afternoon nap, and could not sleep through that, either. The thought of saint sex with her was too powerful to shake. The thought of marrying, *before* the saint sex, had flown away with Saint John, now safely in heaven or in a statue off somewhere.

But something terrible had happened before his joy roll. He had been stricken with horror. WHEN - WAS -THE -EVE - OF - ST. AGNES? There was no clue in the fore play poem, except it was a damned chilly night.

So just before closing time he had found a bookstore, and rushed into it, with shoes and coat, and his pajamas he had not had time to change out of. "I have - HAVE to know when it is St. Agnes Eve!" he gasped.

"Oh, my God," said the frightened clerk, not sure whether 911 was better than total surrender.

"I must know the date of the Eve of St. Agnes!" Michael lamented. "My God, what if it has *passed?*"

He looked so distraught and grief stricken the clerk decided he was just unstrung, very handsome, and not a threat to cash or chastity. "Now my dear man," she said, feeling sorry for him shivering in his pajamas she could see under his unbuttoned coat - and he looked so filled with terror that he had missed this Agnes Eve woman, she thought he was going to burst into tears.

"There, there," she added kindly. "Is this lovely Agnes Eve in the city - THIS city?"

"She's not a saint *today* - she passed on some time ago. It is really an evening named for her." Michael was getting his thoughts together.

"Oh, how nice. What did she do?"

"She stayed a virgin."

"Well, God love her!"

Michael shivered, and realized, finally, he had not really completed changing out of his pajamas, mainly because he could see them still on his legs. He was very embarrassed, but he was also very determined that all of the Keats' fore play should be put to some use, no matter how many years later.

"I wonder if the *Farmer's Almanac* would have the date?" the clerk asked.

"This has to do with a love poem, not farming," said Michael, "And a full moon."

"Whose the poet?" asked the virgin-admiring clerk.

"John Keats, if you have ever heard of him."

The clerk turned herself on as if it was the Fourth of July, and cast off her age for a calf sick MARY LOOK.

"Not you?" groaned Michael. "Not you, too?"

"Why - how could I have forgotten! That poem made me marry a terrible bastard, but I still love it! THE EVE OF ST. AGNES BY JOHN KEATS - a sensual - lyrical tribute to love!"

"It's damned fore play!" Michael contradicted.

The love radiated clerk looked at him in horror. "It is no such thing - with all of those angels -"

"All I want to know is the date - THE DATE - when all of this lyrical fore play went on! WHAT IS THE DATE OF ST. AGNES EVE?"

"I know. I remember now."

"And it is -?"

"It's January 20th."

Michael gave the Keats'- smitten woman a hug, and tears of joy came into his eyes. There was time! He had time to prepare for her St. Agnes Eve arrival, and their Saint feast and their Saint sex! "Life is so good," he breathed, as he rushed away. At the signal, a car bumped into the rear end of Betsy. She received no more than a nudge. He smiled and waved at the man behind him who had the car that had done the nudging. "Life is GOOD!" he yelled to him.

"Why in the hell is that?" the man snarled.

Michael took two days off - one day to clean up the house so it was shining and perfect, and the next day to prepare the Saint sex feast.

He moved all of his clothes to one side of his closet to make room for her clothes to come. He had bought HIS and HER towels, mauve with the letters purpled to arouse her Keats' purple riots of poetic passion. He bought more violets wherever he could find them. He cleaned the fuzz balls out of the refrigerator and stocked it with champagne. *What was in the sex feast?* He poured over the poem, and took it right along to the gourmet section at his local grocery. He said to a clerk busily dusting the gourmet items, "I have a *Saint* feast to prepare, and I have to have - let's see - candied apples, quince, plums and a candied gourd. Isn't that some kind of a pumpkin?"

The clerk was willing to help, but he was quickly dispatched by motherly shoppers who found everything he could use. They smiled at him affectionately; they were thrilled he was into the spiritual in buying for a Saint feast.

"Now what is this manna I have to have?" Michael asked.

"I think Jesus was looking for that in the Bible," said one.

"He *created* it," contradicted the other lady.

"He just called it down from Heaven," growled a third.

Michael found dates and jellies, which he hoped would do by

being smoother than a creamy curd, but he found sugar in them, and chemicals, so he put them back on the shelf.

"I make my own jellies with honey," said another. "I can bring it to you before tonight, if you wish."

"Young man, I have my *fruit* sweetened jelly in my car, made from *organic* fruit from my yard. I was taking some to my daughter in law, but I can give it to you now, and give her more later."

Michael thanked her, took some and added cheese to the Saint feast. Sour dough bread would have to do for the manna.

He worked all afternoon making the food right, and he rushed out for more fresh violets which cost him more than the food, and put them around the food on a great silver platter that should have been a silver basket, but no store had one that was large enough for his mantra meal.

Michael nervously poured over the poem again. *Lavendered* sheets? But they were *blanched* sheets - he took this problem to the nearest store that had sheets. Sheet color had nothing to do with it; he needed a lavender SCENT. No one had it, so he found lavender soap, and rubbed it all over his white (blanched) sheets. He put the pieces that were left in the mauve bathroom. It should have violets there, too, so he rushed out and bought some, all of his violets now probably costing as much as the mauve tile job, but fresh violets were for the color of her eyes. And they were John Keats' favorite flower and probably the girl he loved had blue violet eyes, too.

Soon he and Betsy had gone to so many places, Betsy was out of gas, and he was out of time, for the moon of the night that turned her into a sex goddess was already rising in the sky. *Hold on, hold on* he commanded the moon, for he had to fill his silver bucket with ice and the huge bottle of the most expensive champagne in the world.

He showered, shaved, brushed his teeth, combed his hair every ten minutes, smiled at himself in the mirror, brushed his teeth again, although they were white and perfect, but he kept having this feeling that he had not tidied up *their* closet, that he had left something in it awry, which his parents had not ever learned to accept in his childhood toy closet. No. The closet was as neat as a pin, along with the rest of *their* house.

His social indecency and he were now bonding in perfect harmony.

He left his Tiffany hall lamp lighted. There was no use to stay *downstairs* and wait for her. When the moonlight got strong enough, she would make a beeline for his bedroom, just as she did at the Tick house. He smoothed out the lavendered sheets again, smelled them to see if they were still lavendered. He had a time choosing the color of pajamas and robe, trying different combinations, and then settled on wine for both. He was more nervous than he had been in all of his life. What if she did not come? What if the full moon, now full on *the Eve of St. Agnes,* no longer drove her into sexual frenzies? What if she really had caught on *he was not John Keats?* Still - the bouquet of violets and the plea for loyal atoms should swing her back into that direction.

Of course neither had been delivered, but Michael did not know it.

He went into the mauve bath and gave the violet bouquet in it more water, when it was already drowning. He looked into the mirror and combed his hair again. *Had he left his front door unlocked? My God, had he not left* the front door open, so she could jump up the stairs to ravish him? He ran downstairs, taking two at a time, in a real terror.

He wasn't stupid. He had left the front door unlocked.

Back up the stairs again, and up and up went the moon, and it was getting stronger and stronger, as was the bonding between him and his social indecency.

The grandfather clock struck below. *Where was she?* He had everything - *everything* - ready.

He went to his windows, looked out at the night where the pale enchantment of the moon met the pale enchantment of the bay. He blessed every light crossing its bridge, and every soul following that light. "Godspeed," he said to them all, his eyes moist - so smitten was he with love and its tenderness toward all life.

She did not come to his neighborhood, to his house, to his bedroom, and the ice melted around the best champagne in the world, and finally, its huge bottle bobbed around in warm water as the bathroom violets were doing in their death throes. The platter of bread, candied fruit, dates, nuts, and cheeses survived, but the violets around their edge were shrinking all up.

It was a disaster. He had seen himself tenderly take her to himself, in all ways, and he had memorized some poetry to go along with the wonder of it all - and here he was alone with his dreams, desire - and despair.

The indecent was miserable and passing it on.

*What had happened?* Had he read all of the fore play wrong? He scrambled for his Keats' volume, and went right to *THE EVE OF ST. AGNES*, already underlined in its key portions.

*What time was the sex?* There was the banquet, which was by his bed except for the manna - no lute to play - he could no*t* or *would not* do that - the wreathed pearls slipping from her hair, the unclasping of warm jewels one by one - loosening of the fragrant bodice - rich attire rustling to her knees - half hidden, *like a mermaid in sea-weed* - Oh, John Keats, you were good, VERY GOOD! He read on. Here it was. Damn, the lover made love to her under a SETTING MOON! When was that going to be? When would this damn moon set? *Fade?*

It was too much. It was too awful, and she was not going to come to him anyway, for she had figured out, at last, he was not John Keats, and the violets and atoms' plea had not changed her mind. Women were fickle. They flirted and flirted, and never gave away their hearts. They kept them only to stay alive so they could smell their perfumes. He had drunk all of the champagne. He looked up at the moon, still light as hell, and he yelled to it, "Set - you *son of a bitch.*" It glowered back - a big snarling snake eye. He went downstairs and got all of the wine for tomorrow's plan and drank it all up too, and right in the middle of the lavender scented *blanched* sheets, he passed out cold.

This is how Mary found him. It was St. Agnes Eve when he was going to turn into sculptured stone of passion, not with drunkenness. "This is the second time you have done this to me!" she yelled, throwing a wine bottle so it barely glanced off of his head. He sat up and rubbed his head with surprise. He looked up at her, and rubbed his head some more. "Why does a full moon drive you into such a frenzy?" he asked.

"What?"

"At the tick house it made you jump on me naked and demand sex, and now when I have the Saint sex feast all laid out for it, you arrive to throw a bottle at me!"

She looked at the food and the shriveled violets, and her face glowed, softened, grew totally angelic. "You remember! *My God, you remember!*"

He continued to rub his head. "You threw a bottle at me!" he mourned.

"Well -" she began.

"Well - *what?*"

"Well, it is not as if the bottle was *full*," she said.

# Ten

The next morning they were married. He gathered the violets that had survived, and she carried them as a wedding bouquet.

"I *read* about you two and the violets," he said

"You read about John Keats?"

"From a huge thick volume. And his effect on women is amazing."

"You read his poetry?"

"Some."

"Why?"

"To lure you into this day. Our marriage."

"How?"

"Well, *you* cleaned up my mantra feast."

"Humoring my madness."

"Any way I can," he said tenderly. Anything necessary, he thought.

Michael had chosen the beauty of the church for their marriage more than for the intellect of its minister. He heard Mary talking to the minister, but all he could do was dreamily look at her. "I want you to conclude the ceremony by reading this sonnet to us," she was saying.

"A what?" asked the puzzled minister. "A - sonnet?"

"Yes. It is a favorite sonnet of mine. By John Keats."

The minister looked at Michael, still puzzled. "A friend of the family?" he asked.

"Is he ever!" Michael said.

The minister suddenly remembered what a sonnet was. "I remember now. I read one for a couple by that little Portuguese girl."

"That was from Elizabeth Barrett Browning's *Sonnets from the*

*Portuguese*," said Mary. "Her husband called her his little Portuguese -"

"Oh, whatever," said the minister and hurriedly married them. Mary handed him the sonnet, and the minister rushed through it.

### LAST SONNET

Bright star, would I were steadfast as thou art
Not in lone splendor hung aloft the night
And watching, with eternal lids apart,
Like nature's patient, sleepless Eremite,
The moving waters at their priest like task
Of pure ablution round earth's human shores,
Or gazing on the new soft-fallen mask
Of snow upon the mountains and the moors
No-yet still steadfast, still unchangeable,
Pillowed upon my fair love's ripening breast,
Awake forever in a sweet unrest,
Still, still to hear her tender-taken breath,
And so live ever- or else swoon to death.

The minister handed the sonnet back to Mary, wiped his glasses, rubbed his nose. "Hmm," he muttered. "Hmm. Was it dirty? What did it say, anyway? Do you know what it means?" he asked, looking at Michael for help in the jungle of the unconscious. "My wife is the poetry expert in our family," smiled Michael, and he saw that tears were still in his bride's eyes.

"John Keats tied the power of his love for a woman to the eternal light of a star - *Love has no limit of time*," said Mary.

"And the power of love's ablution - tying in the moving waters with their priest like task of ablution - with that of love," said Michael. He had liked that sonnet himself.

"And the seeking of time between lovers - forever - or swoon to death - the choice being -"

"The unchangeable," said Michael.

"In love," added Mary.

"Oh," said the minister. "Oh," he repeated. *What a strange but handsome young couple.*

In joy, they moved her things into his house, and what they

could carry, they did, and what they could not carry, movers would later move. She could not help but notice that he had left room for her furniture, as he had left room for her clothes. Then they did their first food shopping together, and at his grocery store they met some of the ladies who had helped in his mantra meal. They looked at Mary, and she showed them her wedding ring, and they became moved to tears of joy that the Saint feast had brought Michael such a beautiful bride. God bless young lovers, they thought, and went home, and those who still had an ambulatory husband served him a better meal than usual, with even a surprise desert.

Michael and Mary ate a light meal together in their kitchen. Later, he lit a fire in their bedroom fireplace, and he brought up some new wine from the refrigerator, but he did not bring up the ice bucket, for as he recalled, he had thrown it out of the window, possibly at the moon to bring it down. "This is such a beautiful house," Mary said. "I thought you did not have any money with all of your free cases -"

"I don't have any cash now. My money and what my parents left me is in this house. And it has a good sized mortgage," he added honestly.

He used the bathroom first, and when she emerged from it, she had on the same gown she had taken off at her uncle's. He turned out the lights, for they had the light of the fire, and they had the light of the rising moon. He kissed her tenderly. He caressed her tenderly, and he called her, "My dearest, dearest girl," over and over. She returned his kisses with her own tenderness, caressed him and moved closer to him within each new caress. There was such a passion and such a joy in their sexuality, their being alive and together. "I will be your lost poet," he said. "I will be whatever you will, for I love you so." *I would make death - life, winter a song of spring - time - timeless -*

She grew so far beyond what she had been; she was lost in the delight of acceptance. *Giving is receiving into numbers numberless -*

His penetration was at first painful, but it was union, the magic of two becoming one in the purity and the sanctity of their love for each other. "Not one atom of myself did I withhold from you," she whispered. "Ever."

"Nor I - you. Forever - into lives I always denied, and beyond what I always believed. I would hand you the moon, and give you the Evening Star to wear next to your heart -"

"You did that already."

It was lust of lovers long traced among the stars. It was love cresting beyond any possibility of containment, and finally, in fulfillment of every desire, came the sweetest respite and the sharing of what had been, was, and would always be, within the miracle of human love.

The car lights passing on the bridge became one stream of light.

The sky and the bay became so united in light it seemed as if sky and water were one.

The grandfather clock chimed the night away and its marking of hours was not heard by either of the newly married couple sleeping upstairs in each other's arms.

# Eleven

Mary filled the sunroom off of their bedroom with ferns and violets and other marvels. When he left for his office he revealed his inner joy that they shared the house, their lives - their bed. She charmed him in all ways. He waited for the bad to come, for instinctively, he distrusted such happiness. He had lived a life with no required peaks, so he would not have to plunge into the deep valleys that made them peaks. But nothing bad came to them. There was no awaiting tragedy stalking them. They wrote Aaron of their marriage, and Mary said she had quit school and needed no more money. In time Aaron replied and agreed. Meg and Molly were delighted, but Meg was at a loss to see how Michael could not be John Keats. "He does not *have* to be," Mary wrote. "He must not be anything more than what he is right now."

"But, Mary," wrote Meg. "You were *so sure.*"

"And I am who I am," Mary wrote back. "I do not have to be Frances Brawne, for I do not have to be anything more than I am right now, for it is so <u>wondrous</u>."

They had three extra bedrooms with baths upstairs, and one bedroom and bath downstairs, and she wanted them all used by the unfortunates Michael knew and liked. She got them to help her with the work, and the cooking and shopping, and his house was run with such efficiency he stopped worrying about its large mortgage.

What is this joy, he thought, of greeting her at the door of *our* home, of smelling the magic of her foods in the oven? What is this joy of seeing her face, hearing her voice, touching her and loving her in all ways? What is this joy that you think can be no greater, but gets so, anyway?

What is this love, she thought, looking at him asleep by her, remembering his kisses, his words of endearment he always said with his voice deepening in emotion. What is this love that makes the tiniest thing so important when it is shared between us? What is this love that makes my heart sing when I see Betsy bringing him up the drive? When I want to find and cook the perfect healthful food for him? Why do I have to kiss his closed lashes awake? Trace his beautiful lips with my finger, before I kiss them?

She got pregnant right away. They both wanted this, were overjoyed at this, but she had a hard pregnancy and a doctor that did not get himself concerned about it at all. He seemed to live for one thing, and it was not a patient. It was golf. When she saw him he was always dressed for golf. She did not like him at all. But he was a doctor and would deliver her child, and women had had children in cornfields or other fields, without a doctor in sight. Also, he was not expensive, and that mattered a lot. What harm could he do?

As it turned out, she had no idea.

She was thrilled to be pregnant, but the ecstasy of it did not reach her body - ever. There was something about her carrying this baby that was all wrong. She began to see the doctor as Aaron, for he smiled so much and told her everything was fine, that she was so *young* and so *healthy.*

"Michael - I have this feeling that something is wrong about my having this baby."

They were in bed, and she was in his arms as she always was before sleep. "What do you mean?" His voice was anxious, and she did not want to lay any burdens on him. She knew how hard he worked, and how much he worried about their finances, even if he did not tell her about them.

"I shouldn't have said anything."

"You are keeping more food down."

"Yes. I am."

"I don't like that doctor. Do you want to change?"

"He is all paid for. The birth is all paid for."

"That makes no difference. Do you dislike him, too?"

I *hate* him, she thought. "I think the baby has not turned and he tells me - he - she - has, and that I am young and strong and birth will be a breeze."

"What do you think? Money is not a factor about this. Change. I would feel better."

"It will be fine," she said, hoping it would be.

"My dearest girl," he said, and fell asleep before she did.

She listened to the musical chiming of the grandfather clock, and it was midnight, the old time of Aaron terror. She clung closer to Michael and was comforted by the warmth of his body. *I am safe, loved, sheltered and sustained with love! I am safe!*

Another perfect day arrived. Her soul sang with it, but her stomach began to reject sustenance again.

*It was just too damned good,* Michael worried. There was a new dread hanging over him because she became pregnant so soon. Everything was moving too fast, as if they were taking the plunge into the ocean right off the sea cliff on Aaron's shitty road. She had insisted upon their guests, and she continued to cook for all of them, and for him, when she was too ill to eat adequately. She kept the house as if no one lived in it, really becoming obsessive about its perfection, he thought. As the baby grew, she lost more weight. Their guests began doing all of the work for her. She filled up with the baby, and Michael filled up with terror. "I am never, never going through this again," he moaned to her. "That means - *we will never, never get pregnant again.*"

She smiled, and looked so ethereal about it, he shuddered. "If we could just call this whole thing off!"

"If I do - *so call* - die, Michael - I will *not* become non existent."

"I don't want to hear this," he said angrily. He felt tears in his eyes, and let them touch his face. "You must not leave me! You must *never* leave me!"

"My mother and my father would not lie to me. Time is an illusion, and love makes it so. That is the *center* of our creation - love - I will always be with you, Michael. If my body dies - in the end - that is a small thing -"

"A small thing? Death is a *small thing?* Don't talk to me like that!" he choked. "Don't give me the eternity shit and your living for me from a grave! Your body a *small* thing - its death - a *small* thing? If you do not change doctors, I will!"

She did not hear him, or even see the anguish on his face. "I understand completely what he meant by truth being beauty. The truth of beauty is - it is *timeless*."

"Love is timeless - beauty is timeless - the soul is timeless - I am not interested in the *timeless!* I just want to get the hell through this *now!*"

"It is all about union - being of the *all* - the magic casements into the *real* individuality. That is when you expand beyond it! From the selfish *me*, you become the glory - of the *we!*"

"What?"

"You are the tide to God my parents *knew*, and *are knowing -*"

"They are dead."

"The glory of the all - all of the light of love endless - oh, Michael, remember, in the end, *it is all so perfect!*"

"My dearest girl, you are scaring the hell out of me." He kissed her face, held her; she was so thin. "It is *perfect* for me with you beside me every night. It is *perfect* for me when you come down the stairs to me, or come up the stairs to me. Now! Now! I want what is now and that is all I want now!"

She sat up in bed, and looked at him intently. "I would suffer so if you ever believed me *dead*. That I am not rejoicing with you in hearing a bird sing - seeing another dawn - the sun making jewels on water - the moon making magic another night. The truth of beauty is in its sharing. That is what makes it timeless!"

"I do not know what you are talking about. I just don't want you speaking to me from some damned grave."

"The point is that I will *not* be in a grave," she said. "What is joined in love, Michael, can never be torn asunder."

"What loving God would allow death?"

"What loving God would not? When a garment is used up, you naturally take it off, for it serves no more. That is what we do with our body. When it is used up by age, or pain - we discard it - and if we discard it when we are young -"

"Well? What?"

Mary thought for an answer.

"Why - for the young and the healthy and the contented?"

"I don't know. I guess man has been asking that since the young die before the old, the healthy before the ill - when the prime has been reached - *that is it* - when the required time here is spent -"

"For babies? Small children?"

"It is part of a larger plan that we now do not know - it must be like lives strung on light - each a pearl alive with the reflected light of its source - and if one light winks out - the totality remains, and all of the new pearls to come -"

She was serene within her own image and sighed in content.

He groaned. "My God! Strings and graves, pearls dropping to who knows where - a light winking out - *winking out* - as in a second? Your second could be an eternity of loss for me! Where does light go - but into *darkness?*"

"And where does darkness go - but into *light.*"

"Can we have the baby by Caesarian?"

"No. I feel that would be worse."

"What does the doctor say? Oh, that's right. He says not to worry; you are young, strong and so healthy."

She lay back down and snuggled against him. They were silent and worriedly awake. She prayed, *Dear God, let our lives be but pearls upon a string of divinity, but do not let me leave him now!* But when would she choose to leave him? In what time ahead would *that* happen?

"I will *not* go through another pregnancy - ever - ever- ever!" he gritted and looked up at the night sky, tears touching his face as silently as did the light of the Evening Star now shining directly down upon them.

Within the next night, as she heard the clock strike Aaron's time, the midnight hour, a sudden onslaught of agony tore into her body and it made her scream. Suddenly, with no gradual arrival of labor pains, as she had been told was the norm, her sheets were drenched, not with just the water breaking, but blood.

Michel went into immediate hysteria, and it was the lone remaining guest that finally got her down the stairs. Michael had helped dress her, but had failed to do the same for himself, although he did get on his shoes. They did not match, and he had on no socks and his jacket over the pajamas hid very little of them. He got into Betsy and roared away to the hospital, and on second thought, realized he and Betsy were alone and came roaring back for Mary. The last male guest was Hal - Hal for what, she tried to remember, and he said, "Michael, let me drive."

"Breathe, breathe," said Michael to Mary and Hal said, "Michael, get into the back seat and do the same for yourself."

Hal was also in his pajamas, but more neatly so, and his robe covered the pajamas all up, so he was in better shape than Michael in all ways. "We can drive back for our clothes later," said Hal.

"Mary," said Michael. "Pant! Pant!" and he got into the back seat and panted like a puppy.

*I never knew there could be pain like this! What is tearing me in two? Lions? Fire? Both!* She bit into her lips until she could taste her own salt blood. She gripped the side of the door, until her fingers whitened and it looked as if her hand was bone.

"Hal, you are going too damned fast, except for going too damned slow!" yelled Michael.

"I cannot be doing both," reasoned Hal, reasonably.

"You can!" Michael moaned. "Mary, we should never have had sex! We will never, never have sex again!"

"What does Hal stand for - Hal? Halworth? Halberry? Hal - Hal?"

"You got it, Mary, just plain old Hal. Hal stands for Hal. At least as long as I am around."

"Good," groaned Mary, not wanting to leave a mystery behind.

"Don't talk, Mary. Just be strong," Michael wept, disintegrating before them both in a most astonishing way.

*This beast tearing me in two will kill me. It will have my life in this unbearable agony.* The bleeding seemed to have stopped.

At the reception desk, if that was where they were, for Hal was away parking the car, Michael seized the nurse there and said, "My wife needs help *now!*" The nurse detached herself, or Michael did, and she was as calm as she was centered - centered on the medical bedrock of *incoming funds.* When that had been cleared away, *already paid,* there was the familial background, and what was now coming from Mary onto the floor, did not seem to be a problem. "If you ask one more question," said Michael, "*I will kill you.* Now where is the golf goof?"

"Oh, *Dr. Jones!*" said the centered nurse. Still, even if this distraught father to be was handsome, and might at times become charming, the nurse did not like her life threatened, for she was in *her* personal domain of power. She saw that his shoes did not even match in color or season, and she thought, I don't have to take any shit.

"My doctor-" Mary moaned. "Get my doctor right away." Michael caught his sagging wife, and so many new horrors were pouring from her, he grew light headed, and had to cling to the counter of the nurse from hell.

A young volunteer helper arrived, bubbling with the Christmas season. "Now, now," she smiled brightly, putting Mary into a wheel chair. "Christmas is almost here! Maybe you will have a baby like Jesus!"

Mary moaned.

"Now just relax. *Relax,* and everything will be fine! The key to giving birth is *relaxation!*"

Before Michael knew what was happening, Mary was being taken from his sight. He started to go after her when more nurses stopped him. "There are preliminary things - then we will come for you," they said, both as cheerful as the eagerly keen teen.

"Will you get her doctor?" Michael pleaded. "She is in such agony. Something is terribly wrong."

"Oh, no, *everything is fine,*" the nurses said positively and in unison, and left after Mary and the keen teen.

"The doctor is coming, and *everything is fine,*" repeated the guardian of the hospital gates, happy now that the mess before her desk was being mopped away, and deciding that Michael was the handsomest man she had seen in her life.

Michael groaned, and his face was drained of color. "Do ALL nurses ALWAYS say everything is fine? Why do those words uttered here and now, fill me with terror?"

Hal came in, saw Michael, and decided to drive home alone. "I will come back with clothes for you, Michael," he said, "and even a matching pair of shoes."

"Good," said Michael, and he sat down, and looked at the floor at his feet. He put his head into his hands, and he openly wept.

Before his eyes, her precious blood had been mopped away. He kept hearing her, as if she were with him and saying, *Dearest, don't let me die.*

He looked around him. The hospital was night dull, uncaring, impersonal. It was as if in here, whether people came in to die or to live, it made no difference at all. Gray people, hauntings of themselves, came to the admitting desk and they left. Voices sounded, a sign of life, and then this sound of life faded, and there was only the elevator bell, and that faded away, too.

*Oh, God - help her!*

Time passed. The walls were the same. The smells around him were the same. The lights shining above him were the same, but they weren't, for he knew, deep in his soul, that his dearest girl would die and leave him alone, taking away the wonder of life.

He found a nurse who said Mary was fine. She was producing a healthy baby because she was so young and healthy. Fathers just got in the way. She was fine - everything was fine - just *relax.*

"Now all you have to do, to have this wonderful *perfect* baby," said her happy teen age helper, "is just to relax. Relaxation is the way to have an *easy* birth. Relax! I *keep* telling you that! A baby in time for Christmas! How wonderful Christmas is almost here!"

"Relax," repeated Mary, and thinking - you just try that in the middle of a school of sharks using your insides for a feeding frenzy. There were still NO contractions. The agony was constant. It reached as high as it could and then went higher. "Give me something for my pain," she panted. "I am being torn apart inside."

"It is because you are not *relaxing!*" said Miss Jingle Bells.

"Go get me something for my pain!"

"I can't without the doctor saying I can."

"Then find the doctor! Don't you think by now that I need one?"

The bright sprite tidied up the room, smoothed down Mary's bed, raised its crib sides all around her. She went to the mirror and tidied herself up, too, and had second thoughts about the wonders of sex when they resulted in such messes all over the floor. Satisfied with herself, she gave Mary another Jingle Bells' smile. "The secret is to relax - *re-lax!*" she said, just as if she had not said that before. "And I will get your doctor right away! Also, the prep nurse should be *right* here -"

Closing the door behind her, she left.

The doctor never came. Neither did the prep nurse. In fact, the sprite forgot where she had put Mary, because she forgot all about Mary, as she was so filled with Christmas cheer to come, and had pushed from her mind all negative things about sex.

Mary writhed, and pressed the bell that was to summon help, but no help came. She was being savaged by a birth that would not come. She could see the clock on the wall near her bed. She had been alone in the sprite room since twelve forty AM, and it was now six thirty PM. Her baby had constantly pushed and pushed trying to be born. She had pushed and pushed trying to help him. And with each push came the tearing of her flesh by the devouring sharks, and what they left was being burned at the stake. If she had the strength to crawl over the cage bars, she would have stopped the agony by jumping from her window. But she did not have the strength. The hair around her face was covered with vomit, for every time her baby pushed to be born, vomit ran from her mouth and her nose. Now her pillow was soaked in it. She had not stopped bleeding. Her mattress was soaked with blood. She could feel it and see it - sticky red, and it probably was dripping down on the floor by now. Her hand had never stopped pressing the buzzer for help. No one came. No one would come. They were probably telling Michael she and the baby *were fine* for she was *so young* and *so healthy,* and had learned to *relax.*

Well, she thought, a hospital is indeed an appropriate place to die. They have a place to store the garbage. Or maybe burn it, too, after it has become garbage. That would be so much better than to burn garbage when it still was alive, which was happening to her now.

*And so I die. And the pain will be gone, and I will be with my mother and my father - but, oh God! How can I leave my love when I have found him again- when from the tide beyond time he found me? Don't let me die! Dearest - keep me alive!*

Around and around, and more and more slowly, went the clock. Then gently, tenderly, in its own sweet way, went the clock. Around and around went the walls, the ceiling and the lights above- so softly, so *sweetly*. Everything was enchanted - so shining with energy that was pure love and its joy. She wanted out of her fire -tortured body, and with a slight shrug she got rid of it. A voice came from somewhere growing increasingly distant - it said, "I fear we have lost her!"

"She *died?*" a man asked in disbelief and he held an inert woman in a hysteria of anguish. She paused in her departure and looked down on a spent drama. The inert woman was what she had been she was sure, but it was like a used up little rag doll that meant nothing at all to her. But the suffering man wept and said, "I will not accept this!" This was Michael, and she held him and she kissed his lips and she said, "I am not leaving you, my dearest - I am *joining* you! Don't you hear the beautiful music of the dance in the next room? Don't you know we will meet there?"

The music was so sweet she could not resist its source.

She entered the room and it was bathed in light and dancers there were mere shadows at first, and then gradually, very gradually, they melted into people, alive, vibrant, and they had pleasure from the music and she ached to join them in the dance. But she had no partner. She stood quietly in the outskirts of the ballroom, and she wondered if she were shadow or if she were substance. *Where was he?*

She saw two young girls, teenagers - *young* teenagers, sitting near the fire and drinking punch, its crystal bowl on the table near them.

They were chattering, in a happy *silly* way, and by the light of the candles burning in the ceiling fixtures, one of them drew her attention. She was tiny, the tiniest girl she had ever seen, but she was the prettiest girl in the room. There was a sweet poignancy to her, like a sweet half remembered dream. Or she was a childhood toy - a *treasured* childhood toy.

Mary looked above her. The ceiling was very white, very ornate, with some kind of a classical Greek design carved on its edges - early nineteenth century style - and so were the clothes of the dancers - and the two lively girls - and the one she was more and more drawn to. She was dressed in a pink lace empire gown, waist to her breasts in the style, and in her dark brown hair she had pink bows - two - *she must be quite a vain little creature. She does not like being so*

*tiny, and that is why she draws her hair so high on her head, with
cunning little curls around her face, and her pretty blue eyes.*

What she studied, she *became.*

What had fascinated her, she - *was.*

It was as easy as slipping into a new gown.

A handsome young man, a small handsome young man came
up to her, and bowed in a most gentlemanly way. "Would you like
to join me in this dance?" he asked. He had the most beautiful eyes
and one of the most deeply and beautiful masculine voices she had
ever heard. He looked into her eyes and smiled. "I must first
introduce myself. My name is John Keats."

# Twelve

As they danced and he held her, she was conscious of great strength, and great physical power. He obviously was having trouble with this new dance, the waltz, but he didn't step on her or her long gown, and that was nice. He was familiar to her because her mother had rented the quarters next to his good friends, the Dilkes. She and her family had rented the Charles Brown side of the duplex, Brown being another friend of John Keats, with whom he had been hiking in Scotland for the summer. He had often visited Brown and the Dilkes, he and his ill brother, Tom, and as she badgered Mrs. Dilke to tell her everything she knew about this young man, she could feel his unseen presence all around her in their rented rooms. But it was more than that; she had read his poetry. She had fallen in love with his poetry. She wanted to meet the poet.

As they danced her body grew warmer and warmer, as if it had not lost all of its blood in trying to have a child. The music of the new waltz enchanted her with such a delight it almost equaled the delight of his strong hold upon her.

Around and around the great room they went with the other dancers, and to her, in her growing joy, they all seemed to be dancing within varying hues of energy. The more her body was held by his, the more they were within a shimmering aura of rainbow color. In some strange way, she thought of reality within the myth and the symbol of the snake in the Garden of Eden presenting Adam and Eve with the forbidden fruit, the *illusion* of knowledge.

This dance was a life, and it moved around the energy of centered love. It was an enchanting and magical dance and dream, radiating from the center of love endless. *Howrfect is the plan!*

The centered light created the very shadows - themselves.

Now, moving from the reason to the result, she was firmly anchored within it. She loved being in his arms. She loved being so close to this man she knew was a poetic genius. "I have a shock for you," she smiled. "I know all about you. Mrs. Dilke told me all she knows, and I read your volume of poetry." She wanted to impress him with more facts. "Published March 3, 1817, by Olliers."

"Ah," he laughed. "*You* were the one who bought it!"

The waltz ended. He would not let her go, nor did she want to leave. She just stayed close to him until the music began again.

While they waited, and held, the other dancers were changing partners, or going for punch or wine. Some even quietly left the room. They still all seemed to be moving within varying colors.

She studied him closely, but no more than he was studying her. "I have a shock for *you*," he said softly, wanting no one else to hear. "I hate to dance. And I hate this dance for the veterans of Waterloo, because I hate the Redcoats and all they stand for."

"So why did you come here?"

"To ask you to dance. I heard about you from -"

"Mrs. Dilke," she said, moving with him as the music began again. "I like Mrs. Dilke," she said honestly, and she liked her even more now.

"She is a lovely, lovely lady," he said, holding her tightly, firmly, exuding power over her she loved. "Miss Brawne, you have beauty that takes my breath away," he said suddenly.

"I am glad you think so," she laughed. The dance continued. He was unsure of the steps, but she was not. "Why do you hate the poor Redcoats?" she asked.

"They are the arms for a heart of injustice." He looked at her in such admiration, her heart all but stopped. "But one had better never be around you, Miss Fanny Brawne!" He was not jesting. In truth, he had turned very sober about Redcoats even being *around* her.

"They won't be," she said truthfully.

We cannot be strange to each other, she thought. I was attracted to him before this dance. I dreamed what he would look like, how he would speak to me. She knew all Mrs. Dilke knew about him. From Mrs. Dilke's account, a rare, tender, and brilliant young man was created, and she was eager to meet this man who had given up

111

a financially secure life as a surgeon, or even a physician, to write poetry. He had dedicated his first slim volume of poems to Leigh Hunt, his friend, and one of the most radical liberals of the time. The great Tory *Quarterly* and *Blackwoods* refused to even review it. His work received only one small write up in the *Monthly Review*. In it, some astute writer had noted that he had found in this poetry, by such a *young* man, the "rapturous glow and intoxication of fancy, a revelry of the imagination and tenderness of feeling that forcibly impress themselves upon the reader." The Olliers brothers did not push his book at all. *They are afraid of Tory power*, she had long decided to herself.

There was a longer pause before the next waltz, and they shared punch and their growing fascination for each other.

This dear girl, he thought, with her pink lace dress, the pink ribbons in her dark hair, has the most beautiful eyes I have ever seen. When I heard about her very intelligent mind, and how she reads German and French, how she loves poetry, I wanted to meet her just for *conversation*. But now that I have seen her, no words from her, no matter how brilliant, wise or musical, will be enough for me. He was smitten with desire for her, an actual craving to hold and to kiss her. He smiled ruefully at himself, for he had teased his brother George at his falling in love so soon, and making his life his wife's. Well, what you mock you must live, he thought, and what George had felt for his girl, must be a whisper of what he was feeling for this one. He had an immediate sexual attraction to her, and this had to be carefully hidden, for the society around them regarded such attraction to be assigned only in heaven, where, happily, there were no bodies to do anything about it. He had never been really attracted to *any* girl before - this way. He did not want to be attracted to any girl, this way, or any way, because he never intended to marry. He was going to devote his life to writing poetry. It brought him his need to live.

*Had* brought him his need to live.

Now all of that was changed because of this enchanting wisp of a girl. *I want to live forever and share all of it with her!*

He was born October 31, 1795, she was told. This is September 1818. That means he is short of his twenty-third birthday.

She was born August 9, 1800, he knew from Mrs. Dilke. She is *just* eighteen. She is so young, but his brother George was married to a girl even younger, and had taken her away with him to America where they were going to get very rich right away.

Now John Keats and Frances Brawne sat the next dance out, and each one knew that they had fallen in love, and both found you do not reason with that feeling at all. It just was. *His hair is the most beautiful shade of auburn, his nose so handsome, so perfect, his dark brown eyes have so many lights in them, so much soul. His lips are full and perfectly formed, and their kisses will be gentle and marvelous, and when I think of these kisses, I had better think of something else.*

*I am spellbound. It is as if a woman has risen from the magic of perilous seas in fairylands forlorn - as if a goddess who enchants every wood and every sea has come to me to be my own! She is what inspires poetry - already she is enshrined within music so clear to my heart -*

"I am only five foot two," he said. "My brothers are tall, but I am only five foot two. I hate it."

"Why?"

"It is ugly. I am called that *little* poet. I hate it," he repeated. "I hate it," he said again.

"And I am five foot exactly," she replied. "Do you find that ugly?"

"I could find nothing about you that isn't *perfect*," he said, and she was amazed that his voice actually trembled.

"And - my dear Mr. Keats," she said, "I find everything about you incredibly handsome. I know this is shocking, wicked to say, but I say what I think, and this upsets my dear mother very much. I do what I want to do, and that upsets her more. And - I do not like the Redcoats either!"

He threw back his head and laughed so heartily and so merrily, he induced smiles from all around, as he usually did, so pleasing was his personality.

"My brother George is five foot ten. And so is Tom, my poor dear brother, dying - I - now - know - he had the luxury at least of not being a *midget*."

He was holding her hands, and anyone watching such a scandal could talk about it all night. "That is something, my dear Mr. Keats, you never were, nor ever can be," she said.

"Why not?" he smiled, relieved that she did find him adequate in appearance, and that wonder had come into his life beyond what he found even when he wrote. "Writing poetry is a need I cannot give up."

"Good."

"I will probably die a pauper."

Her beautiful eyes glistened. "If you impoverish yourself to write, you will leave the *world* richer."

He looked at her with even more light coming into his dark eyes, that she had not thought possible. *What high beautiful cheekbones he has. He must look like an Indian of America, he has such a fierce falcon look - and yet the lips are so tender. The beauty of this man's soul shines in his face. And he has such broad shoulders - he exudes strength - he has such a perfect athletic build. I have heard how women are attracted to him. I have heard how he always is detached from any flirtations with them. More than one girl has told me how charming and brilliant he is - how glorious, and he does not know it at all - worrying about being five foot two!*

"He has this wall of *reserve* -" she had heard girls say. "He has this wall of *privacy*," another said. "He lives alone in his own world," they all agreed. Sadly, too, for many had wanted to share his world.

"Will you share your world with me?" she asked suddenly and boldly.

"Will you share *yours* with me?" he replied instantly.

"Yes."

"And the world is already more beautiful," he said.

It was. They danced again, and among the dancers and the varying rainbow colors of energy, they were alone, except for all that made the wonder of all things wondrous.

The dance ended. Candles were being capped. "I don't want to go home in my friend's carriage," she said.

"Nor do I want you to!" he said huskily. "Let me walk you home. The moon is full. It will be a beautiful walk."

"It is a long walk," she said.

"I just walked six hundred and forty two miles in Scotland," he replied, and he fetched her wrap, and put it around her slight body. "Are your shoes comfortable?" he asked, an important matter seldom considered by a man.

"Happily, yes. They are old and worn in," she laughed, but she would have walked anywhere with him this night of a large old moon and new magic, if she had no shoes on at all.

As they left the ballroom of Hampstead, the music seemed to follow them. All of the violins were silent and put away, and yet their beautiful music lingered all around them. He felt it, too. "Beauty," he said "has such a long echo."

The moon absorbed the night. He took her hand, and they walked to her house by a narrow lane where no coaches would clatter by them, no coach horns would sound, and they could hear the soft hooting of a night owl. A slight breeze rustled through the leaves of the trees that over arched their path and through them a star or two would glitter as if they were walking among them. They passed a farmer's unlighted cottage, its thatched roof a square of moonlight, and its orchards nearby bearing apples for the slow oozing of the cider-press. "I don't know whether I prefer spring to autumn," he said. "Within each, I think that is the one I prefer."

A stream wandered noisily near them, moonlit to rush back to the shadow of the trees. "The English countryside is so glorious," he said, still warmly holding her hand. "I love it. I love its every part."

"But it is the full moon on the ocean that entices you," she said. "And you are haunted by the power of opposites. I read and have *memorized* your *The Castle Builder*."

He stopped, dumbfounded. "I had sent that to Reynolds," he said. "It was never finished - published -"

"You forget that Mr. Charles Brown copies everything you show him that you have written, and I found it in his desk, and I read it and learned it." She laughed, teasing him and the shock upon his handsome face.

"You *memorized* it?"

"Well you had better believe it. Listen to some lines -

O that our dreamings all, of sleep or wake,
*Would all their colors from the sunset take -*"

"That is not *The Castle Builder*," he interrupted.

"Brown had that title on it."

"He was wrong. Those are lines from *The Enchanted Castle*."

All right - *the Enchanted Castle*. These are the lines I love -
It was a quiet eve,
The rocks were silent, the wide sea did weave
An untumultuous fringe of silver foam
Along the flat brown sand.

Now, John Keats, I am going to finish the lines I do *not* like, for they are too hopeless. You want *our dreams to be*, and I quote -

From something material sublime
Rather than shadow our own soul's day-time
In the dark of night -"

She shuddered. "That is so *depressing*."

"I get blue moods," he said, honestly. "I can write that spring has a triple morn to sing, and then I remember how my father was killed so young, how my mother drowned in her own blood, and I could not keep her from dying, even when I stood at nights outside of her bedroom door with my uncle's sword - thinking I *could* fight death away - and now I *know* that I cannot stop my brother Tom from drowning the same way - in his own blood, and he is not even nineteen!"

They tarried on a bridge and watched the stream foam white as it rushed over rocks beneath them, carrying a small branch. "Into light and into dark we go," he said, "caught like that - flotsam - where?"

"To the - now," she smiled.

"Yes," he smiled back. He took her hands to his lips and kissed each one tenderly, on the palm. "I thought I could only give my heart to my quest of beauty, but tonight, *right now*, Frances Brawne, I give it to you."

"You give your heart to me?"

"Yes."

"And I give mine to you," she replied. With no hesitation at all, she repeated, "And I to you." *How can this be so fast, and so new, and so old?*

"My dearest girl," he said huskily, and it was as if he had said this before and would, surely, say it over and over again. He breathed in the warm air and looked all about them. "*We* cast forth the beauty of this night," he said softly, "and *we* make magic all of its shadows."

She laughed happily. "We can do that?"

He held her hands to his heart. "We can do anything."

They walked slowly on and time and the night within it were their own.

"You wrote that there is *no* standard law of earth and heaven," she said. "Even through fancy - that it is a flaw to *try* to see beyond the limit of the self, because, and I quote, '*It forces us in summer skies to mourn, It spoils the singing of the Nightingale -* '"

"I was in a blue mood, and I wrote that."

"No law of earth or heaven? Even through the *imagination?*" Those lines had shocked her, for her spirit was buoyant, and she thought of the self as limitless. "I do not believe that at all."

"I don't either. I told you I have a dark side to my nature and when I am in it - I write about it."

"What do you *really* believe? Why are we here?"

"To become individualized."

"How?"

"Through growth. I think we are here to grow and to reach beyond the finite and all of its pain and all of its sorrows. I think we have to find our way beyond what we know as our self -"

"Where to?"

"Into the sacred."

"What is that?"

"Into the truth of beauty."

"What is the truth of beauty?"

"It is limitless."

"How do we reach beyond ourselves into the limitlessness?"

"Through creation. Through the casements of the mind into the world of creation where fancy roams free to record a sound forever echoing, a kiss forever to be given, a song yet to be sung, youth yet to love, or die, all frozen - and forever perfect."

"But that is life yet to be realized."

He looked up at the Evening Star shining beyond the wayward moon. "Or ended," he added softly. "In a moment of perfection, of perfect love and perfect joy, I would rather die than live and lose them."

"I do not believe love ever dies."

He looked at her. "I know I have fallen in love with you. Would your love equal mine?"

"Yes. I think I fell in love with you before we met."

"How?"

"Through the beauty of your poetry. I think it echoes the light of your soul."

She saw tears glisten in his eyes. "My love for you is as pure and as constant as the light of the Evening Star above us now. I give that star to you. Whenever you see it, in all of our years together to come, remember this night when we fell in love."

She looked up at the star. "I accept your gift. I will never forget," she said.

Tenderly they kissed. The first was so rapturous a second had to follow, and then a third, and she pressed against him for a closer embrace and he moved swiftly away.

"I want more," she said.

"So do I," he said roughly. "And I think, my dearest girl, that more with you would never be enough!" His voice trembled.

He led them on, and for both, it was into a world of magic.

"Everyone," he was saying, "wonders why we are here, to live, to love and to die, and poets make all of this into poetry, musicians into music and painters into paintings. The business men might do it in collecting their money, the politicians more power, and the soldiers with their swords and rifles, but I think the purpose of our creation is personal growth, and the greater the growth, the greater the individualization. What we come from - we do not return to - the same."

"*Return* to?"

"In realization -" and he stopped, and breathed in the air again, the sweet smell of night dew freshly fallen on meadow grass.

He is such a tender man, she thought, but she had heard that as a school boy he not only won all intellectual prizes, but every athletic contest, too, being an amazing pugilist.

"Why didn't I meet you sooner?" he asked. He felt time pressing him -time that was not patient enough to give him a long life. He thought of his mother, his brother dying right now, and a sudden breeze made him shiver as if the night had turned cold when it had not.

"Do you believe in God?"

"Of course, because I believe in the perfection of creation - "

"How?"

"I *know* - without *belief* - that we are atoms of light - intelligence – souls - perception, flung into the dark by a centered energy - God - if you will. But we are separate now, to seek an individual identity, and experience, if we can, the rapture of our source, for within us remains the energy of what created us. There is a return to divinity, in realization, and when we move from it, we miss heaven on earth."

"Heaven - is a form of consciousness?"

"How can you really *think* who you are? You *experience* who you are. I believe that man is his own greatest mystery, and the unfolding of that mystery might be eternal, but the rapture is in its seeking."

Their path came out of tree shadow. The stream flowed brightly by them again, no more than murmuring moonlight. From nearby came the hooting of the night owl and the soft rustling of a red squirrel, unique to England, and then there was only the sound of the stream.

"This vale of earthly pain is the vale of soul-making," he said. "Souls acquire identity and a unique personality - *here*. How can these sparks, that are God, have a separate identity and possess the individual bliss of *individual* seeking, but through the medium of this world?"

He kissed her, stopped them in their tracks and kissed her, and with her instant cooperation, kissed her again and again. "My dearest girl," he said. "The path to Paradise regained is through the heart."

His lips were so gently seeking and his kisses so sweetly giving. She stayed within his arms to feel his heart beating against her own. Again, he stopped the kissing, and they walked on. "Not merely is the heart the Hornbook to individualize a soul," he said, "it is really the mind's bible, and it is the very essence from which the mind or intelligence takes *its* identity. As various and as many are the lives of man, so various become their souls, and thus does God make individual beings, identical *only* in bearing the light of His own essence."

"You are not an orthodox Christian!" she laughed.

"My dear beautiful girl," he replied. "I am not *orthodox* anything."

She thought, I never want to reach home and see him walk back to his home, rented from postman Bentley at Number One Well Walk. All I want to do with the rest of the night is have him kiss me and not stop until there are two moons in the sky!

But he had stopped the kissing, and she was to find, that he always would.

When he left her at her door, she took his hands and held them against her face. "You were so right," she said.

"About what?"

"The path to paradise is through the heart."

# Thirteen

When John Keats reached his quarters at 1 Well Walk, Hampstead, the moon afforded enough light for him to talk to his landlord Bentley, who had stayed with Tom for him. They went outside and stood by Bentley's horse. "He slept all the time you were gone," Bentley said. "Tom is such a gentle nice lad. It is a shame your brother George couldn't have helped you with his care, going on to America -"

Bentley saw Keats cringe, and was immediately sorry for his words. He knew how painful Tom's dying was for Keats, for these two brothers were always so close, but he also remembered that Keats would brook no criticism of George.

"Mr. Bentley, thanks for staying with Tom," Keats said softly, and Bentley could see that his friend was very agitated. "Do you want me to stay, lad?"

"No. Thank you, but no. I will have to get through what is coming the best way I can."

Inside the house, he undressed, prepared for bed without lighting a candle. There was always the terror for Tom, and for himself, that Tom would suffocate in another hemorrhage. He had moved his bed to be near his brother's, and as he got into it, he heard Tom struggle to breathe, and tears of agony streaked his own face. *Just to have the right to breathe! Should not all living things have that right?* In Tom's labored breathing he heard that of his mother, and he had to push that pain from his mind. He lay still, watching placid moon light change the dark corners of their room. *Go gently, dear Tom, my little brother I watched over since you were born, and I thought I could stay the death of our mother with an old rusty sword I held outside of her bedroom door all night! I couldn't, and I can't stay your death either, no matter the love between us.*

Life was so strange, wonder surely at its heart for it to bear so much pain. *Where will you go, shy gentle Tom? With our mother and father, and Granny Good?*

Now feeling his face still wet with unashamed tears for Tom, his heart yet sang with the enchantment of the dance with Miss Brawne. How can one feel so much pain and exult in its opposite? He still felt her body close to his, felt her soft lips, how eagerly they met his own, and he felt again the touch of her breasts when he embraced her, and he wanted all of her totality, as he wanted to give her all that he was and could ever be.

So magically the moon made radiant about him and about Tom what had once been shadow, and as magically had she won his heart. He was a man, with a man's sexual desire, and yet, she was a goddess, to remain ever untouched by any mortal man. Enchanted with the full moon as the goddess Diana, pure forever, he was in the throes of his poor *Endymion,* so trashed by the Tory press - a man lusting for a woman of the earth, and in love with a goddess so remotely above him.

The opposites remained within his heart as it did the night, dark to light and back again to dark, or dark, back again to light, and he felt the ecstasy of his love for a woman and the agony that for Thomas Keats, that ecstasy of love would never come.

The next day he began the distasteful and arduous task of trying to persuade Richard Abbey to allow a visit from their sister, Fanny. Tom wanted to see her before he died, and John wanted this for Tom as desperately as did Tom, and he also wanted his cherished little sister to meet the girl who had stolen away his heart so suddenly, and so totally.

Abbey hated Tom and John Keats as much as they hated him. He saw them as wild and filled with passion as had been their mother and father, who had so openly allowed their love for each other to show, to even a superior man of dignity and means like himself. John Keats had constant visions of himself pulling off Abbey's head and the superior smile/sneer that never once had reached his cold flint eyes. Without his head he would only have his fat body, glutted on the money that was left to the Keats' children and left in his charge until they were of age. Meanwhile, he was spending it all on himself as fast as he could.

With sour and dire warnings to Fanny Mary Keats, Abbey allowed the visit by early October. Of course she hated Abbey more than her brothers did. From the time she was seven, until she came of age on her twenty-first birthday, she had to live with him and his odious wife who were her guardians in their own particular home of pure hell.

His *dearest girl* and his cherished little sister took to each other right away, as Mrs. Dilke had taken to his girl, and the friendship between Fanny Brawne, Fanny Keats and Mrs. Dilke had been formed for the rest of their lives.

When Tom was fortunate enough to sleep, Keats took his girl and little sister on a long walk, always a cherished pleasure in the country lanes of England. As they walked, John holding his girl's hand, and taking it to his lips when he felt like it, which was very, very often, Fanny Keats smiled with joy. At fifteen, she hoped that some day she would meet a young man as handsome as John, with the innate sweetness and tenderness of her brothers John and Tom, and a man who was not afraid to express, as John was doing now, his delight in love. But she also knew how private John was about his deepest feelings that slipped out in his poetry, shone in his eyes, but were *not* expressed to friends, no matter how close. The fact that he openly displayed his love for Miss Frances Brawne in front of Miss Frances Keats, was the greatest compliment he could pay his sister.

They walked among the bright falling leaves that made summer gold of their path, passed low lying dales all but hidden in mist, and when they climbed up into hills of sunshine, flocks of swallows took to the skies. Farm apple trees were heavy with moss and ripened fruit; bees droned lazily among nearby flowers and he thought of themselves as honey makers, too. A sudden breeze rose and became a strong wind. "Stop!" he said. "The tide - let's share the tide!"

Together they stopped to watch the winnowing of the wind through fields of golden wheat and waves made in the tall green corn. "The poetry of the earth is never done," he said, and squeezed his girl's hand, and he grieved that Tom could not be sharing in this.

"Fanny," said Fanny Brawne to Fanny Keats. "I want to know more about your brother."

"John was never one for *half feelings,*" said Fanny Keats. "Granny Good said our mother and our father were like that, too, and they had a marriage made in heaven."

"They did," said John. "Indeed, they did."

"Our mother was so filled with *life,*" said Fanny Keats. "She was Frances Jennings -"

"Whom Abbey despised because once he saw her beautiful legs, and I wager he stood on his head to see them," said John Keats.

"Our mother was the daughter of John Jennings who successfully ran a coach line and bought his own livery with *very* comfortable living quarters over it. I forget its name."

"The *Swan and the Hoop,*" said John.

"A handsome ostler was hired, named Thomas Keats, from Lands End, Cornwall."

"They fell in love," said John. "They were married October 9, 1794, and they were married in St. George's Church, Hanover Square, in the London west side."

"John was born October 31, 1795, George on February 28, 1797, and Tom on November 18, 1799. Another son was born - Eddie, who died in infancy, and I was born June 21, 1803. Grandma Good had been Catherine Keate from Yorkshire, and she married John Jennings in Cornwall in 1770."

"Fanny, stop all of this family history," said John Keats to his sister.

"Fanny, go on. I want to hear it all, and do not let Mr. John Keats stop you again," said Fanny Brawne to Fanny Keats.

Thomas Keats bought the *Swan and the Hoop* from his father in law, and did so well with it, he moved his family to a nice house on Craven Street, City Road, one half mile north of the stable. John had been born over the stable, but the other children were born at the nice Craven Street home. The business continued to prosper, but when John was seven, when he was riding home on a stormy Sunday night, his father's horse crushed him to death against an iron rail.

"That lying Abbey tells he was drunk," said her Keats bitterly. "He hated my mother and my father, and he hates Tom and me -"

"And me," added Fanny Keats, just as bitterly.

It was in 1802 that the Keats' children lost their father. He had wanted the best school for John, who clearly had a superior mind. "He would have sent John to Harrow," said Fanny Keats. "And then on to Oxford, or Cambridge."

Mrs. Keats married a Mr. Rawlings after a year, for she was lost as to running the business, caring for her small children and their house.

"Mr. Rawlings *beast*," said Fanny Keats, "abused her. All he wanted was the business, and she had to flee with us for her life. As her husband, he now got the *Swan and the Hoop* for himself."

"Thus business matters are settled in England," said her Keats, and fury was in his eyes. "A woman counts for nothing."

The Keats' children moved to their grandparents' home in Ponders End.

"It was a fine home, very large," remembered her Keats.

Then their grandfather died there in 1805, and he left a tidy sum of money for his wife, and his children and his grandchildren. The money that was not bequeathed outright was held up in the Court of Chancery, and that would eventually take twenty years to settle, after the heirs were all dead. Then came the mistake Grandma Good made that would make all of the lives of all of her grandchildren a nightmare of cruelty and poverty. "Abbey, the oily slick smiling slime," said her Keats. "He talked our grandmother into letting him be our guardian and control the estate left by my grandfather, and he has sat on it like a brooding hen even before Granny Good's death four years ago. He does not want us to see our sister, or for her to even write us, or receive mail from us! And he has the power to stop this."

"That is because he is stealing our money, and when I am twenty-one, I am going to take him to court and they will put him in jail." (This indeed, did happen)

"What he doesn't steal, he puts down a rat hole," said John. "We are hard pressed for coal to heat our quarters, and usually we don't have it -"

"And John always has to ride on top of a coach, and never can afford a fast mail carriage - or have a thick warm coat, or even warm boots -"

"His excuse is that I am supposed to use my surgeon and apothecary license and get rich - he wouldn't even release the money for me to go to Edinburgh and study to become a physician. Of course then I might be too respectable for him, with the word Doctor before my name -"

Her Keats was engulfed with such fury, Fanny Brawne moved nervously away from him.

"John has no *half* feelings," his wise little sister repeated, and again, to Miss Brawne, he looked like a falcon like Indian of the new world. It was in his nose - his eyes - so fierce -

"I just hate injustice," he said quietly. "*To anyone.* Tom may not be dying if he had been able to keep decently warm."

"I want to know about the schooling - where all of this flowing of beautiful poetry came from -" said Miss Brawne.

"Poetry does not come from schooling," her Keats gently contradicted. "It comes *spontaneously,* or it had better not come at all. It comes to you - *almost half remembered,* and then it should strike the reader the same way - something of beauty uniquely *his own,* and now remembered, and enjoyed again."

Miss Brawne snuggled close and looked him lovingly in the eyes. He began to laugh in delight. "All right, all right! Fanny, tell Miss Brawne here about my school days."

He had started a fine school in 1803 run by an excellent headmaster, John Clarke. It was the Enfield School and George came along later. By the time George arrived, there was no hazing of any kind of another Keats. John had taken care of any hazing immediately, proving to have the best boxing skills in the school, and apparently in the whole general area. At a theater, an usher pushed Tom, and brother John landed him so urgently upon his seat, it was said, for a week, he stood up for meals and other life necessities. John heard about a butcher that liked to torture kittens for his customers' general amusement, and he visited the butcher and put him into a nap behind his counter, took the kittens home, and the butcher did no more torturing of any animal.

"I boxed because I am so small," said her Keats. "Is this story about me to go on?" he impatiently asked his sister.

"Yes," she replied.

"Most certainly," said Miss Brawne.

Annoyed, he walked away from them, and sat on a fallen log, and looked out at a new band of swallows skimming the sunset.

Her Keats excelled in every athletic contest. He then became obsessed with reading, digested every book in the school library, and in the Clarke library, for he and John Clark's son, Charles Cowden Clarke, became close friends.

"*Everyone's* a friend to my brother," said Fanny.

"Except for Richard Abbey," said Miss Brawne.

"Well, he's not in the human race," countered Fanny Keats.

When Granny Good had turned the care of her grandchildren over to Richard Abbey, in 1810 Abbey could not wait too long to see that John was jerked away from his studies, where he had won all the school prizes and achievements for scholastic excellence.

"His mother died in 1810 - my Keats said something about standing watch outside of her door -"

"Oh," said Fanny Keats, looking nervously over at her big brother, absorbed in how the rosy light of the sky was bathing the earth in the same color.

"Tell me! Tell me!" Miss Brawne pressed. "He can't hear."

"I knew our mother and John had a - special kind of bond. I remember when she was in her bed, so ill, that whenever John came home from school, he read novels to her, and stayed by her bed all night to be sure that she took her medicines -"

"Go on!"

"I think that John thought - that if he could stay awake all night and guard her door - when she was very bad - that he could stand between her and death."

Fanny Keats stopped and looked toward her brother with such affection, Miss Brawne thought - *there is such love in this family.*

"Miss Brawne, you must never tell my brother, I told you this."

"All right. I will not tell him or anyone."

"Our mother died when he was at Enfield School, and when the head master told him this, he curled up under the head master's desk, and - wept."

Fanny Keats' eyes became wet. She wiped tears away with a raggedly handkerchief. "No one hazed him, mocked him, or even talked about it. You see, John wept, because he believed if he had been outside of our mother's door, death would not have taken her away."

*Oh, my dearest, my Keats* - "Go on. All of his life up to the time we met at the Hampstead Ball for the veterans -"

Abbey took her Keats out of Enfield and apprenticed him to a surgeon, Mr. Thomas Hammond, who lived near Granny Good on Church Street, Edmonton. This was in 1811, three years before Granny Good died, and John in his free time always looked in on her. Tom and George had been put to work in Abbey's Coffee and Tea warehouse as clerks. "His place of business," Fanny Keats sneered, "is at 4 Pancras Lane, London, but of course the Duke and the Duchess of Deviltry, live in the suburbs on Marsh Street, Walthamstow, where I had to go and live with them when Granny Good died."

Her Keats studied under Surgeon Hammond for four years, and then persuaded Abbey to allow his studies to be concluded in London at Guy's Hospital. He found cheap and shabby lodgings near the hospital at 8 Dean Street, on the first right turn for him after crossing the London Bridge. He hated the dirty cramped and noisy winding dark streets, but his brothers lived across the Thames in quarters at Abbey's warehouse, at 4 Pancras Lane. George hated being a clerk for Abbey, and Tom soon was too ill to work. Her Keats had entered Guy's Hospital October 1, 1815, on a Sunday, paying a fee of twenty four pounds. He became a dresser under surgeon Mr. Lucas, and saw quickly, that Mr. Lucas killed far more people than he helped. He was soon doing the surgery himself, with brilliant success. In the meantime he was taking the required courses on anatomy and physiology, two on the theory and practice of medicine, two on chemistry, and on *Materia Medica*. He dissected specimens, attended medical lectures, and on the side of his notes, appeared flowers, and snatches of poetry. One day, he had told them all, during an endless lecture, which he already had grasped and understood, shafts of sunlight came through the windows, and in the moving particles of light, he created in them magical beings of his own fancy. In January of 1816 he moved to St. Thomas Street, and began to read Coleridge, Woodsworth, Shelley, Jane Austen, but the poets were his passion, and he began to attempt to write more poetry himself. He would get his license for being a surgeon and an apothecary, and maybe go on later when he could, to become a physician, and dabble in poetry as a pleasant hobby.

1816 was a very important year for her Keats in other ways that changed his whole life around. He met a young painter, Joseph Severn, who became a good friend. His friend from Clarke's school, Cowden Clarke, introduced him to Leigh Hunt's liberal paper, *The Examiner*, and Burnet's *History Of Our Times*, and her Keats became a passionate supporter of civil and religious liberty. Both John Clarke and his son were liberals, and Abbey hated them for this, considered them anti –England, and thus anti-God, and jerked Keats out of their school as soon as he had the power to do so. Cowden Clarke had introduced him to an idol of her Keats, Leigh Hunt. Hunt was living in Hampstead in the Vale of Health, and his small home was always filled with the liberal writers and poets of his day, and at his house John Keats met Shelley, Coleridge, Lamb, Hazlitt, another poet a year younger than himself, John Reynolds, and the new artist making a stir in London, Frederick Wordsworth Haydon. Here he also met the great William Wordsworth, whom he worshipped for his poetry, as he had worshipped Leigh Hunt for his belief in the innate right of man to have the inalienable God-given rights stated so eloquently in the American Declaration of Independence. Hunt published Keats' *Sonnet On Solitude* in his *Examiner* on May 5, 1816. This, said Fanny Keats, made her brother decide to support himself by writing poetry. He completed all of his medical studies, and passed his medical exams with flying colors on July 25, and refused an offer to work for Tottenham Surgery. That autumn he wrote *I Stood Tip Toe Upon a Little Hill*, and found that the best part of his writing came when he had broken away from the old stereotypes of poetry. He wrote a delightful sonnet for his brother Tom, on Tom's seventeenth birthday, November 18. The three brothers moved into 76 Cheapside, London, and lived amiably, even happily together, all filled with dreams of a bright future; Tom would get in good health,

George was dreaming of going to America to get rich, and John was dreaming of becoming known among the English poets of his day. His hopes had been high; the Olliers were bringing out his volume of poetry in March of 1817. But the Cheapside lodging had proven too smoky for Tom's health, so they moved to the rural 1 Well Walk by April of 1817. Traveling in the Isle of Wight, her Keats wrote to his brothers at Well Walk that he would cease to exist if he could not write poetry. Tom joined him at Margate, and John began his doomed *Endymion*. He consumed himself with this for seven months. By May Tom's ill health continued to keep him from working for Abbey; George quit working for Abbey because he hated him and the work, and was going to America anyway. Abbey thought they were all mad, Tom for staying ill, and John's brother, George, moving to a land of savages, and being John's brother, and he hated Fanny for being John's sister, John for being John, and quitting medicine and thinking he could ever write decent poetry. Actually, there was *no* decent poetry. Abbey did not approve of poetry. If it did not pay that was bad enough, but he was sure that all poetry was dirty. Then George told him there were piles of money to be made in America. That was in his favor, for Abbey loved piles of money more than most men, but going to AMERICA for it? Being roasted by naked heathens, associating with restless chair-rocking - tobacco-spitting lame brains who twitched, spit, rocked, and on the Fourth of July, blew up their towns or set them on fire with rockets because they had not had the good sense *to remain British*. They had shot up good British lads disguised in women's bonnets from the windows of *outhouses,* cowards who fought hidden behind trees and not marching into battle in a decent red uniformed line. Abbey hated everything American. George Washington should have been hanged as a traitor to God, and Thomas Jefferson, with the rights of man vulgarity, should have been shot, but that would have been too good for him. Abbey and John used to have yelling matches over the merits of the American Revolution.

Through the Leigh Hunts John had met Charles Brown and Charles Wentworth Dilkes. Charles Brown was living comfortably on his brother's inheritance, and Dilkes had a fine family pedigree going right back to Sir Francis Walsingham who had served under the great Queen Elizabeth Tudor. Some Dilkes were now living in some castle in Warwickshire, and Charles Dilkes had a good job as a clerk in the Navy Pay Office, and was successfully publishing his own newspaper, the *Athenaeum*. Charles Brown was a bachelor, and he and Dilkes built a large comfortable double house together, the Dilkes' family taking the larger quarters, the two homes sharing a common yard with a beautiful plum tree.

When the Keats brothers moved to 1 Well Walk, Dilkes was twenty-seven, had his only child, Charley, and a lovely warm hearted wife who was utterly charming about being late every where she went. But when she did get there, she was so charming about it, everyone was glad she had arrived at last. Dilkes took to John Keats immediately, for John Keats met no one in his life who did not like him, with the exception of Richard Abbey, the detester of anybody. Dilkes and John Keats loved the poetry of William Blake and enjoyed reading it together.

"Here on, I know about him, from Mrs. Dilkes," laughed Fanny Brawne. "And I know about the women who send him poetry, sea shells and even a laurel wreath or two."

John heard this, and joined them, laughing, and when he laughed, the glory of the sunset was more glorious.. He put his arm around his girl's waist, and the other arm around the shoulder of his sister. "I have never been so completely happy," he said. "This day was a poem to autumn."

As he helped the girls down from their hill, they heard the call of a robin, the bleating of lambs nearby, and high above them, the twittering of another band of swallows skimming the last light of a perfect autumn day.

# Fourteen

"The phrenzy of the POEMS was bad enough in its way; but it did not alarm us half so seriously as the calm, settled, imperturbable drivelling idiocy of ENDYMION. The old story of the moon falling in love with a shepherd, so prettily told by a Roman Classic, and so exquisitely enlarged and adorned by one of the most elegant of German poets, has been seized upon by Mr. John Keats, to be done with as might seem good unto the sickly fancy of one who never read a single line of either of OVID or of WEILAND. *(I read German, and read OVID in the original,* thought John Keats as he read this, August of 1818) His ENDYMION is not a Greek shepherd, loved by a Grecian goddess; he is merely a young Cockney rhymester, dreaming a phantastic dream at the full of the moon. Mr. Hunt is a small poet, but he is a clever man. Mr. Keats is a smaller poet, and he is only a boy of pretty abilities, which he has done everything in his power to spoil. And now, good-morrow to 'the Muses' son of Promise' ..We venture to make one small prophecy, that his bookseller will not a second time venture fifty pounds upon anything he can write. It is a better and a wiser thing to be a starved apothecary than a starved poet; so back to the shop, Mr. John, back to 'plasters, pills and ointment boxes,' ..But for Heaven's sake, young Sangrado, be a little more sparing of extenuatives and soporifics in your practice than you have in your poetry." Author, or authors — SIGNED Z.

Thus *spoke* the reactionaries of the Tory press.

Actually his publishers, Taylor and Hessey, 93 Fleet Street, never wavered in their support of him, or the belief in his genius, and this loyalty remained after his death. And in their day, his poetry had never paid for its publication.

In late September of 1818 the Tory *Quarterly* appeared, with its expected attack on John Keats. This venom was actually not signed either. The author admitted he did not read beyond the First Book of *Endymion* in which he did find some powers of language, rays of fancy, and some gleams of genius - but this young man was a disciple of the new school called Cockney poetry that consists of incongruous ideas (new ones) told in "the most uncouth language."

The third review had come out in June, but was not seen by John Keats until his return from his long hike in Scotland. Another spook author did this one, too, in the *British Critic*. He told the story himself, and added lines to the poem to make it total nonsense, and then blasted the poet for this idiocy created by himself in all of his snobbish glory.

The last paragraph noted that the poem contained 4,074 lines, was printed on very nice hot-pressed paper, and sold for nine shillings, and that the poet was something between a boy and a man.

So the two most important reviews of the England of George the Third had spoken and decreed the *cockney lower class* poet, John Keats, into the dust bin of English poetry. Frances Brawne read the poem and its reviews before she met the poet, and fell so quickly in love with him. She wrote letters to the *Morning Chronicle* expressing her outrage, and letters like hers continued to that paper into October. In the October 3, 1818 issue, one reader wrote to the paper, "Beauties of the highest order may be found in almost every page."

The Whig *Edinburgh Review* remained strangely silent, and did not review *Endymion* until two years later.

Her Keats had so many changes added to his life, he did not have the passion against the unsigned venomous attackers that she had. In January of this year, 1818, his London doctor, Mr. Sawrey, had assured him that Tom was getting well. In the meantime, while George took Tom to Devonshire to leave London smoke, he was supposed to end *Endymion*, but he and his moon struck shepherd, torn between the pure goddess he loved and the same goddess as a sensual earth woman, did not get along. He just could not finish the third volume. Yet when he joined his brothers in Tiegnmouth,

Devonshire, and attended Dawlish fair with another good friend, barrister James Rice, he rattled off a humorous and bawdy doggerel that she found amusing but which she was not supposed to have even read. In fact, he was angry that Charles Brown had shown her his scribbled copy, and how Brown got the copy from his own, her Keats did not know. Brown seemed to always find some way to copy everything John Keats wrote, as if he were an invisible sprite hovering over the John Keats' candle, desk, and paper.

In rare light spirits of this time, her Keats had written:

> Over the hill and over the dale.
> And over the bourne to Dawlish.
> Where Ginger-bread wives have a scanty sale,
> And ginger-bread nuts are smallish.
>
> Rantipole Betty she ran down a hill
> And kicked up her petticoats fairly
> Says I, I be Jack if you be Jill.
> So she lay on the grass debonnairly.
>
> Here's somebody coming, here's somebody coming!
> Says I 'tis the wind at a parley.
> So without any fuss, any hawing or humming
> She lay on the grass debonnairly -
>
> Here's somebody here and here's somebody there:
> Says I, hold your tongue, you young gypsy.
> So she held her tongue and lay plump and fair
> And dead as a venus tipsy.
>
> O who wouldn't hie to Dawlish fair
> O who wouldn't stop in a Meadow
> O who wouldn't rumple the daisies there
> And make the wild fern for a bed do.

John suffered now and again from the sore throat that had forced him to leave Charles Brown and their Scottish hike. When he arrived back to 1 Well Walk on August 19, it was clear now that Tom would not recover. Whenever the doctors told him he was doing very well, there came another ghastly hemorrhage. In August came the savage attack on him through his published *Endymion - Blackwoods*, followed by the *Quarterly* after the *British Critic* copy was given to him when he had first come home. Within all of this pain, fears for Tom, missing his brother George, gone to America, his own sore throat coming and going, but getting worse at each return, he wrote to his publisher about his failed *Endymion*.

No one was more critical of his poetry than himself. He wrote that his own self criticism "has given me pain beyond comparison beyond what Blackwood or the Quarterly could possibly inflict- and also when I feel that I am right, no external praise can give me such a glow as my own solitary reception and ratification of what is fine." He recognized that *Endymion* was slip shod, but he was thankful that he had had the power to attempt the poem and by himself, that if he had asked advice or trembled over every page, none of them would have been written. "The Genius of Poetry," he wrote, "must work out its own salvation in a man: It cannot be matured by law and precept, but by sensation and watchfulness in itself. That which is creative must create itself. In *Endymion* I leaped headlong into the sea, and thereby have become better acquainted with the Soundings, the quicksands, and the rocks, than if I had stayed upon a green shore, and piped a silly pipe, and took tea and comfortable advice. I was never afraid of failure, for I would sooner fail than not be among the greatest."

And thus her Keats judged himself.

With Brown still in Scotland, not being able to mention the caustic reviews to Tom, who could now not even greet him at the door of Well Walk, he had found his beautiful young girl, and he had the Dilkes at Wentworth Place, and it was with them that they spent what time they could when Tom was sleeping his life away, reprieved for awhile of coughing it away. One of the Bentley's stayed with Tom. There would soon be a time, her Keats told her, that he could not leave him at all.

The Dilkes invited them to dinner to celebrate his birthday, and there she went into a rage at the Z signatories who did a hatchet job on the poetry of John Keats for the glory of crown and empire. "The Tories do not believe in a middle class," she said, as they were drinking claret before the fire. "They want everyone but themselves to be peasants defending their manors, and working their fields as the blacks do in America. Let us begin with the first half of the Z – ers - those that cannot sign their name to their *spewed venom. Mr. John Lockart,* son in law of Sir Walter Scott. He went to Cambridge to get a degree in self- appreciation which he imparts in Greek or German to make it stronger, and when he managed to meet Goethe in Germany, he thinks that was through the personal intervention of Jesus Christ. Now the other half of the Z- ers - *John Wilson,* son of a wealthy Glasgow trader who went to Cambridge so his vanity and conceit and stupidity could equal Mr. Lockart's. The two of them together could not have half the mind of my Keats, and certainly not a *glimmer* of my Keats' courage, for when Hunt's *Examiner* asked them to reveal their names in print, they did NOT!"

"My dear girl," said Keats, but he was pleased at her wrath. Everyone in the room already knew what she was saying, but she had to say it again. "Those Tories hate anything new to the world since their own births, and I do not think their mothers *finished* what they were doing - giving birth before their minds had arrived!"

The Dilkes laughed in spite of themselves, but no one laughed harder and with more merriment that her Keats. "Miss Brawne, you are a shocking young lady. Imagine, an unmarried young lady knowing about things as the *birth* of children -"

She wanted to kiss him, and could not until the Dilkes left them alone after dinner, for her Keats was increasingly private about his passion for her. She did not feel that way at all, and her family, her mother, her sister Margaret, and even her baby brother Sammy, knew she had found the man of all of her dreams. In truth they heard about it almost every day.

The Dilkes went upstairs to the comfort of their bedroom fireplace, after saying their goodnights, and receiving their thanks for his birthday dinner. "I am sorry Abbey would not let your sister come also," said Mrs. Dilke. "He is such an inconsiderate selfish man."

"Stay and enjoy the fire," said Mr. Dilke. "It would be a shame to waste the heat, for you and Miss Brawne are going to have a long cold walk back to her house."

They did enjoy the fire, and alone in the back parlor, overlooking the communal garden, they sat on the floor, and soon, his head was upon her lap, and she was stroking his hair, touching his brows, and his lips with her hands. "My *dearest*," she said. Even with Tom so ill, it was hard to find the money to heat his room. His own coat was too thin, his boots worn out- his always having to take the slower coaches and ride on top made her grieve. She never knew him to complain about himself. He was always worrying over Tom, George, his sister - and she looked down at his perfect face, and ached to hold his lips to her breast. "Tell me again about why we are here, and where we are going," she said. "And tell me about human love - and why we cannot get married -"

"Oh, my dearest girl," he said huskily, his voice trembling as it always did when he was deeply emotional. "If I could build an enchanted castle for us; if I could cast a secure life at your feet -" He stopped, and his eyes were wet. "I have to give you more than the sharing of my poverty," he said. "I have to bring us a good living with my poetry. I have to try - and I have to believe that I will succeed - that we will marry."

She was silent, deeply moved, and they remained in silence, but the fire did not. It crackled cozily and merrily. A wind grew outside and the night would be cold, and the walk to her house, colder still.

He sighed unhappily, his face melancholy, his eyes haunted. "My dearest girl - you absorb me in spite of myself. You have become an *obsession*."

"I love you," she whispered.

"I could not *exist* without you. I could not breathe without you. I cannot reason away the reason of my passion for you. Fanny, you have consumed all my old wishes and all my old dreams - I will never be able to bid you an entire farewell."

She bent down to kiss his beautiful lips, and then she held him to her heart.

"Withhold not an atom of what you are from me!"

"I wouldn't! I couldn't! I want you to take me in all ways, and I do not care if we marry or ever can!"

He suddenly moved from her, as if she were one of the glowing coals of the fire, and had landed on his breast. "Don't talk like this to me," he said hoarsely. "I am in torment enough!"

His eyes were so alive with the passion of such anguish it was startling. "My dearest heart -"

He moved farther away and shivered, as if they were already out in the night's cold. "It is time for me to take you home," he said roughly. He put on his thin inadequate coat, and helped her put on her very adequate one. "I am glad that your family was left comfortably well off by your father," he said sincerely. "I could not bear for you to ever be cold."

She tried to be as close to him as she could as he walked her home, a mile from Wentworth Place. If she could shield him from the cold, for the wind had grown bitterly hostile, and it sent dried frozen leaves against their legs. "I want to get married on Christmas Day," she told him, holding his hand within her own. "You know how we love the Elizabethan season of Christmastide. I know you could move in with us now, wherever we decide to finally live."

"That would be too hard on me to do that," he said. "I want our own home. I do not believe a man should marry a girl and move in with her mother."

"It would just be for a while."

"Then we can wait for me to earn the money to give us a home."

"I don't want to wait. I feel that if we do -"

"If what? That my poetry will in the end will fail us?"

"Oh, my dearest Keats. Your poetry will never do that!"

"It has already," he said grimly. "*Lamia* may do no better than *Endymion*."

They passed houses that still cast a faint light into the street. There were no police in London, only the "Watch" who walked their beats in twos or threes, armed with sticks and lanterns, and shouted out each hour of the night. They had just come to Hampstead, and tonight they passed two who were huddled in their sentry box for warmth. Near them, the street was lighted with a flickering oil lamp, and as they knew her and her Keats from his walking her home at night, they shouted a cheery greeting. "John Keats - it's too cold for lovers to be out this night! And when snow comes, it will be worse, even for a poet and his girl!"

She felt his hand tighten in hers, but he smiled with his charming way of greeting everyone. "Maybe when the snow comes," he laughed, "I will pull my beautiful companion in a warm sled!"

Now they were at her house, the front room lit with the lamp her mother always kept burning in the window. They kissed where it was dark enough for their kissing not to be seen, and as usual, he was the one who ended the embrace. "My dearest girl," he said softly. "I think I will have to stay home alone with Tom from now on."

"Can't I come and help you with him?"

"No. I know what is coming. I saw it with my mother's death, and I have studied enough medicine to know how tuberculosis kills. I will take care of him alone. I would not want you to see it, my dearest girl."

One more kiss, and then another, and after the last, he all but ran away from her.

In his own bed now, he thought of his lips upon the soft swelling of her breast, how he had felt the gentle taking in of her breath. He had written to his friend Bailey in November of 1818, "I am certain of nothing but the holiness of the Heart's affections."

How true that was, but could he have known how true, before he had fallen so deeply in love? He wondered now if the beauty of the earth, each season, would even be, as he had written, *if human souls did never kiss and greet?*

In the warmth of her room and in the warmth of her bed, she looked out the window to see how the wind was blowing the tops of the trees against the cold glittering of the stars, and she thought of how he regarded the sanctity of human love. Love came from the heart, he said, and the mind had a time to reason it away! Dreamily, she said some of his lines from THE THRUSH'S SONG.

> O thou whose face hath felt the Winter's wind,
> Whose eye has seen the snow-clouds hung in mist,
> And the black elm-tops 'mong the freezing stars
> To thee the spring will be a harvest-time.

He spoke of this night, this wind and these elms moving in shadow against the stars -

To thee the Spring shall be a triple morn,
And he's awake who thinks himself asleep.

How he and Tom suffered in their chilly rooms. Tom would not know another spring. And he would soon die and know no more cold, no riding outside in a blizzard on the top of the coach, no money to heat their rooms against one more winter.

*Help my dearest darling*, she prayed to God, way up there beyond the wind-blown elms, beyond the stars and the stars beyond them.

Their clock chimed the midnight hour, and as it did she was comforted by what he had written in his sonnet to Homer.

*There is a budding morrow in midnight.*

# Fifteen

Tom died in his arms, December 1, 1818. It was just at sunrise and John Keats held the still form of his dead brother, and looked out at the light growing into another day. He could fancy Tom within it, sturdy and strong, as he had never been in this slight body, and he would be walking to their mother and their father, who were probably doing the new waltz, for then they could hold each other in the public eye, without Abbey watching them, and trying to look up his mother's skirts to argue against beautiful legs for women. And Granny Good would be greeting Tom, too, maybe with sweetmeats or minced meat for the Christmas coming - in what house? John placed them all within his father's fine home on Craven Street, City Road. He placed within this house the old warm fires, burning all night long to keep every room warm for morning breakfast.

He looked around now at their own bedroom, the cheerless cold of every dark corner in which no fire shed light or the rays of the sun had yet to reach. Gently, he lay Tom back down on his bed, wiped his face, closed the eyes, and the body looked so peaceful and so relieved to be at rest, and free from the phlegm and the blood bubbling up through its mouth and its nose. "Godspeed," John said gently. "Go happily into the new light, my dear Tom. Go happily."

John put on his coat, and closed the door on Well Walk behind him. He vowed he would never return to open that door again. It was a closed one, like so many closed doors of his life. He boarded with Charles Brown at Wentworth Place, and Brown arranged for his things to be brought to his quarters there and for the removal of Tom's body.

Tom was buried December 3, at St. Stephen's Church, Coleman

Street, London, where his grandmother, and his father had been buried. His *dear girl* was with him. And she was with him as much as she could respectably be, all of that month. He bore his grief so quietly. She knew what he felt inside where he kept his emotions hidden, but he could not stay their eruption into his eyes, or into his poetry.

She liked Charles Brown, not as much as she liked Mrs. Dilke, or Fanny Keats, but she liked his fondness for her Keats. The two had gotten along well in their Scotland hike, and there was no reason to assume they would not get along as they shared Brown's half of Wentworth Place.

Charles Brown was born in 1786, and now he was thirty- two, bald, with side whiskers and spectacles. He was husky, strong, had a loud infectious laugh, and had the deepest appreciation for the poetry of John Keats. But of Keats' passion and love for Miss Frances Brawne, he did not know for a long time. As it grew more and more intense, her Keats' wanted it still just between him and what he always privately called her, either "my dearest girl," or "my beautiful girl."

The home of Charles Brown had two sitting rooms, one front and one overlooking the common garden. John Keats was given the front sitting room, facing the road and a beautiful view of Hampstead Heath. Upstairs there were two large bedrooms, one front, one back, and her Keats had the front bedroom, over his sitting parlor. There was a third bedroom, very small, for company

"If someone were to ask me about my Keats," she said to her mother, "what would I tell him?"

"That he was made in Heaven, and has never left it," said her mother, smiling wryly.

"And that he has the face of a Greek God," added her sister, Margaret.

"And that he tells me these great stories of King Arthur," said little brother, Sammy.

Fanny was helping her mother with the Christmas dinner three days before Christmas. The meal had to be perfect, for on Christmas Day, they would be engaged to marry, and she had decided this would be right away, and *Lamia* could take care of herself or be damned.

"You really want to marry him," said her mother, but really posing a question.

"Yes," she replied. "We could marry right now, and he could move in with us - we have the room, and the money -"

"He has already told me he would never do that. He wants to provide you with your home himself."

"Until he can! Mother, I do not want to wait!"

"Fanny, it isn't just you doing the marrying!" replied her mother.

They were making mincemeat for pies, and the spicy smells of its bubbling on the fire filled the whole house. "But he cannot go on eating with Brown at chop houses-"

"Fanny, they are two grown men. Your Keats is a very determined and strong young man. You will NOT have your way on this. I would wager everything we have on it."

Later while Fanny bathed and dressed for his arrival for supper, she gave herself more warm water than usual, and lay in it, and watched the mist from the warm bathroom form on the frosty windows. *What are you, my Keats? What do I so love?* What would she place first? His intellect? She was sure that he was a genius, so easy all mind things were to him. And who could take the light and the shadows of life on earth, and weave them into such a haunting magic? *It's his infinite tender and gentle nature. No, it is his courage; he does not flinch away from any horror. No, it is his humor. He is a fun-loving delightful companion for the rest of my life. No, it is his integrity. His mind probes into all of the injustices against the weak - he will take them on some day, as he tells me he will do. First my poetry, money to live on, then I will do something that will leave my world a better one, he says over and over, in varying ways. So I love him for that. And it is his total lack of affectation, and his innate dignity. Hadn't Cowden Clarke said that if he had been born in squalor, he would have emerged a gentleman? It's his independent mind, his passion for his casements of fancy, beyond the limits understood by the mind. It's the poetry in his soul, the way he sees women as beautiful and as goddesses - it's really - his ability to stretch beyond all of the dark corners of what is seen as real and is not.*

Tender lover, with a rollicking zestful humor, sensitive to the rights of others - well, she thought, snuggling down in the cooling water, I cannot go through the list again, for this water will be ice, and I frozen in it - an ice maiden he will put into a poem.

But so deeply in love she was, she went through the list of his perfections again, until the water had turned cold. I just love you *in all ways,* John Keats, she said, shivering her way out of the bathtub.

What do I love about her, he thought, as he walked from Wentworth Place to the home the Brawnes rented on Downshire Hill. He passed three men on watch now, all huddled snugly in their sentry box. "John Keats!" one yelled, always liking to see the young man walking to court his young lady.

"Still the same!" laughed Keats. "And not an inch taller, either!"

"But still a-court'n," said another sentry. He liked the young man, too, and you would never know from his plain and friendly manner and his strong husky looks, he was some kind of a *published* poet.

"Still courting my beautiful girl!" Keats laughed, and waved a cheery goodbye to them, seeing his own breath caught in the cold air, and wraith-like, vanish before him.

What do I love about my beautiful dearest girl, he asked himself, deepening his pleasure as he told himself why he adored her, cherished her, and would love her for all eternity. If there were no eternity, his passion for her would create one. *I will haunt all your days and all your dreaming nights,* he promised her as he walked head-down into the bitter cold.

"I know women cannot love as deeply as men," he had told her.

She had not liked that at all. "Being as you are not a woman, John Keats, how would you know that? Didn't you say your mother worshipped your father?"

"Yes, but I worry about *you -*"

"What? *What?*"

"You wear those pink bows in your hair - and I think you *like it* because men find you beautiful!"

His jealousy was not one of the things she had listed about him in her cooling bath.

Now he went back to a woman's *inherent* fickle nature in his mind, and it helped him forget how miserable he was in his thin coat, his threadbare boots. Women were not deep like men. *That will just have to be accepted,* he told himself, with the wonder of the rest of her.

Why do I love her so? Why does she hold my heart within just her smile? Is it her rare and fine intelligence, the fact that she reads French and German, loves Shakespeare as I do, and loves the theater as I do? Is it because - for a woman - she has a tender and a loyal heart? Is it because she has the same passion against injustice that I have? But she loves so to dance, and how the men look at her - oh God, how can I bear the ravishing of her by their look of desire - *My dearest girl,* his soul cried, as his body felt craven and empty with his passion for her.

And there she was, greeting him before he could ring the bell, and covering his lips and his cold face with her warm kisses.

And she was so perfectly, perfectly beautiful.

The house was warm, and tantalizing smells from the kitchen filled all of the downstairs rooms. She had his favorite wine, claret, and allowed him to pour it for her, and for him. Her eyes sparkled with joy. Her hair shone under the candles of the crystal chandeliers. The smell of roasting fowl with onions and herbs came to him, the smell of bread baking, a specialty of his girl and her mother. A fire burned in the dining room fireplace, and one danced in the parlor. He assigned Tom to such a place and to such a joyful moment, too, so he could feel joy of his own.

Little sister Margaret helped with serving the food. Sammy sat by him, and wanted more Arthurian enchantments, but this time he told him of Elizabeth the Great and of the great white swans always in front of her castles when she was in residence. "She wanted to always know the waters were clean enough for them," he said. "She did not allow *any* waste to be dumped in the streets, streams or rivers. *Ever.*"

By candlelight and firelight they ate, and were warm and shared a joyous meal. Church bells of the Christmastide season rang, and their sweet sound always made the season sacred to him, and this season was sacred to her, because in it she knew they would become engaged.

After dinner her mother saw that the children left them alone in the front parlor, and as usual, they sat on the floor in front of the fire, and as usual, his head ended up on her lap, where she could more easily caress his hair, his lips, with her fingers.

"I think the joy of God is increased with our own," he said. "Knowing the glory of love - in all of its aspects, body and soul - is the highest tribute a man can make to his creator."

"Tusk, tusk, you vulgar young anti-Tory man. They do not acknowledge that we have bodies, those nasty things they have traded for empire and pound!"

He laughed. "Then you are a shocking young lady to love a shocking young man."

"As much as I *can*," she teased. "Even with my *womanly fickleness*."

He looked up at her, the lights in his eyes, so unique to him, an expression of love. She kissed his forehead, and he brought her lips down to his. They kissed and then they remained still, too content for even a word. The fire was high and warm, the windows around them completely frosting over from the cold outside. "Stay here, tonight," she said.

He stretched, stirred, and smiled. "Where?"

"With me."

"Where?"

"In my bed."

He moved rapidly away from her. "You must not talk like that or *think* like that!"

"I think like that all of the time!"

"My dearest girl - you are *not* supposed to have thoughts like that!"

"Well, if a lady denies that she has them, I would say we have a lot of lady liars."

"But men are the more vulnerable - attracted -"

She became angry. "You know better than that. At least in your *poetry* - you now better than that!"

"I will have no more than kissing until we are married."

"And we cannot get married until your poetry supplies us with a home!"

"It will." He came back to her, and kissed her many times. "It will."

"How *do* you write a poem?"

"The poem writes itself. I believe I have a secret guest who writes through me."

"Who?"

"My *secret* guest. And there must always be a mystery left for the reader - let him expand beyond the writing into what it brings to *him*. The light I have found -"

"You gather to pass on -"

"That is what the joy of creation is. But I wrote to Woodhouse that if I wrote poetry all night and burned what I wrote all morning, and no eye would ever see what I wrote, I would still write again from my yearning to write and in my joy in creating -"

"What?"

"A new world - magic that was previously unseen. Yes. Light to light - as if I can garner a star – our Evening Star - and say, dear lover, this is also yours!"

"Our Evening Star," she said, her eyes wet.

He touched her face, her lips in a tender caress. "Our Evening Star," he repeated. "And our love is as constant, as eternal, that no night can deny, nor no dawn diminish."

The moment held. It was as pure in energy as was the Evening Star hidden above the snow falling outside.

The church bells of London began to peel. They thought of all the Christmas seasons past when those same bells peeled out the celebration of the best in man, and they both thought of marriage, the completion of their love within a new life created by them both, of a life from that life, and their being old and filled with content before another fire - and new Christmas snow would fall on new homes, and the lights within them would shine, just as they were doing now, sweetly sanctified by the season.

Sammy had come in to ask a question of his sister's love. "All I want to know," said Sammy, sensing his mother on his trail, "is if she kept the rivers so clean, what did Queen Elizabeth the Great do with all of the puke pots?"

# Sixteen

They were engaged that Christmas day of 1818. They secretly exchanged rings, and locks of hair. "You must give me your word, that this engagement remain private between us, until just before we marry," he said.

"I give my solemn promise," she said, having put his ring on a hidden rope of pearls that she wore under her dresses. "Here, it is next to my heart, and I will wear your ring *all of my life*." She had more wondrous kissing, and he even allowed it to go on - more than usual, and held her more closely - more than usual - and it was so exquisite, it seemed as if all of England had fallen in love with them in that Christmastide season. The church bells were constantly peeling from one snowy street to another, from one snowy village to another, and to her, still from years long past into years to come. Warm tavern windows fogged against the outside cold; warm house windows the same, with smoke from the chimneys and Christmastide smells from their kitchens, and horses passed with bells ringing merrily, and the mail coach horn, and the horns of passing coaches in snow banked lanes - it was life, and all of the wondrous sounds of its sharing. They walked their now favorite path between Hampstead and Highgate Hill on Milfield Lane. "It is too cold for us to be out," she said, warm herself, but knowing he could not be in his inadequate clothing.

"I am too filled with joy this season, my beautiful girl, to keep myself confined to one room, one house, and even one city!"

"If you are not in London, where are you?"

"I am in Heaven – Eden – Paradise."

They passed sloping meadows iced with the winds from northern and eastern Europe; the sky remained bitingly clear, the hedgerows gleaming with snow. This Saturday coming, he would dine at her house again, coming with the Dilkes. "We are so lucky to have found each other," she said. "Oh, my dearest Keats, we are young, and have such a wonderful life yet to share!" She all but twirled around him in pure joy. She slipped on a patch of ice, and he caught her, kept her from falling, and they kissed ardently, and he did not even look to see if they were on 'their' lane alone. "Saucy silly girl," he teased. "You fly around in all directions, bows flying from your hair -"

She stopped his words with a kiss. "Marry me," she said.

"I will, I will!" he laughed.

"Don't wait for *Lamia* to shed more skins, if that is what she is doing. Write SHORT poems to sell, and then we can get married right away!"

He laughed so hard at her he slipped, and as she could not hold him up, he fell and looked up at her, still laughing. He finally regained his feet, and they walked on. "You know Tom's money stopped with his death," he said, turning as sober as fast as he had turned mirthful. "Abbey will not release any. He says he will keep it until Fanny becomes of age, and then there will be none left."

"That horrible man, not letting her spend Christmas with us."

"Think how it is for her; all I can give thanks for is that their house is warm and stashed with food, for he does not get as fat as a hog on good thoughts."

"Last Christmas was the happiest day of my life," she said, feeling his ring under her dress, now warmed by her warmth.

"It was *our* day," he said, his voice trembling with emotion. "I have started a poem for us. We are the lovers in it. Well - I have *the idea*. Next month, I am going to start writing it."

"Maybe it will allow us to marry - if it is about us as lovers - maybe it will sell, make you wealthy, me your wife, and you - with claret and plum puddings - and warm, warm fires in *every* room!"

"I'm happy, my dearest girl. You have brought such joy to me."

"Wait until we are married, and we don't have to have any more *goodbye* kisses!"

"That will be delightful," he said huskily.

She had dreamed this every night before sleep, and so had he, even awakening from a dream of holding her in his arms, and still feeling her fragrantly warm and soft against him. *She haunts all of my days and all of my dreaming nights.*

On New Years Eve of 1819 there was a grand ball in Hampstead. Her Keats had the return of his sore throat and could not go out into the cold. She went to the ball alone, and although he insisted that she do this, he did not like it at all. He wrote a rather poor sonnet to her telling her so.

He also took himself away from Hampstead to visit the old father of Dilke, and then in the middle of January he went to Chichester with Charles Brown. He arrived there on January 20, and there he began his great choral hymn to love, and all of its opposing forces. It was not more than a sketch, and he named it *The Eve of St. Agnes.*

On his return to Wentworth Place, he walked to see her, and was cheered on by his allies of the town night watch. "We thought you deserted the pretty lassie!" one yelled.

"Only when I am dead!" he had replied. And probably not then, he thought. She opened the door at his ringing of it just once, and flew into his arms with such ardent kissing, she almost knocked both of them down. Little Sammy came to see the activity, and growled because he wanted to get right into the Camelot court tournaments. "Why do you two ALWAYS do that?" he whined, and was going to whine some more about it, when his mother jerked him out of sight.

"I have begun our poem!" her Keats said, his eyes glowing.

"Finish it here! We have an extra bedroom - oh, write our poem here!"

"I could not write *anything* around you!" he said, remembering she had been the belle of the ball at that odious silly dance on New Years, with all of those arms of imperialism around her waist.

"Why not?"

"And you went to that dance and danced with all of those cruel colonizers -"

"You TOLD me to go!"

"You did not HAVE to!"

She stamped her foot, and he noticed her shoes always matched the bows in her hair. Silly women.

"MEN!" she snapped, shaking her head.

"WOMEN!" he snapped back, and put his scarf around his throat, though it was too thin and worn to do much good.

They glared at each other from a growing distance.

Sammy had sneaked away and joined them to find out where Lancelot really came from. "Now *this* is more like it!" he said approvingly. Neither his sister, nor her beau heard, for from their kissing slop they had become very mad at each other.

"I am going home to write our love poem ALONE," her beau growled, and opened their front door so wide that all the cold, stored up from the winter so far, blasted through their house and dampened the downstairs fires.

She did not see him all of the rest of the month, and all of the next month. In her bath, made as hot as she could stand it, using all of the kettles for the dishes, she began to subtract all of his wondrous wonders until the water became too cold to bear.

In his quarters he wrote feverishly, and became so united with her within his poem, he was burning not only with the power of creation, but also with the passion of sexual love.

This was to be his first successful long poem. It was perfect; his glaring immaturities were absent. As his life would hold the worst possible pain, contrasted with the greatest possible joys, his poetry before *The Eve of St. Agnes* had born sublime writing and poor writing. Now came this long sensuous lyrical utterance in a tribute to spiritual and physical love. He worked it over and over, until it rang of beauty - to him. He took the tale of St. Agnes, who was a Roman virgin who had converted to Christianity. In A.D. 306, the Emperor Diocletian condemned her for her conversion. She was to be raped in the public stews and then executed. But the rape was not allowed. By thunder and lightning, they were not allowed. Her virginity was miraculously preserved. Her life was not. After her execution, her parents had a vision of her among assembled angels with a lamb by her side, as pure white as snow. Through the centuries she would take under her care virginal girls, and on the eve of the day, sacred to her memory, January 20, the girls who had done certain rites, fasting all day, and going to bed fasting, who had never even kissed a man, would dream of her lover, and he would come to her, bring her sweets, and take her as his bride.

But he was not writing the choral hymn to St. Agnes. He was writing to the woman he loved; he was writing a sensuous poem to youth, to love's passion, set to moonlight and music, sharp contrasts of fire and shadow, cold and warmth, silence, the blaring of silver trumpets, despair, ecstasy, gluttony, chastity, death stalking life, the dream within reality, and the reality within the dream, and as the lovemaking scene approached, the colors within the poem intensified, colored in imagination by pure moonlight, and the sexual and spiritual consummation rocked the Puritan pulpits of the day.

He had written of love's entrance into a castle of death, and all of the contrasts of life in that castle, and of the escape from it of the lovers, out into a howling storm, but in the castle they left behind lay nightmares of witch and demon and large coffin-worm, and "the Beadsman, after thousand aves told, for Ay unsought for slept among his ashes cold."

"It will do," said the author as he wrote. "It will do."

Abbey now refused to allow Frances Keats to see or write to John Keats. That radical young man, trying to be a poet, would be a bad influence. Poets did not make money. Only wealthy men could be poets as they could afford to be stupid.

February came and went, bitterly cold. He stayed inside away from the walk to her house. He re worked *The Eve of St. Agnes.* He tried to go on with *Lamia*, but like all women, she was unfaithful to him. Yet she had to be created to bring him some money, so he could at last marry another unfaithful woman who had gone to a New Years' ball and danced with all of the Redcoats there, probably in that pink lace dress with its silvered train, and the pink bows in her hair, framing her beautiful sparkling eyes, and those colonial rapists had felt her breasts against their chests, when they danced too close, which he was sure they did. That any other man would ever know the softness of her lips, or her breasts, or ever do with her what he ached to do, even in his poetry - he just found the pain to reach his sore throat and make it worse, and into his chest, where it was now attacking his right to breathe.

His cherished friend from his school days at Enfield School,

Crowden Clarke, visited, and insisted that he read aloud his new - really unfinished - poem. "I think *The Eve of St. Agnes* is the best thing you have done, Keats,'" he said, in obvious approval.

"Poor men that get tangled up in such passions," he replied gloomily. "She is going to lead him into a life of torment! That storm outside will be *nothing!*"

Crowden sighed, sharing male misery was a pleasurable habit with him. "Well, they were put here along with us, so we have to make the best of it," he said.

"My mother adored my father. I remember that more than anything else - from my childhood. Now why can't - well, ALL women be like that?"

"It just is not their usual nature," said Clarke. "I had a good and loving mother, too. Would becoming mothers make them any better? That is a thought, Keats. Maybe we should make them mothers right away, and then court them."

He saw his friend shudder. "It is this awful tormenting yearning for just *one!* Why can't I just platonically love her? Why can't we do that? Clarke - it is HELL!"

"I know. I know. Since Eve gave Adam the poisoned apple and drove us all out of Eden - what is it about this - mysterious - *one?* What about her is so tantalizing?"

"Every single thing!"

"Oh! That kind puts us at a grave disadvantage."

"I know. I know!" his friend moaned, getting closer to his meager fire. "Why can't they always be as warm as wool and look like teapots?"

"Because life is not fair to man once he meets a woman who has - this - *every single thing,* as you say. My Keats, you must just be strong and resist her as you would a rip tide of the ocean!"

"Clarke, I am not in a rip tide. I am at the bottom of the ocean."

He was in a deeper blue mood when Clarke left to go live with his retired father in Ramsgate. They never saw each other again.

If he used his apothecary license, he could make a good living. But he wanted to write, had to write, and would die without writing. But he would die without her, and never once, by suggestion or sentence, had she suggested he earn a living as a surgeon, and then they could marry, and he could go on with his writing as a hobby. Damn *Lamia*. She was getting more and more unpopular with him. Why didn't she let herself be finished and not stay coiled around his throat - like a throttling, malevolent, giant snake?

In his quarters, with *The Eve of St. Agnes* mostly done, he gloomed and he groused. He abandoned the beautiful *Eve of St. Mark*, and never would finish it. He read *Palmerin of England* and underlined passages he liked, even when he had borrowed the book from Taylor. He marked what applied to him.

> Some men in love commend their happiness,
> Their quiet sweet, and delicate delight.
> But for the sweetness other men have felt,
> I came too late, my part was elsewhere dealt.

He wrote George, and his sister in law, Georgiana. He never would admit in writing his love for Fanny Brawne, but he did put her in his letters, as heartless as she was to him. "Brown and Dilkes are considerate and kind. Miss Brawne and I have every now and then a chat and a tiff." He wrote of the failure of *Endymion*. In a year or so, he might try the public again with more poetry. "I have no doubt of success in a course of years if I persevere -" He had not a prayer now with the powerful *Review* or the Tory *Quarterly*. He wrote George he might practice medicine, that he should study in Edinburgh and get his physician's license, but he added, "I am afraid I should not take kindly to it -" still - "it's not worse than writing poems, and hanging them up to be fly-blown on the REVIEW shambles."

He found a way to contact his sister, and wondered if they could secretly somehow meet at Abbey's Walthamstow garden, and she could teach him how to dance. Just a few common steps, and perhaps how to properly bow, too, "And I would buy a Watch box to practice them by myself."

Miss Brawne sent him a note wanting to see their great love poem. He sent a note back saying that he had not finished it.

He continued journal letters to George, taking on new ideas and new paragraphs without dating them. He got away from

Hampstead, and *her*, who flirted so outrageously with other men to kill him. He visited the home of John Taylor, one of his publishers, on 93 New Bond Street, London, charming the whole household as usual, coming back to Wentworth Place on the twenty sixth of February. There had been no note sent to him by the *her* of the traitorous heart.

So the misery of February was gone, and his three sentries for the nightfall over Hampstead huddled in their sentry box and rubbed their hands together, and blew out frosted breath, and wondered why the poet Keats had stopped his walks by them to court his girl. They liked to see them as a couple passing by together, and she was as warmly friendly to them as he was, and could they now be married? Did he no longer have to walk to her house?

"We should know if they are married," said one. "They should at least let us know how the courting turned out."

Yes," said another. "We should know what happens on our watch."

"It is not that we are not interested!" said the third. "The street is lonely without him - always his cheery greeting -"

March came, and along *their* walk to Highgate Hill on Milfield Lane he thought the hedgerows would be yellow with daffodils, and there would be more yellow from the celandines in the verges. The sap was running high, and other young men, with a *true* woman, as true as their mothers, would walk *their* lane. The blackthorn would be in blossom, the hazel dangling its catkins, hazel shoots to be used later to secure thatch to a roof, to hold up pea and bean plants - and there *she* would be, with her Redcoats three, seeing all of this, and her pink slippers would match the pink bows in her hair, and she would be wearing her pink and silver ball gown with the train behind it, and he gleefully saw one redcoat step on it, one trip over it, and one tearing it off as he fell headlong into a pile of shit placed there by a huge bull, which had come loping gloriously along, just to do his potty.

He vented his spleen against orthodox religion in a letter to George. The clergy thinks it has the power to sanctify, indoors, and outdoors if the weather is not too bad. "A parson is a Lamb in the drawing-room, and a Lion in the vestry. The notions of Society will not permit a parson to give away his temper in any shape - so he festers in himself - his features get a peculiar, diabolical, self-Sufficient, iron stupid expression. He is continually acting - his mind is against every man, and every man's mind is against him. He is a Hypocrite to the Believer and a coward to the unbeliever. There is no man so much to be pitied as the idiot parson." A Redcoat, created for the purpose of nothing, "is not half so pitiable as the parson who is led by the nose by the bench of bishops and is smothered in absurdities - a poor necessary subaltern of the Church."

"A Man's life of any worth is a continued allegory, and very few eyes can see the Mystery of his life - a life like the scriptures, figurative - which such people can no more make out than they can the Hebrew Bible." About Jesus Christ he wrote that his greatness handed down by others was - "written and revised by men interested in the pious frauds of Religion. Yet through all this I see his splendour." He added, that he, himself, "was straining at particles of light in the midst of great darkness." He had written earlier to George, when Tom was yet alive, and he had not yet met *her*. "I hope I shall never marry. I feel more and more every day, as my imagination strengthens, that I do not live in this world alone, but in a thousand worlds. I melt into the air with a voluptuousness so delicate that I am content to be alone. These things, combined with the opinion I have of the generality of women who appear to me as children to whom I would rather give a sugar Plum than my time, form a barrier against Matrimony which I rejoice in."

While John Keats thought of his old desire to live alone and unmarried in his private thousand worlds of light, and how frightened he was to dare to publish anything he wrote again, Richard Woodhouse, who had found him his publishers, and probably remained his best friend, wrote to a woman about his writing. *Endymion* was written by a very young man, but when Milton and Shakespeare were his age, they did not write nearly as well. Shakespeare's earliest work, *Venus and Adonis,* was not as good as *Endymion.* "Are we to expect that poets are to be given to the world in a state of maturity? Are they to have no season of childhood? Are they to have no room to try their wings before the steadiness and strength of their flight are to be finally judged of? I can only prophesy. And now, while Keats is unknown, unheeded, despised by one of our arch critics, neglected by the rest, I express my conviction, that Keats, during his life will rank on a level with the best of the last and the present generation, and after his death will take the place at their head."

And while Woodhouse was glimpsing the truth about the genius of this young man, Miss Brawne was busily taking all of her bestowed on him glories of looks, talent, and, especially, character - away in her increasingly chilled baths. He had no business scolding me for going to a dance, she thought, and scorning me for wearing bows in my hair - *who does he think he is?* And as she shivered in the water, the one thing she could *not* take away from him was the expression in his eyes when he looked at her, those lights of love from his very soul.

Then, as she subtracted, she immediately began to add, and soon she had so many things back on her *good* list, she decided if he did not come to see *her,* she would walk over to Brown's and see *him.*

He was adding to a journal letter to George in America that he happened to date for once, March 19. "This morning I am in a sort of temper, indolent and supremely careless -" He told George that all passion within him was asleep.

The following March days dawned in warm glory. There is no spring like the springs in England, she thought. No wonder we have magic woods with kingdoms of fairies in tree shadows, castles of dreams along our rivers, and the ghosts in ancient castles along the ocean cliffs where shades of knights still fight for their king, or their lady love. A peasant before sleep knows he, too, can hear the retinue nearby of the great Elizabeth Tudor who has come again to be among the most humble of her people.

He was at his desk downstairs trying to deal with *Lamia* but covering with bullshit the whole Imperial British Army, those walking with her on *their* Milfield Lane, those that danced with her in Hampstead - those that came to Hampstead and even *looked* at her.

In fact, so deep he was into creating the bullshit mound higher and higher, he did not see over it as she approached down the carriage walk to Wentworth Place.

He was adding maggots and flies on the boys in Red Coat red and did not know she was with him, until he felt her arms around his neck. "You can't be HERE!" he gasped, always seeing such vivid mind pictures, he was terrorized she would step right into one of the shit mounds he had created.

"I can, and I am," she laughed, and when he turned from *Lamia*, and what had taken her place, she was twirling in front of him like a little girl - just as he had seen his little sister do, when Granny good made her sweet meats.

He put down his pen, and looked at her. She stopped twirling and looked at him. She wore a bright yellow dress, to go with the spring daffodils outside. She had yellow bows in her hair to match her yellow shoes. She looked so beautiful he thought he would never breathe normally again. She even had put down a packed lunch near them, and he could see she had remembered claret wine for him. "You match the morning," he said, "- the sunshine of spring."

She laughed joyfully, and without any apologies for dancing with the colonizer criminals, and the walks with them in Milfield Lane after the dance, or on Sundays, she began to kiss him, and just about push him out of his chair and away from his desk. He began to return her kisses, and found that he had written such a great lie to George. His passions had not gone to sleep.

He held her and kissed her so ardently, all taken from him during her cold baths came back tenfold. Probably no man in the world would ever have the adoration in his eyes when he looked at her, between kisses. No man in the world would have such strength and such tenderness as one of the other. No man in the world would ever kiss her lips as he did, and send fire all along her veins.

"Brown is home," he said. "He might come in here."

"To copy our love poem? I think he copies everything before you finish writing it."

"I haven't finished writing it." And whether Brown came in and found him in the secrecy of his passion or not, he began to kiss her lips, her throat, and right down to the swelling of her breasts.

This cannot end, or be halted any more, she thought. I will see that he *can not stop*, that I am compromised, and he will *have* to marry me.

Finally, pushing himself away from her, he put on his scarf, and a jacket. He picked up her picnic lunch. *We are going to eat this thing near the lane, or on the lane, and there had better be a hell of a lot of people walking by. How can I deny what I have to have much longer?*

# Seventeen

There were many people about enjoying the perfect morning of a perfect spring day. Many knew him, and smiled their affection. Some even stopped, and said they enjoyed his poetry, even if they were not supposed to. More and more young ladies were smiling at him, and she loved this. She was so certain of his love and total adoration, they all could smile and flirt to their heart's content, but the lane they walked together was theirs.

They talked long and joyously of his beloved William Blake. They agreed that heaven was in the face of a flower, and universes in a grain of sand. There were no avenging angels guarding Eden with flaming swords. No. Angels joyfully opened their golden wings to shelter those who realized they had never left Eden after all, that God could not banish what he was, that a melody lives within song.

He was breathless with happiness. *Spring has a triple song to sing.* He thought of a line from his trashed and scorned *Endymion*.

> Now I have tasted her sweet soul to the core
> All other depths are shallow.

He quoted it to her. "My dearest girl, I wrote that for you before we ever met!"

"My poetry for you, John Keats, is hidden within my heart - I can't ever express it but with my love."

He held her hand, and he did not care now if it drew looks. "The highest good that mankind can know is the truth of love, shedding its own light. It equals the miracle of the Evening Star."

"Which we already have given to each other," she smiled.

"That will see the ending of night with the light of a new dawn."

The day remained clear and warm. A breeze rose to move through the meadow grass below, and through the trees bordering their path. "Feel the *tide*," he said softly, "feel the *living* tide!" They stopped and watched the wind change tree shadows. He would not move on until the wind died, and its play on light ceased. It was so dear to both of them.

"Now we can go on," he said, for the wayward breeze had wrought its changes and was gone. One small cloud passed to leave the sky a glorious unblemished blue.

He chose the place for them to share lunch.

"It is too close to the lane," she said.

"I don't know whether it is close *enough*," he said mysteriously, opening the wine, and pouring some for each of them.

"We will get the food dusty and dirty staying here," she complained, already vaguely picturing his ravishments of her, but clearly picturing the subsequent marriage. He would move into her bedroom and her bed and be able to kiss her to sleep, and into awakening. She began to tingle all over with the thought of what he would do when she had him beyond the point of pushing away from their kisses.

She had brought roast fowl, bread, cheese, wine, and oranges from Spain. She had brought plenty of claret. She would get him to drink it all by himself, and then they would go to hiding shade and hiding ferns and she would put his lips on her breasts and he would succumb and ravish her, which he clearly wanted to do, anyway. Dear God - *please make him ravish me!* She saw herself lying on the grass among the tall thick ferns that had so helped out Rantipole Betty on her way home from the Dawlish fair.

Things were looking good. The lane traffic had stopped. "I want to move away from the path," she said. "There are too many people here."

"There is no one here but us," he said, looking puzzled.

"But there will be - might be- "she insisted.

"Why don't you drink your wine?"

"I am saving it for you." Too much wine was supposed to bring out the *beast* in men, her mother always said, and how she wanted to unleash that beast with all of her heart and soul. She kept filling his glass including what had been in hers. If there was a beast in him he could not control it would soon arrive. It had to.

He got the food out and ate most of it. She was too busy plotting out their mutual ravishing to eat. He never before drank more than one glass of the only wine he liked, claret, but now he did, and it seemed to make him sweat on his forehead and around his eyes. Finished, he put all of their dishes and glasses away, and lay back on the soft grass near the lane, as if he did not care who saw him lying on it. His eyes remained open, looking up at the cloudless sky. How long did wine allow the beast to survive? How long did she have before the wine and its longed for beast would disappear – vanish - *be gone?*

She moved closer to him. To lie down by him would send him flying to his feet, and she didn't want that. At least one of them was down in the style of Rantipole Betty of the Dawlish fair. "Tell me about our love poem," she said. Often his own poetry inspired wondrous kissing.

"No."

"What is it about?"

"When it is finished, I will read it to you."

"I bet Brown has read it!"

"Only what is unfinished - I want you to hear it when it is completed."

"Why should I be different from Brown?" she semi-snapped, because her ravishment plan was going nowhere, as if she knew where to send it in the first place.

"Well you ARE different," he smiled. "And thank God for it."

"What do you mean?"

"You are prettier. You are beautiful, and poor Brown is not."

"Didn't *Endymion* love a woman as a goddess, *and* a seductive SENSUAL wood nymph?"

"And look what happened to him, the poor devil."

"I am trying to get you to tell me the necessity of SEXUAL love. Which did *Endymion* want? SEXUAL or divine?" *Sensual seductive* and *sexual* - all unladylike words which she hoped would arouse the male beast she fervently hoped to be still present.

"Both. They are the same, aren't they? I do not consider sexual love a so- called - dirty - part of spiritual love. I think the union of a man with a woman in spiritual love must be no less than the rapture of union with God - maybe one is a small pattern from the other -" He thought on that, and looked adoringly at her.

*I am getting somewhere now!* But she did not know just how. "That is beautiful. Go on," she said, moving closer to him, but still not daring to lie down beside him.

"A man's love for a woman, and its fulfillment, and a woman's love for a man, and it's fulfillment, is a *spiritual* as well as a *physical* necessity -"

"Of course! Of course!" she broke in, with a little more enthusiasm than she had intended.

He went on calmly, and her heart sent his ring into twirling under her bodice.

"And the orgasm of union - spiritual - physical -"

"Orgasm?" She did not know what that was. "What is that - this orgasm?"

"It is - the rapture of union," he said. "The tide of creation - for does it not result in creation?"

"Just how?

"In union. The two - one - two become - *are* - one." He was looking dreamily up at the sky.

"Orgasm - this rapture of union - is this better than kissing?"

He cast her a look of love that made her feel on the entrance to Heaven. "Oh, my yes," he said softly. He looked away and up at the sky again and content and a tranquil joy were on his face. "We must reach primal light and add to it - the center of all creation must grow with us -" He was giving this deep thought. "God - ever growing - the soul of man seeking the same? Do you think of God - as growing?"

"I am more down to earth." She certainly was, along the lines of Rantapole Betty doing what she could do with a lush grass countryside.

"If we are light from light, life from life - our growth is a part of the divine plan -"

God was on His own. She was sinking out of sight in her own divine plan. "Are we extinct in love?" she asked, feeling more and more so.

"Love is not *extinction*. It is *extension* of the self into its eternal center of love."

"We are centered in God's love? Isn't this pagan and wrong? It certainly is against the church!"

He sat up and looked at her as if she were back in the cradle. "I would HOPE so!" he said. "Do you believe, even REMOTELY - that the Christian churches have left very much of Jesus within them? What is more important to them, Jesus, or Satan? Which gives them the most POLITICAL power, Jesus or Satan? How dare they pawn heaven and hell off on us, as if they were pieces of *church* real estate? The miracle is that a sacred and enlightened man like Jesus can shine through all of the centuries of hypocrisy and fraud, and vile murders and corruption of church *politics!* And as for the so called *pagan* savage who has the earth for his church, the wind for his voice, and the sun and earth united within his soul, does not the same evening star that blesses the flocks of our fields - bless him? Can he not travel his *own* trail after death to live among the stars?"

She did not need a discourse on Jesus and Satan and Indians of America traveling up to the stars. She wanted what she wanted. She got up, and walked off the path, into the high ferns under the oaks that formed deep shade among them. He had picked up the picnic basket and had followed her, and she saw puzzlement upon his face. "Fanny, what are you DOING? Where are you GOING?"

"I am no longer your beautiful dearest girl?"

"Of course. But where are we going? Why do you want to stumble through these thick - entangling - ouch - ferns and - *ouch,* blackberry patches?"

There were quite a bit of thorns, unexpected ones, painful ones, but somewhere there would be soft ferns and soft grass and no prickly berries.

He stopped her. She had torn her dress; he had torn his pants, and he did not have a lot of pants to tear apart among blackberry shoots. "FAN- NY!"

It was no use. She was just dumb. She didn't know how to find herself a ravishing in any place or at any time. She pressed against him and began to sob in frustration. He put down the basket, and amid the prickling thorns he took her within his arms, and caressed her hair away from her face, as she liked to do for him, and he soon was kissing her face, her lips, the tears that streamed from her long lashes. "My dearest girl, what is it? How have I hurt you? What did I say - do?"

"You won't let me be Rantipole Betty!" she wailed.

"Who? What?" he asked, lost, and hurting, too, from the thorns and his desire for her.

"*Over the hill and over the dale and over the bourne of Dawlish,*" she sobbed. "*So she lay on the grass debonnairly. O who wouldn't rumple the daisies there, and make the ferns for a bed do!*" she quoted in between sobs.

"Oh, Fanny - oh, my dearest girl - oh my God! You should not have been even shown that bawdy thing! It was a - silly joke for - I don't know why I wrote it. But YOU should never, never have seen it!"

"I want to lie *plump and fair and as drunk as a venus tipsy!*"

He led them back to the lane, or near it, safely away from ferns and thorns, and his sexual arousal. But he only left the ferns and the thorns behind. "Those were just silly words," he said. He held his arm around her waist, kept her close to him, and she could feel him trembling against her. "I want you to do what a man does to the woman he loves and who loves him for this orgasm union with God," she sobbed, taking her handkerchief from under the bodice of her dress, where his ring was rising and falling with the racing of her heart.

When she finally looked at him, tears were in his eyes. He slowly moved away from her, and then lost to her, the world, any common sense, he began to beat his hands viciously against a tree, and he beat and beat them, and punished them into bleeding, and would have gone on destroying them if she had not screamed, and stopped the bloodletting.

She held the poor bleeding flesh to her face, her lips. "How could you," she sobbed in horror. "How could you do such a ghastly and *horrible* thing?"

He took his hands away from her face, her lips, and took his worn scarf from his throat, and he bandaged them and stopped their bleeding. He sat down on a fallen tree, and buried his face in his bandaged hands. "My God, my dearest girl, don't you know how I ache - day and night - to possess you - to make love to you? To do what I have been in torment and agony to do since I first tried to do that damnable waltz with you?"

He walked away from her, deeply shamed, and he found another place to sit, and he looked at his hands, and bent over himself in obvious pain, and he finally hid his face in his hands again, and she could hear him weeping.

She went to him, but he pushed her away.

So in this warm and glorious day of spring, in their first meeting for what had seemed forever since January, she stood alone, and he sat alone, and he cried as long and as bitterly as a man could, as he had openly wept when he crawled under his schoolmaster's desk after he had heard that his mother had died when he had not been outside of her door to keep death from taking her away.

She was cried out. Her sobbing and her need for him in all ways had worn her out emotionally and physically. She just looked at his agony now, and she thought, *I cannot bear to see him suffer like this.*

Finally, he worked through his outburst. Finally, he was able to stand, and he took the picnic basket from her, and carried it without a word during the walk to her house. It was dark enough for the three night watchers to be on duty. It was warm enough for them to be walking on her street, calling out the time.

They all greeted her Keats with such affection; she smiled and loved them all. He greeted them so cheerily they never even saw the blood on his bandaged hands. At her house, she bathed his hands, and kissed them.

"Don't," he said. "I don't want you to be as enslaved by love, as I am."

"But I already am."

"No. I don't want to believe that. I cannot accept that."

She was wrapping his hands with clean bandages. "Why not? Why shouldn't I have the love for you that you have for me?"

Again, his eyes became wet. "I would not want you to have the pain I have from it."

"Love - is pain? This rapture of orgasm you were talking about?"

"My God! Stop saying that! You don't know what you are saying – all right. Let me explain to you, for I am sure your mother never has, and would not, if you asked her. I love you, and you love me - but we have had no -"

"Orgasm of rapture."

"I told you to *stop* saying that!"

"You say it! If you can say it, I can, too!"

"But I know what I am saying, and I don't say it every five minutes anyway."

She was not going to be pushed around because she wanted kissing of all kissing from him. "We have not had - what then? That word I am supposed NOT to say, and what my mother will NOT explain to me?"

"Fanny, you are so persistent. Our love - has brought us joy - in a loving COMPANIONSHIP. We take long pleasurable walks on the heath and on Milfield Lane to Highgate Hill, and we talk - read poetry together - and we hold - and we kiss - but we have had *no* - orgasm of - rapture."

"Union with God?"

"Union - between US. I said that total consummation of love between a man and a woman in love must be the SAME rapture that the soul seeks in union with its own source."

He was shaking, and he was sweating, and this was not going to get him out of what he had begun with her - not at all.

"John Keats," she said angrily. "You seduce me with kisses - and holding me and - really loving me, and then you finish it all off with these DISCUSSIONS of the joys of spiritual AND PHYSICAL LOVE, and then you bring in your God streaks and Eden angels not holding us from Eden at all, Eden being, I guess, where the one soul was separated - and always this seeking and finding UNION, UNION, UNION for us, hopefully ten thousand years from now if *Lamia* is EVER finished, is printed, sells, and now you are switching to this total CONSUMMATION of love - in that ORGASM OF GOD RAPTURE!"

"DON'T SAY THAT!"

"So now I CANNOT *say* the orgasm word and the consummation word? When YOU CAN?"

"Fanny, not so loud! What if Sammy is lurking about us as he always is?"

"He will think you are telling me where Lancelot really came from!"

He laughed. "And he would be correct."

"All right. Now YOU must explain to ME this rapturous orgasm of consummation that we are YET to have. And stop that sweating and shaking. You have to tell me, because I have never believed that men should know something and women cannot."

He looked out at the darkening windows, down at his hands, and crossed one leg over the other, as he always did when he read. "Your mother has never told you A THING about the sexual union of a man with a woman?"

"Of course not! She didn't even tell me about - about you know, what women do each month - I found out about it when it just happened."

He swallowed, and closed his eyes, as if he were in the middle of *Lamia* who evidently caused him trouble unending. "Well, in all species of life there are males and there are females, bugs, flies, ants, *everything.*"

"John Keats! Do NOT patronize me! I want to know this orgasm of rapturous consummation BETWEEN YOU AND ME!"

"WILL YOU STOP SAYING THAT?"

"If you would be kind enough to tell me all about it, I would not have to say it OVER AND OVER again - asking you to EXPLAIN!"

"WHY are you such a stubborn girl?" She had told him not to sweat and not to shake, and he did it, so unreasonable he was. He sweated and he shook, and she still did not know what was ahead of her in their God orgasms of rapturous consummation and he did, and she would be dead before anyone closed her mind to what it wanted to know. "There is this union - between a man and a woman. He makes TOTAL love to the woman he loves, and she makes TOTAL love to him -" he stuttered. And stopped.

Her temper gave way. She was about to take all of her bandages back, right off his hands, and they could bleed right down to the first floor, too. "HOW? HOW?"

"My God! Oh - damn. Your mother MUST have told you!"

"Is making love - kissing? Kissing my breasts - as you once kissed my breast over my heart?"

"Partly. Partly," he choked.

She liked this God rapture to come better and better. "There is more of what I like so much?"

"*Much* more," he said hoarsely as if his sore throat were back and was working at striking him dumb.

"Maybe you kiss me somewhere else, too?"

He suddenly looked down at his crossed legs, and was up and going out of the door. "Ask your MOTHER!" he gasped, and he was down the stairs and out of their house before she could stop him.

Close to her house his three companionable watchers of the night and safety for Hampstead were lighting whale oil lamps. One of them was shouting, "Eight by the clock, and all is WELL."

John Keats almost jumped over him. "The hell it is," he snarled.

The three stopped their safety patrol and its necessary thoughts. They looked at the house, obviously of his girl, and joined in eternal male bonding. "Oh, we don't mean about THEM," one said. "Nothing's EVER well with THEM."

"No, Mr. Keats," said another. "We was talking about revolution."

"Over here, Mr. Keats. We was saying there is no revolution here in England, as there was over the ocean - you know. All is well - HERE."

John Keats hurried down the street, waving at his friends, and they noticed for the first time the bandages on his hands. "Are they biting us now?" one asked.

John Keats had given Miss Fanny Brawne very poor advice as to discussing various raptures with her mother. For little Sammy had been pressed against the bathroom door to hear all he could of what went on aside from the slop kisses. He had since birth a lively and curious mind, and now he thought he might learn something more from his sister's beau, who seemed to know everything in the world. He had to learn more about King Arthur and his court that was still going on in the Bodmin moor in Cornwall. Just as he had learned enough to accompany his mother back to his bed, in which she had just tucked him into three times, he also learned to take care of his own interests. He just could not stay in bed with his sister's beau in the house. There were just too many interesting things to hear when John Keats was around. Now, as Sammy pressed harder against the bathroom door, his mother jerked him right out of his seated position and dragged him down the hall and into his bedroom. There she threw him upon his bed, and yelled, "Sammy Brawne. If you get out of this bed ONE MORE TIME TONIGHT, I swear upon the Holy Bible, I will go through your father's things, find his belt, and whip you with it!"

"You had better NOT," said Sammy, as spunky as his sister Fanny. "I found out what I wanted to find out about King Arthur's court - I found out from Mr. Keats what NO ONE else knows!"

His mother was blowing out all of the candles of his room she left burning when she was not mad at him. "And what would that be - you wicked non-hearing and non-obeying boy!"

"I found out at last where Sir Lancelot came from!"

One more candle to go, and then Sammy and the dark were on their own for the night. "Now why would Mr. Keats talk to YOU, hiding and listening outside of our bathroom door?"

"He was talking to FANNY, and I heard. Sir Lancelot of King Arthur's court, now at Bodmin moor, came from the God-like rapture of orgasms of – TOTAL consummation!"

Mrs. Brawne straightened as if shot, and Sammy was spared the last candle and its light, for Mrs. Brawne had not the breath to blow it out.

# Eighteen

April came with the scent of bluebells carpeting the forest depths with pale lilac. There was now the blooming of his favorite flower, the violet, and when he found them, he always gathered a bouquet for her. "They go with your eyes," he said.

April and May of 1819 opened the flood gates of their love treasured even beyond joy.

In April the Brawne family moved next door to him and Brown; the Dilkes had rented their house to them, having gone to live in Westminster for their son Charley to go to Westminster School. In April, the fire of creation, that had begun with *The Eve of St. Agnes,* rushed into a torrent of master writing for John Keats, despised by the critics.

He worked all day, but he and his girl always took their walk at the day's end, *their* walk on *their* path from Hampstead to Highgate Hill, on Milfield Lane. There they passed wild ponies, fallow and roe deer, foxes and squirrels and rabbits, all shy, but not as shy and as the badger and hedgehog. Those emerged at night, when the moon was large, while the thrush sang its evening song. "How I love the English countryside," he said over and over. "All of the old myths and the legends of magic beings live here, and a beautiful woman walks with us, spring, in her gown of soft green and lilac, and summer will walk with us, too, in her gown of gold, as gold as wheat and bee honey, and fall in her gown of reds – bronze – flaming with the summer gold still lingering in the crowns of the trees-"

"And winter in her furs of ermine."

He shivered. "I dread winter, for in it I am never warm enough."

Her Keats always worked many creations at once, from the unfinished *The Eve of St. Agnes,* to *Lamia,* and now he struggled with *Hyperion*. He was to have four great poetic failures. His first - *Sleep and Poetry*, his trashed *Endymion*, *Hyperion*, and *Otho the Great*, whom her Keats hated so thoroughly, he could hardly share his company when he tried to push both of them along for money. "Otho is not arriving *spontaneously*," he grumbled. "I don't think he intends to arrive *at all!*"

On April 16 he came to her house, and left her a sonnet he said he had written just for her. It was to be incorrectly labeled his *last sonnet*, for he later sent her the original from the *MARIA CROWTHER* on which he was sailing away to Italy to die. But now she read it and she wept, and she copied it and kept both copies the rest of her life. He had linked her and his love for her with the splendor, the steadfast and unchangeable light of *their* evening star, the sleepless eremite of purification round earth's human shore.

So was love – the purification of light from light, gross within an earthly life, and seeking its roots, its heart, the glory of being.

How had he said it when they became engaged on that sacred Christmas night of 1818? *Their* Evening Star – their love as steadfast – and the Evening Star brought light to the night and lingered into the new dawn, forever and forever into each new day. *I will love you John Keats as long as my soul creates new lives, for once a soul has found its other half – it will be whole and craven no longer. You are my completion; you were with me in Eden, and I was of you and you were of me before one soul became two.*

All of the while, unknown to both, the chiming for them of the midnight hour had already begun. Their day, their days together, were ending.

Now he rushed into the short period left for his writing. He wrote to George of it, and he told George of a dream he had had - where he was in a lightless iced grave of hell, but in it he had found bliss and joy, for his lips were kissing the lips of a woman he adored, and in their union they soared together above the grave and all of its iced darkness, warmth to warmth, bliss to bliss. They soared so high they rested in the treetops. Suddenly, all about them, the treetops burst into incredibly beautiful flowers. A gentle wind wafted among the flowers, and it lured them into following it, and they did, traveling as light and as free as a cloud.

He told her the dream, so deep was its impression.

"What does it mean?" she asked

"I kissed the lips of a woman and we soared beyond death as one -"

"The flowering tree tops?"

"We soared above the tomb - hell - into shared and *blooming* beauty."

"Was I the woman?" she asked softly.

"We were too close for me to see - with my kiss - we were one."

"Above a tomb to where trees bloom-"

"Yes."

"It could mean your poetry will bring beauty beyond our death - yours and mine - maybe you will unite us forever with poetry that cannot die."

He smiled and kissed her and touched her lips with his hand and kissed her again. "There is no wish that I could hope for more, my dearest girl."

"We leave all the flowers in bloom - as light as a cloud -"

"Above here, where youth grows thin and dies and new love cannot last beyond tomorrow -"

"That is gloomy."

"Death is gloomy. My mother dying so young - poor Tom dying before he knew kisses like yours -" His eyes became wet, and his voice became deeper than she had ever heard it. "I will never give you a complete farewell, dearest girl. I will never graciously accept death as our dance master - the dance here is so short."

"Don't be in a blue mood! We are here and warm before this fire, and the plum tree is in bloom and in it the nightingale will sing tomorrow and the tomorrow after that! My love, marry me! We have room in our house; we are not short of money. Isn't it marvelous now you don't have to walk to my house a mile in the cold? Isn't it marvelous that we are in love, your sore throat is gone, and the girl you love is begging and begging you to marry her?"

"It is marvelous," he said, looking at her with those special lights of love in his eyes, which she really saw as soon as he took her hand in the waltz for the veterans of Waterloo.

The year became one of joy, the pure magic of two in love. They went to the theater, attended lectures on Shakespeare and poetry, shared claret feasts with the Dilkes, and his friend and admirer, Richard Woodhouse, and he always had more stories of Camelot for little Sammy. Sammy had learned to tolerate the slop kisses, as he did not have to sneak around to see them, mainly as his mother held a death sentence over his head if he did.

On April 28 John Keats wrote his haunting masterful *La Belle Dame Sans Merci* in which he took the old ballad form and put it into a new atmosphere in such a unique and thoroughly astonishing way it opened new unexplored paths for English poetry. His ending with *kisses four* was unhappily changed to *So kissed to sleep.* His society at the time would be humiliated to have a damsel not only involved with kisses FOUR, *(all at once?)* And there was the problem of the wild, WILD eyes, so they had to be changed to wild SAD eyes. By the time the changes for Puritan purity were demanded, he was too ill to fight them, so he allowed the gross butchering of his much finer writing.

*Ode to Psyche* introduced the great odes, to be overshadowed by *Ode on a Grecian Urn, Ode to Melancholy,* and her favorite, *Ode to a Nightingale,* that were all written in May.

*Ode to Psyche* was experimental, with some good lines, some weak ones, but the casements appeared:

> And there shall be for thee all soft delight
> That shadowy thought can win,
> A bright torch, and a casement ope at night,
> To let the warm love in.

His odes followed his own unique pattern. In the music of his poetry, he had no equal. In pure sensuality of word, he had no equal.

In May he was happier than he would ever be again. He closed a letter to George: "This is the third of May, and everything is in delightful forwardness; the violets are not withered before the peeping of the first rose."

May was England's magic month. The trees and the meadow were at their most emerald green. Wildflowers bloomed to overflowing in both pasture and wood. In verges and hedgerows cow parsley was moonlit lace; dandelions marked the English school day, opening at its start, and beginning to close at its end. Lilac of the cuckooflower, blue of the speedwell, pink of the vetch all created rainbows of soft color all over the land. Butterflies carried the color of summer to come on their bright wings; bees buzzed deep in pollen to make honey in their cold clammy cells.

First he showed her *Ode on a Grecian Urn*. Brown had already copied it, and it was always his favorite.

His *Ode on a Grecian Urn*, she thought, was more than a *distant, dispassionate* look at a carving of timeless beauty. The duality of his personality appeared in it, as it always did in his poetry. He presented two worlds. There was the outer world. Here was a perfect piece of art, a *still unravished bride of quietness,* a *foster-child of silence and slow time.* Men, or gods, maidens, are all on their way to a pagan sacrifice. They carry and play pipes and timbrels. The heifer to be sacrificed wears garlands and the carving depicts a wild ecstasy. But what are they all pursuing? What do they struggle to escape? The answer was not in the poem for those caught just in its outer world. Now the outer world of such wild exultation, frozen in time and to a magnificent carving of stone, inches into the inner world of questions. Why are they coming to the sacrifice? To what green altar does the mysterious priest lead them? Why have they left, *forever,* the towns by river and sea, or mountain built with peaceful citadel? *Not a soul to tell.* Timeless, the pipers will play sweet tunes forever; the spring green boughs will never lose a leaf to winter; the lover about to kiss his beloved will always be strong and young, and his beloved fair. Now, her Keats reached even more into the inner world to find that of his reader. The kiss is never to be consummated. The ceremony is never to be reached or completed. No one knows why, or why the journey was even begun in the first place.

From timeless beauty he took the reader into what creates it. *"Heard melodies are sweet, but those unheard are sweeter"* - let the pipes speak not to the sensual ear, but *"pipe to the spirit ditties of no tone."* She reveled in the beauty of his words, their spiritual truth. The *unheard* melody is sweeter - beyond all physical confines, as are the *ditties of no tone.* Where do the forever-stilled pipes play? *They sing forever through the casements of fancy into the soul, heard beyond sound, into the beauty and the truth of the timeless.*

And *there* is the triumph of this still *unravished* bride of *quietness*, she thought. She teases the mind from thought, as must thought be teased from what is eternal.

You do not reach the eternal by thought. You reach the eternal by stretching beyond thought into its master and its mentor, the soul. The truth of beauty is it stretches into the eternal and awakens again, the first light of creation.

He took the thought from his introduction to his trashed *Endymion*, and concluded with this truth he had found for himself.

> When old age shall this generation waste,
> Thou shalt remain, in midst of other woe
> Than ours, a friend to man, to whom thou say'st
> "Beauty is truth, truth beauty," that is all
> Ye know on earth, and all ye need to know.

There was no doubt in her mind, that this was a masterpiece that would live as long as man read poetry.

He had written an ode to beauty, object and poem merging in a calm unrippled clarity. Now he was to write an ode to magic, her favorite, and immediately learned by her, and through it she reached him when he was with her, and when he was not.

She insisted that she saw him write it, that he did this on the fifth of May. A nightingale had built her nest in the plum tree, high above the common garden at Wentworth Place. She loved to hear the bird sing, and she knew how he stopped to hear every bird song, and listened with the same rapture that came to him when he watched the tide of the wind making patterns in meadow grass, corn, or summer wheat. From her own back kitchen window, she saw him leave his quarters, and go outside with some papers in his hand. The bird began to sing. She listened and opened the windows wide for the song and the breath of such a sunny day. He went back inside, and came out with a breakfast chair and sat under the plum tree from the time she fixed breakfast, they ate, and she had cleaned up the kitchen. He had begun writing on his scraps of paper, and she reasoned that he was not out there for more than two hours.

Then he took himself and the chair back into Brown's house. He went into his sitting parlor, and Brown came into it. "Did you write another poem?" he asked.

"Yes." He put four scraps of paper among his books.

"May I see it?"

"I want to take it over to Miss Brawne first."

"Oh. Is she getting *that* important to you?"

"Yes."

And Brown knew John Keats well enough now to know his private affairs were private, and he would not change on it, even with him.

She was the first person to read it. He brought it over to her for their evening before the fire, and had not even mentioned it during their walk in the twilight of that afternoon.

He handed her the four sheets, and told her how to go through them to read the poem. There were five scraps, then two half sheets, and he had written clearly without *one* change, after he had abandoned another beginning.

He watched her read, and she saw that his hands were shaking. As she read, she became lost within a magical shimmering of life, its passions, sensuality, hopes, sorrows, wine, song, dance, love, death, yearning to die, and pass on into beauty, and a final triumph to be found, merging *beyond* awakening or sleeping. He had made into a poem his humanity, and the conclusion was the triumph of his union with the timeless. The casements appeared again, the bird's singing *that oft- times hath charm'd magic casements, opening on the foam of perilous seas, in faery lands forlorn.* The nightingale's song ends, lost over meadow and still stream, buried deep in the next valley glades - and the poet is back to his sole self, but he does not know if the song is a vision or a waking dream, for he is one within the timelessness of beauty. *Fled is the music- Do I wake or sleep?*

She put the poem down, and tears came to her eyes.

"THAT bad? My God, what will the *Quarterly* do? *Blackwoods?*"

"No hungry generations will tread on this," she said. "You always say we are here to strain after the pure light we once were - my Keats - you merged with it - the sanctified of heaven before any light sullied by this earth -"

"I thought it was good, for it came in one long rush, like the song of the nightingale. My secret guest wrote it, I am sure. I could hardly keep up with him."

"My darling, dearest man," she said. "You and your secret guest wrote a masterpiece. You might equal this, but never - never can you outdo this."

His eyes grew their - what she called *soul* lights. "Thank you, my dearest girl," he said, his voice trembling.

"You have taken your life, all of its pain, and you have transformed it into pure enchantment - right into where there can be no pain, no human suffering, beyond time and place, beyond awakening and sleeping - where death can do no more than consume itself."

"You live within everything I write, my dearest girl. Thou art my heaven, and I thine eremite," he said huskily.

She read the poem aloud. "The melody," she said. "The lush sensuality of words - the song heard by Ruth heard now - the life she lived - lived again- and you take the reader, and he says, *here is pure enchantment, and, I too, am a sorcerer of magic!*"

They sat before the fire in the silence of perfect sharing. She had brought his favorite claret, and they each had a glass, and they watched the glasses glow with the light of the fire. "I am so happy," she said.

"So am I, my dearest girl," he replied.

Yet, when the poem was published, before its inclusion in *Lamia*, he used the pseudonym CAVIAR. He did not want falling on him again the wrath that *Endymion* aroused. He was afraid of his own name, being known by the Tory magazines and papers as a liberal.

As the ending of May approached, so did the specter of Brown renting out his house. He did this every summer and her Keats would have to move somewhere else. He still would not consider moving in with her family. And in this period came another ode, the *Ode to Melancholy,* so filled with symbols of death, she hated it. In it love and death were one! He denied the calm serenity of the Grecian urn. He denied the final spiritual triumph of his *Ode to a Nightingale.* Now her Keats said grief abides forever in beauty, death in joy, melancholy in delight.

She dwells with Beauty-beauty that must die;
And Joy, whose hand is ever at his lips
Bidding adieu; and aching Pleasure night,
Turning to poison while the bee-mouth sips;
Ay, in the very temple of delight
Veiled Melancholy has her sovran shrine.

It was enough. She would never read any more of it.

He had nine months allowed him for his great writing. But May ended with his poor *Ode to Indolence* that she disliked more than his *Ode to Melancholy.* "Why are you denying what you are?" she asked him angrily.

"I never have *believed* what I know," he said gloomily. His sore throat was back. Brown would soon be away and her Keats would have to find new living quarters. "No, I will not move in with your household."

"Move in with me!"

"The torture of living under the same roof with you," he told her, "and not having you for my wife, I do not want."

"Then marry me!"

"Not as a pauper!"

"Where will you go?"

"Somewhere to write something I can sell and we can get married."

From America, the land of promise, came terrible news from George. The journey taken by him and his bride from Philadelphia to Pittsburgh was a horror, as if the journey from England to Philadelphia was not bad enough. He had to buy his own horses and a carriage, but he could not rebuild the terrible roads. He was forced to float his horses, his carriage, and all of his belongings on a keelboat, some six hundred miles down the Ohio River. Somehow he had ended up in a place called Henderson, where he had met a very friendly man named Audubon, for whom a bird society would be named. Audubon had a boat that ran things up and down rivers for people to buy, and he sold some shares of the boat to George at a very reasonable price; understandably so, George said, because the boat had already been sunk and was on the bottom of some river. So now George was in desperate need of money. Her Keats had foolishly loaned money to Haydon, which he never had returned.

Now, husbanding his own meager income, her Keats took the Portsmouth coach from London, the slow coach, on which he rode on top, from eight in the morning from the Angel Inn, London, to George Inn, Portsmouth, arriving at seven o'clock in the evening. All through the ride, he was chilled by a violent storm. He reached Shanklin on the Isle of Wight on June 28, and he was overwhelmed with longing for her. His friend, solicitor James Rice, was with him, and her Keats went to work to finish *Lamia*. "I never knew before," he wrote to her, "what such a love as you have made me feel, was; I did not believe in it; my Fancy was afraid of it, lest it should burn me up." He also tried his hateful struggle with the great beast, OTHO THE GREAT. On July 25, Sunday evening, he poured out his love to her again. "You cannot conceive how I ache to be with you; how I would die for one hour. . . my dear love, I cannot believe there ever was or ever could be anything to admire in me especially as far as sight goes . . . you absorb me in spite of myself - you alone. . ." And then came the morbidity that hurt her so much. He wanted to possess her so much, and keep such a joy, he would like to die at that perfect moment *before it could be lost.* That was in his Bright Star Sonnet to her written in the previous glorious April, and now she could tell by his letters he was sinking into a hopeless despair that they would never marry. On August fifth he wrote that he was striving to keep his thoughts from her, and could not do it. "Upon my soul, I cannot say what you would like me for. . ." In the next day's letter he planned a trip that they might take and spend a pleasant year at Berne or Zurich. After seven and a half weeks at Shanklin he went to Winchester with Brown. He had half finished *Lamia*, and had completed four acts of OTHO. At Winchester he worked on the fifth act of his despised play, did not go to see her, and had not even written her four days after his arrival, and when he did write, it was not a nice letter. He acknowledged he had not written and said he had no excuse for it. And then - "Remember I have had no idle leisure to brood over you." And, "My heart is now made of iron."

She knew how exquisitely sensitive he was; she knew the agony he felt at their continued enforced separation, spiritually, mentally, and physically, so she saw right through his heart made of iron. Now he had to write, write, write, even when it did not charm or enrapture him. "If I fail, I shall die hard," he wrote.

It was such an outcry of deprivation, she held the words to her heart, remembering how gently his lips had sought it. Now that her Keats had gone away for the summer, little Sammy was allowed more freedom to roam. He was by her now, as she read his letter. "Does he tell us more about Sir Lancelot?" he asked, wondering if she was crying because she missed that, or those slop kisses he still thought disgusting.

She rumpled his hair affectionately. "Sammy, listen to me. If you ever want to see in your room at night again, do not mention ANYTHING here about Sir Lancelot!"

Her Keats did not write to her for a month. His OTHO he sent on to its miserable conclusion. He never should have written for the theater at all, but Brown had persuaded him that doing so would be the path to riches. She was to hate all that he had written in his desperate struggle to provide for a marriage between them. Writing for money, he had silenced the glory of his hidden guest. He could have written more glorious odes, another *Lamia*, and she later read what he had written of *The Eve of St. Mark*, and she thought another tragedy of his short life, and to the reading world, was that this was an unfinished masterpiece.

While they were separated, he finally finished *Lamia*.

She was to read every word. The story line was strong and fresh. It contained passages of sheer beauty. Through a god intervention, a lamia, a snake, becomes a beautiful woman. As a serpent she was desperately in love with a young man of Corinth. He falls in love with her when she has metamorphosed into a beautiful woman, and they live together in a palace with an entrance no one else can see. He wants to marry her, but this would forfeit her immortality, and she refuses marriage. He presses, and presses. He wants to introduce her to his friends as his wife. Finally, she gives in, and loses her immortality. The door of their castle then becomes visible, and they have a great wedding feast. All classes come, including the gross, whom Woodhouse, and Taylor did not like at all, because her Keats put into his lush poem that they were "who make their mouth a napkin for their thumb." At the feast, she knows that a magician in attendance sees her for what she really is, and she makes herself vanish from her lover's life. Without her, he goes mad, and dies. The question raised by her Keats was not answered in the story. Is it better to live in illusion, happily, or live in the truth - in misery?

Richard Woodhouse, and his publisher Taylor approved of *Lamia*. Now he was finishing up his love poem to her, his girl, *The Eve of St. Agnes.*

In Winchester John Keats received another anguished letter from George. His shares in the Audobon boat were indeed at the bottom of an American river, the Ohio, along with the boat. All of the money he had taken away with him was gone. He would have to return to England, if John could not ply their joint share of Tom's patrimony from Abbey and mail it to him.

The day he received the letter John Keats left Winchester at nine that evening and arrived in London at nine the next morning, Saturday, September 11. He wrote Abbey for an interview, which Abbey granted for seven o'clock the following Monday. He was in London, not far from Hampstead and Miss Brawne. Could he go to see her? He just could not. So he called on Rice at his home. He morosely wrote George, "A man in love I do think cuts the sorriest figure in the world . . ." Gloomily, he dropped in on his publishers at 93 Fleet Street, where he met Woodhouse and they agreed to meet the next day for a visit and a long leisurely breakfast. This breakfast visit lasted for six hours, when the two friends parted *the Swan* and later the *Two Necks Inn* where Woodhouse took the Accommodation Post Coach for Weymouth at three.

On Monday, he finally wrote his girl. He had not written her since August 16, and here he was in London and could not see her because it would be too painful under his circumstances.

"I love you too much to venture to Hampstead, I feel it is not paying a visit, but venturing into a fire. I have been endeavoring to wean myself away from you..."

*Just try it*, thought his girl. *Just try it!*

He met Abbey at his home in Walthamstow, and was allowed to see his sister, but only for a short time. He met Abbey again that evening at seven for tea, at his place of business in Pancras Lane. Abbey would consider Tom's estate share for George, and then he began "blowing up Lord Byron while I was sitting with him..." wrote John Keats to his brother. Abbey said maybe Lord Byron did say some true things in HIS poetry now and then, "At which he took up a magazine, and read me some extracts from Don Juan (Lord Byrons's last flash poem) and particularly one against literary ambition."

If Abbey would shake loose with Tom's money for George, he was to send it to some wilderness place in America called Louisville, Kentucky.

John Keats returned to Winchester on Wednesday. He would not write her for another month, but he had finished his love poem to her, *The Eve of St. Agnes*. And he had shown it to Woodhouse during their long visit in London on that Sunday, September 12. On the twentieth Woodhouse wrote to Keats' publisher, Taylor, about one of the masterpieces of English Literature. He had been *shocked* by it. Keats had wanted them to publish *Lamia*, and his odes, and - AND *The Eve of St. Agnes* immediately, and Hessey, his other printer, had said it could not be done now. Keats asked ,"Why not?"

*Lamia* was one thing, said Hessey, and all right, and could be published and read by ladies, as far as he could tell - BUT NOT *The Eve of St. Agnes*. Instead of the hero taking his love away and making her his wife "to be married in right honest chaste and sober wise" as soon as they have declared their love, he lies BREAST TO BREAST on her (this was removed) and then acts "all the acts of a bonofide husband," but of course the heroine thought it was all a dream and that they were married, anyway. Hessy wrote he told the poet, "the interest on the reader's imagination is so greatly heightened... it will render the poem unfit for ladies, and indeed scarcely TO BE MENTIONED to them..."

John Keats had seen the shock and the dismay on Woodhouse's face as he read *The Eve of St. Agnes*. "These vulgar lines will have to go, Keats; they will just have to go!"

"What vulgar lines?"

"They have to be married - and THEN they cannot have this - this -"

"I do not consider the sexual aspect of love evil, bad, wicked, anti-British, or hurting the King. The whole poem is a tribute by me to the beauty of spiritual and physical love within a life of contrasts."

"Keats, this will not do. Not at all."

"Those lines stay in, and they WILL do, or there is no poem."

Taylor wrote a scathing letter against *The Eve of St. Agnes*, which he had not yet read, but Woodhouse had shocked him with just noting what had not YET been removed from the poem. On September 25, Taylor visibly shook in his letter. He grieved that John Keats was flying in the face of decency and discretion, and this folly of his was the most stupid folly he could conceive. "He does not bear the ill opinion of the world calmly, and yet he will not allow it to form a good opinion of him and his writing . . . but I will not be an accessory (I can answer for H, I think) towards publishing anything which can only be read by men, since even on *their* minds a bad effect must follow the encouragement of those thoughts which cannot be raised without impropriety . . ." If John Keats could not write *decently*, if he did not know *right* from *wrong* in moral taste - he would not sanction this infirmity of the poet by encouraging it through its publication. Did John Keats think he could overcome "the best found habits of our nature?" Thus, if this poet would not take out the sexual lovemaking lines, Taylor and Hessey would NOT publish "those parts unfit for publication."

Taylor loved John Keats' *Isabella*. John Keats hated his *Isabella* as much as he hated his damned OTHO THE GREAT.

Taylor liked both of them better than the enchanted *Lamia* who allowed into her castle peasants that used their *mouths* as a *napkin* to their thumbs.

# *Nineteen*

He walked right into their house at Wentworth Place as if he had not been gone at all, as if he had not forgotten to write, or had skipped visiting her on his London trip to see Abbey. And to her, in the sheer ecstasy of seeing and being held by this man she adored, there was not a time that had separated them either. She covered his face with joyous kisses, when he was not doing the same with her face, and Sammy came in and saw all of it, and began to whine in despair. Hearing the familiar whining from her son, Mrs. Brawne was right behind him, smiled in real affection at John Keats, but jerked her baby right out of his sight. "My sore throat is gone; I have finished *Lamia*, whom I grew to like, and have dumped *Ortho the Great*, whom I totally hate, on Brown who thinks he is going to get Edmund Kean to act in it. And in Winchester I wrote an ode to autumn - remembering our perfect day - you, my sister and I shared - looking down from our hill, over OUR lane -"

"Let me read it. Has Brown read it, copied it?"

"Yes. I wrote it before we left Winchester and came back to London."

"You have moved next door?"

"No. I am taking two rooms at Westminster for a time for more writing day and night - I'll probably come back here in November."

"Our love poem - you started last January?"

"Finished. But I do not know if Taylor and Hessey will publish it with *Lamia*. Or that *Isabella* of mine whom they so adore , and I so hate."

He had moved to a chair, and she was on his lap. He quickly decided to a companionable sharing of the floor before the fire, but he did not put his head upon her lap. She didn't care. They were in the same room, the same world, the same life. "Why the opposition to our love poem?"

"There are lines they consider too improper to be read, discussed, thought of, or even *imagined.*"

"That God rapture between lovers?"

He laughed, and stirred the fire, and the coals awakened to light no brighter than that in his eyes. "My dearest girl, I love the way you do not preen and prance around a subject matter. Yes, our poem does have physical consummation between a man and a woman in love, and they are not married, or in mutual comas, or on separate clouds in heaven. I thought that when Woodhouse realized this, he was going to fall into the breakfast eggs in front of us. He turned white. He shook. He swallowed and wondered how best to tell me of the wickedly wicked I had done. He looked so shocked, and so grieved, you might have thought that on my way to meet him I had climbed all the nunnery walls in England and ravished every nun in them."

"And has Brown copied it, too? Our poem?"

"Brown seems to copy my poems before I finish them."

"I want to read it."

"One poem at a time. You read *To Autumn* to me, and I will read *The Eve of St. Agnes* to you."

As she was reading his ode to autumn, she knew she was reading aloud another of his masterpieces. When she was finished, the quiet serenity of the poem possessed her. He had not *found* the beauty - sound, sight, smells, wonder, of the season. He had *absorbed* them and reflected them all back to the reader in perfect tranquility. In *Ode to a Nightingale* he had merged with the bird's song, but here, he was a tranquil observer, one at peace with and of the season, and the poem made no suggestions beyond this. Nothing came between the reader and that day, that warm, wondrous day she so remembered - that day - fruit ripening with sweetness to the core, the engorged bees at work in their clammy cells, and autumn itself, personalized, made into a man sitting carelessly on a granary floor, his hair soft-lifted by a winnowing wind, lingering lazily on half-reaped furrows, then fast asleep, drowsed with the fume of poppies - or - standing by a cyder press, patiently watching the last oozings, *hours by hours.* That softness of that dying day he had shared with her and his sister was so clearly, clearly back, the stubble-plains of rosy hue, the bleating of the full grown lambs, the gathering of swallows - streaking into that sunset sky - she was there again, and would be again and again when she read and re read these lines as she would do long after his death.

He had made that day forever undying. She read again,

> Then in a willful choir the small gnats mourn
> Among the river sallows, born aloft
> Or sinking as the light wind lives or dies;
> And full-grown lambs loud bleat from hilly bourn;
> Hedge-crickets sing; and now with treble soft
> The red-breast whistles from a garden-croft;
> And gathering swallows twitter in the skies.

"I love it, my dearest Keats," she said simply. "Light to light, returned to our sacred source - ten fold."

"You build me up too high, but I want you to go on doing it. I leave you so I can work, and then I come back to you so I can work, but what matters above all of this - is my love for you."

"Is that a part of your truth of beauty?"

"The truth of beauty is that it is timeless, as is my love for you, Miss Fanny Brawne. So the power of human love is as great as the timelessness of beauty, wouldn't you say?"

"You are the poet," she replied, kissing him, and his ardent response was as quick as it was magical.

He read to her all of *The Eve of St. Agnes,* and when he finished, she knew that he had put their love into a masterpiece. It was a celebration of lovers escaping a castle of death. "I am totally enchanted, enraptured, and mesmerized," she whispered.

"Thank you, my dearest girl."

"The constant contrast - the pale enchantment of the full moon, dim silvered twilight and bright color nevertheless - crimson, gold and jet – the brilliant colors heightening with growing passion - the passion *beyond* passion (she was reading the poem now) - *when upon his knees he sank, pale as smooth-sculptured stone.* My dearest

Keats, in this poem we love, and will love as long as man reads – no hungry generations will tread us down- you have made us love beyond this little dream of life here and far beyond it." She stopped and wiped tears from her eyes. "But what would I expect, my love? You gave us the Evening Star!"

"Thou art my heaven, and I thine eremite," he said simply, the key line of his poem.

He meant every word. They held and even a kiss would have been intrusive in that moment of love's intimacy.

*How wondrous is the commonplace, candles and a fire as the night falls, warmth when winter comes - and words of the news, the weather, and the night watchman announcing the time and - that all is well!*

She lingered against him as he would leave, "You are among the greatest of poets," she said.

"If it were only true," he sighed. "And if it would pay in pounds."

By November he was back in Brown's house in Hampstead. He was beginning a comic faery poem in Spencerian stanza, *Caps and Bells,* and it would not be finished. He wanted to do a poem on Leicester and Elizabeth Tudor. He didn't. *Caps and Bells* was to be a political and social satire, but he was too depleted now to write it. He could not marry if he could not write. And now, he could not write. He began to wonder if he had the same disease that had killed his mother and his brother. Doctors always told him he was in robust health. But they kept telling Tom he was fine, too, and Tom had never been well. This month, he imagined his beautiful girl was flirting with other men, wanting other men, and by mid-November, he was so tortured with this fantasy, he wrote some lines on one of the pages of *Caps and Bells.* She found them, and they horrified her. "My God! How could you write this - to me? You are imagining yourself dead, and exulting in *my* agony of *remorse!*"

"I was in a blue mood."

"Well, you do not have to write poetry about it!"

This was one poem Brown was not going to get and copy. Yet she couldn't tear out his page of *Caps and Bells.* She copied the ghastly thing, and hid it in her room. He promised to tear it up so Brown could not get it. She never was to know if Brown had seen it, and had it, too.

And she did not let the horror of what he had written to her, drop. "So you want a *dead* hand haunting me? If you die before I do, you want me to wish that I were dead too, or drain myself of my blood, so in your veins red life might stream again? My dearest Keats, you have been so loving, even when you didn't write letters to me, I understood. I understand why you have to write poetry instead of pursuing medicine - I have understood and accepted and loved everything about you - but NOT your - *This Living Hand* horror! I HATE it!" she almost wept.

As life went on about them in this winter, Elliston, the manager of the Drury Lane theater, took *Otho the Great* with the proviso that it could not be brought out until the following season. Keats and Brown then took it back, offered it to the Covent Garden Theater, which did not take it. So *Otho the Great* was not to be produced.

By December, her Keats' sore throat was back, but they still celebrated, secretly, the one year anniversary of their engagement. That day they dined with the Dilkes. *Lamia* and other poems by him would come out in the next year; he had bought himself a warm coat and thick shoes, and his spirits were better than they had been in November, the time of his ghastly *Living Hand* poem. 1820 would see them married if *Lamia* and its companion poems pushed him into the literary world.

In January of 1820 his brother George appeared for money. He had taken one thousand one hundred pounds with him to America, and had lost it all on an already sunken boat. Tom's estate, after his debts were paid, and counting what had been drawn from it, came to eight hundred pounds to be divided between the three Keats' children. George did the dividing, and the money managing. He gave Abbey one hundred pounds for Fanny Keats, which he and John had borrowed from her money. He persuaded John to let him have his share, two hundred and sixty pounds, for himself to invest into a business he would begin in America. He left with a total of seven hundred pounds - and Miss Brawne knew of it, and said nothing against it, but she never liked George for it, and he did not like her, either.

"He has a wife and a child," her Keats said to her.

So might you, she said to herself.

"He will do well with the money," said her Keats.

It is your money; two hundred and sixty pounds would allow us to marry before you try to enter the literary world again, she said to herself. And the one thousand one hundred pounds on the bottom of an American river was probably partly yours, too.

In truth, George was to finally do well with the money, for eventually he became a managing partner in a successful flour and saw mill. And her Keats' money was returned by George who took it and paid all of his debts, *posthumously*.

I wish he had not taken the money from me, her Keats really thought, but he had never been able to refuse his brothers anything.

On January 28 he saw his brother off at six in the morning on the Liverpool stage, the *Royal Alexander*, which left the *King's Arms, Snow Hill*, at that hour. George had told his brother he did not like Miss Brawne. He was to let him know it again, just as John walked him to the stage. "She - - is just a - MINIATURE replica of you, John," he said in a contemptuous way.

For the first time in their lives the passion that could appear like fire in his older brother's eyes, blazed against George. "Or I, George, a MINIATURE replica of her."

# *Twenty*

When George took the Liverpool stage at six in the morning, January 28, 1820, it was snowing again. There had been a lot of snow in London, but when February arrived there was a sudden warming thaw, and her Keats went into town without his great new overcoat. He returned on the late stage, riding on top cheaper, as usual, and it had turned bitterly cold, with a ghastly biting wind. By the time he had walked to Wentworth Place, he was shivering and feverish. Brown met him, and told him he looked ill, and suggested he go to bed. It was eleven o'clock. "I don't feel well at all," Keats said to Brown, and got between the cold sheets. "These feel like *ice,*" he said, and suddenly coughed. "I have coughed up blood," Brown heard him say. "Bring me the candle, but that was blood from my mouth, I know it." Brown handed him the candle, and they both could see one bright spot of blood. John Keats looked at it and he then looked up at the anxious face of his friend. "I know the color of that blood," he said very calmly. "It is arterial blood. That drop of blood is my death warrant. I must soon die."

He had tuberculosis. He was going to die soon, and in the same drowning suffocation that had taken his mother, and Tom.

The doctors bled him and said there was no evidence at all of pulmonary tuberculosis. They told him to stay in bed the next day and rest, stay indoors two months after that, but otherwise he was in *fine* health. *Where have I heard that before?*

His dearest girl never ceased to visit him, and when they were not together, they exchanged notes. He wrote that "when so violent a rush of blood came to my lungs that I felt nearly suffocated - I assure you I felt it possible I might not survive, and at that last moment thought of nothing but you."

His medical studies alone would have made him realize the truth. He never told his sister about the blood. And for a long time - he pretended he *was* getting well - to his girl - to his friends. But some of the inner agony burst through. He wrote to his girl that if he should die, he had left no immortal work behind him - "but I have loved the principal of beauty in all things, and if I had had the time I would have made myself remembered."

This brought bitter tears, and she said to him over and over again, "You will be remembered as among the greatest of English poets."

"No. No. There is no time for that, my dearest girl. My name was writ on no more than water."

The words brought her pain, as much as did his *living hand* travesty.

And so they both prepared for his death, as much as lovers can prepare. She gave him a ring with their joint names engraved on it. "You are the love of my life, this life, and any that may follow," she said when she gave him the ring.

"I have said this before," he replied, taking the ring gently, as if it wanted and needed to be held so tenderly. "My dearest girl, I will never be able to bid you a complete farewell."

On March 6, he had a heart attack with violent heart palpitations. Two days later, he was too weak to even sit up. The doctors said his illness was all in his mind.

On March 16, the weather was mild, and he was better, so he went to London and dined with his publisher. Home again, he could take no walks. She sat by his chair and the sunset and the gloaming came outside of his windows in such beauty, if they were in it, and if he were well, he would have written another ode to spring. "My dearest girl," he said softly. "I feel like a frog in the frost when eagles are abroad."

He closed his eyes and she took his hand and held it to her lips. "The soul soars above the highest eagle in the sky," she said.

"And mine?" he smiled sadly.

"With mine."

"In the *Eve of St. Agnes*."

"And don't forget you gave me the Evening Star."

"When I am gone and you see it in all the nights ahead of you, look up at it, my dearest, and remember me."

"You are of me. You are not to be *remembered*. I will not remember *myself!*"

The silence was between them again, but not one of joy of lovers already sharing their future together. This silence was one that would fall to all lovers who knew that one was going, and all of the tears of the other could not stop it, or the sun in the sky leaving even the last light of the last of the gloaming.

In April he sent his book of revised poems to Taylor. In May, Brown rented out his house, and her Keats would not move in with the Brawnes, and on May 5, moved to Kentish Town, 2 Wesleyan Place. It had been suggested that he return to 1 Well Walk, the quarters he and Tom had shared. "I just could not bear that," he said. "The ghost of dear Tom, and knowing I will soon haunt those rooms as much as he - *no.*"

He saw Brown off at Gravesend. Brown was going on another hike in Scotland. They never were to see one another again. It had been a hard trip on her Keats to see his friend off, three and a half hours, riding on top each way, and it did his health no good. In May he had to correct the proof sheets for the *Lamia* volume. It would also contain *Isabella, The Eve of St. Agnes* { still unchanged at the author's insistence) and his odes, excluding his poor *Ode on Indolence.* Unfortunately, *La Belle Dame Sans Merci, Meg Merrilies* and fragments from *Ode to Maia* and *The Eve of St. Mark* were not included. The poorer *Fancy, Bards of Passion, Lines on the Mermaid Tavern* and *Robin Hood* were. He did not want anything from his unfinished *Hyperion* included, but it was. He wrote to Brown that if his poems did not succeed, "I shall try what I can do in the apothecary line." June was filled with rain showers; away from his dearest girl, he became tortured with jealousy that she did not love him, and he wrote her agonized letters about it. On June 22 there was another hemorrhage, and as he was too ill to care for himself, the next day he moved in with the Leigh Hunts. By June 27, he had been spitting more blood. On July 3, his book came out printed by Taylor and Hessey, with an apology by them that they had included lines from *Hyperion* against the author's wishes.

*Lamia* sold for seven shillings and six pence under his own name, and *author of Endymion*. His publishers were enthused. Taylor's enthusiasm was now unbounded, even if the lovers in the exquisite lyrical *The Eve of St. Agnes* did what they did. Taylor wrote to a relative, "Next week Keats' new Volume of Poems will be published, and if it does not sell well, I think nothing will ever sell well again. I am sure of this, that for Poetic Genius there is not his equal living, and I would compare him against anyone with either Milton or Shakespeare for Beauties." Hessey was equally happy. He wrote, "For my part, I think no single volume of Poems ever gave me more real delight on the whole than I have received from this. I think the simplicity of *Isabella* will please you much - *Hyperion* is full of the most sublime poetical images and the small Poems delight me very much."

By July 12 John Keats' Dr. Darling turned him over to a specialist, Dr. William Lambe, specializing in cancer and consumption. He recognized his grave condition immediately, and told him he could not survive another winter in England. He would have to go to Italy before winter began.

John Keats already knew he was dying, and had known it since that first drop of blood he had coughed on his pillow, February 3. At the Hunts he was so ill and tortured with jealousy for his beautiful girl forsaking him, he wrote her terrible letters. Whom had she smiled with? "You do not feel as I do. You do not know how to love as I do - one day you may, but your time has not come yet. I am tormented day and night...I cannot persuade myself into any confidence of you." She gave him agonies of jealousy he could not speak of, but he did it anyway. "Do not write me if you have done anything this month which it would have pained me to have seen... If you still believe in dancing rooms and other societies as I have seen you - I do not wish to live - if you have done so, I wish my coming night to be my last. I cannot live without you, and not only you, but a chaste you; virtuous you...Be serious! Love is not a plaything - and again do not write unless you can do it with a crystal conscience. I would sooner die for want of you than -"

He had not finished, because his agony could not be put to paper, or even supported by his body. Later he wrote, "Do you suppose it possible I could ever leave you?"

Her family saw her suffering. Sammy even stayed by her side, and did not go out and play in the warm sun, or in the shade of the plum tree. "He will be well again," he promised, for was not Sir Lancelot living all of these ages past on Bodwin Moor?

"You are only nineteen," her mother told her. "And he is dying. You have to recognize that there will be other men in your life."

"We are of each other, mother. When he dies, he will take my heart with him."

And little sister Margaret began to help with Fanny's share of the cleaning and cooking. When Sammy went to his room to bed, his mother gave him all of the lighted candles he wanted.

My agony is not in dying, thought John Keats. It is in dying and leaving HER. All he had so confidently KNOWN, if not BELIEVED, was rejected because they would soon part. The eternal sparks from God - all of *that* became nothing, and totally based on whether immortality would have them together somewhere else, or in another place or another time. He never thought of his poetry, or how it would do - be hated or be loved. "I long to believe in immortality," he wrote to her. "I shall never be able to bid you an entire farewell. If I am destined to be happy with you here - how short is the longest life. I wish to believe in immortality - I wish to live with you forever. Let me be but certain that you are mine, heart, and soul, and I could die more happily than I could otherwise live."

His third and last letter came from the Hunts. No, she could not go to Italy with him. He did not want her to see him die. Right now it was impossible to think of going to Italy before the winter, because she would not be there. And then his illness brought back the horrible brooding jealousy. He wondered if Brown had had indecent thoughts about her. And then came the anguished cry from his soul - he would have faith if he were within her arms, and at the rapture of it, live forever within that rapture or die within it. This was in his Bright Star sonnet to her, for it was not a new feeling. But then there was hope of a long and happy marriage, of sharing children, old age, and now, all of that was gone.

Hunt took him for a drive to Hampstead. They got out of the carriage, and sat on a bench in Well Walk. As John Keats had never shown emotions to Hunt before, the man was amazed when he turned to him, and his eyes were swimming with tears. "I am dying of a broken heart," he said. The next day, August 10, he received at the Hunts a letter from Miss Brawne. Through a careless error, the letter was not delivered to him that day, and not even found to be delivered until the next day. This was too much for him. He went to Wentworth Place that evening, and after he saw his beautiful girl, he had intended to go back to his old rooms at 1 Well Walk. "I *will* go back to our old rooms," he said to his girl. "I have to. I will."

"No, you won't," said Mrs. Brawne. "You will stay right here with us until you leave England."

"That is correct," said his beautiful girl, her eyes snapping, and her chin set stubbornly.

"I agree," said Sammy, his eyes filled with wonder as always in the presence of Mr. Keats, who still knew everything in the world.

"Very correct," said Margaret, and with one lad and three women blocking his way out, there he stayed, until he did sail for Italy.

He wrote to Abbey to see if he might see his sister one more time before he left the country, but Abbey said no. John Keats wrote Hunt, and lied about his dying. He was going to Italy for better climate, and as for his illness, "Tis not yet consumption, I believe."

Charles Lamb gave his *The Eve of St. Agnes* a lovely review. He said it was a Chaucer-like painting. "We have scarcely anything like it in modern description. It brings us back to ancient days," and "Beauty making beautiful old rhymes." This was published a fortnight after *Lamia's* publication. The *Monthly Review* lamented because John Keats was so original. And at last, the *Edinburgh Review* wrote on *Endymion* and his *Lamia* poems in its August issue, and said that both books were flushed with "rich lights of fancy." The whole review was one of praise.

The sales were moderate, no more than sufficient. Her Keats wrote to Brown the truth. "My book has had good success with the literary people, and I believe it has a moderate sale."

The Tory *Quarterly* continued its venomous attack on John Keats, and praised a peasant poet, John Clare, as living forever among the great English poets. As for the venomous Tory *Blackwoods*, they did not deign to dirty their heaven high minds with reviewing anything written by John Keats - John Keats, born over a STABLE.

He wrote a tender letter to his sister. "If I return from Italy I will turn over a new leaf for you. I have been improving lately, and have very good hopes of cheating the consumption." She had been told, so he mentioned it.

Miss Brawne begged for them to marry, for her to go to Italy with him. When he refused, she begged his doctors to let him stay in her home. "He always does better when I am close to him," she wept. The doctors were still into bleeding him, and now they thought of something as bad. He should not eat. Well, only in an emergency, when it was a TOTAL necessity! Shelley had written him a nice letter, and invited him to spend the winter with him in Pisa. Shelly also said he had read his *Endymion*, and had found in it treasures of poetry. "I feel persuaded that you are capable of the greatest things, so you but will..."

On August 14 he wrote his will, and sent it to Taylor. All he did have to bequeath were a few books and many debts.

He wrote a nice thank you- but no - letter to Shelley regarding the invitation to winter with him in Pisa.

August passed, and in his mind he remembered how the summer wind winnowed through the ripened wheat, and how he had written of the bounty of autumn in an ode, for that September day with his sister and his girl so merrily laughing, and how the earth was so perfect, and his love, too.

It was a year later and he knew there would be no September for him of 1821. This was the last time he would see the approach of fall in all of its reds and golden leaves into the first snows. He knew that in 1821 there would be no spring for him either, beautiful spring with its triple song to sing.

*What did I write? How could I have strained so after the light I once thought I was? I am a frog in the frost. My name will be nothing – my name was no more than writ on water.*

Outside, the ox-eye daisies would still be at the edges of the wheat fields, the peacock butterfly busy among them, carrying the jeweled colors of summer spent. The pheasant - the little harvest mouse would be there, too, pink nose quivering, black eyes searching - *all a part of the English countryside I love so much.*

A cold wind soon rose to chill the early evenings.

He looked out at dark skies and he yearned to be out within the changing season.

The moors in the country would be mauve, pink and purple, the harebell the brightest blue, as if it had brought down a part of the sky to color its very center. The berries would be ripe in the rowan tree, and the bearberry shrub would glow in more fat red clusters of ripening berries. Tender new shoots would be on the heather, and on them the grouse and the red deer would feed. Bitter, bitter cold would soon be coming to the high hills, coming down in great icy drafts that would blow the smoke away from the crofter's cottage as he warmed himself before his fire of peat.

Before the deep snow, the mountain hare would have changed its color to white.

*When eagles are abroad, sleeping wide-winged on the rising and the falling of air currents, here I am - a frog in the frost.*

George had sent him no money. He had no funds to take him to Italy. Then on September 11, his publisher, John Taylor, came to his rescue. He had advanced one hundred pounds already on his trashed *Endymion*. He had never regained that money in sales because of its massacre by the Tory press. Taylor now advanced him one hundred pounds for the copyright of *Lamia*, and gave him a letter of credit for another one hundred and fifty pounds.

Taylor closed his letter to Keats on an affectionate note: "I hope yet to see you as rich and renowned as you deserve to be. Meantime, wishing you a pleasant voyage, perfect health and happiness again, I remain, my dear Keats, your faithful friend, John Taylor."

It was time now for their final departure. He would not let her see him off on the *Maria Crowther*, or go to Gravesend with him. Once he had seen what his illness really was, there had not been any more kisses between them, and not even a close embrace of any kind. He did not want her to get his disease. Now, he was leaving Wentworth Place and their farewell was a private one. He would have had it no other way. He had the old scarf wrapped around his sore throat, and the tightness in his chest in which his lungs were steadily being eaten away, made it difficult for him to breathe. But he did take her hand in his, and on it, he saw his ring, and on his hand, she saw her ring. "My dearest girl," he said. "I wish I could tell you to forget me, but I cannot. I wish I could have been a great poet - I might have been, if I had had the time. If I had had the time, I would have written something immortal to forever keep us together."

She could stay sobbing, but she could not stay the flowing of her tears. "I have to have one more kiss."

He had turned to go, and looked back at her, and never had she seen more pain upon a face. "That, my dearest girl, I cannot give to you." His voice trembled, and sudden tears were swimming in his eyes. "Goodbye. I can never, my dearest girl, accept that this is goodbye for I cannot give you an entire farewell."

And so he left Wentworth Place, and she and her family watched him walk away with long easy strides as if he were not dying at all. Tears came into her mother's eyes, and little Sammy began to cry, and Fanny took him and silently held him within her arms.

What he called his *posthumous* life without her - lasted five months. He would not read any of her letters, for he wanted to die within any tranquility he could muster. On his way to the ship, as usual, he had had to ride the stage top. The *Maria Crowther* sailed on September 19, the year anniversary of when he had written his ode to autumn- really, to one of the happiest days of his life.

He never wrote her one letter, one more note. But he did write to Brown, who lived next door to his dearest girl, and who did return to London on September 18. He begged Brown to be her friend. "The thought of leaving Miss Brawne is beyond anything horrible - the sense of darkness coming over me - I eternally see her figure eternally vanishing. Some of the phrases she was in the habit of using during my last nursing at Wentworth Place still ring in my ears. Is there another life? Shall I awake and find all of this a dream? There must be, we cannot be created for this kind of suffering...I feel as if I am closing my last letter to you.

My dear Brown
Your affectionate friend,
John Keats."

The *Maria Crowther* reached Naples on October 21 and was quarantined for ten days. On October 21, he did not write to her, but he wrote to her mother. "I dare not fix my mind upon Fanny, I have not dared to think of her..." but there was an agonized postscript to her. "Good bye Fanny! God bless you."

They landed on October 31, his twenty-fifth birthday.

He could not bear to write his love to her, but he could tell Brown his feelings. On November 1, he wrote: "The persuasion that I shall see her no more will kill me...My dear Brown, I should have had her when I was in health, and I should have remained well. I can bear to die - I cannot bear to leave her. O, God! God! Everything I have in my trunks that reminds me of her goes through me like a spear. The silk lining she put in my traveling cap scalds my head. My imagination is horribly vivid about her - I see her - I hear her. There is nothing in the world of sufficient interest to divert me from her for a moment ...O, that I could be buried where she lives! I am afraid to write to receive a letter from her - to see her handwriting would break my heart - even to hear of her anyhow, to see her name written, would be more than I can bear. My dear Brown, what am I to do? Where can I look for consolation or ease? If I had a chance of recovery, this passion would kill me...When you write to me...if she is well and happy, put a mark thus + ; if not - ...My dear Brown, be her advocate forever... I am afraid to write to her - I should like her to know that I do not forget her. Oh, Brown, I have coals of fire in my breast. It surprises me that the human heart is capable of containing and bearing so much misery. Was I born for this end? God bless her, and her mother, and my sister, and George and his wife, and you and all!"

The next day he added a postscript, and she was in his last words. "You bring my thoughts too near to Fanny."

Upon November 8, he and his friend, Joseph Severn, who had accompanied him, left Naples for Rome, one hundred and thirty miles and nineteen post stops away. Severn wrote that Keats' listlessness was broken with a fantastic pleasure at seeing and smelling the flowers of the seaside hills. He had found an English doctor, James Clark, who said his whole trouble was not in his lungs but in his stomach. The kindly doctor found the two a lodging in Rome in the *Piazza Di Spagna*.

As his problem was now seen to be in his stomach (the doctors had had it jump originally from being all in his head, then to his lungs, and now fallen into his stomach) he was to ride horseback, take long hikes and leave food alone - as much as possible and still remain alive. On November 30, John Keats wrote his last letter to Brown, telling of the new diagnosis of poor digestion. "Write to George as soon as you receive this, and tell him how I am, as far as you can guess; and also send a note to my sister - who walks about in my imagination like a ghost - she is so like Tom. I can scarcely bid you good bye, even in a letter. I always made an awkward bow.

God bless you!

John Keats."

He was angry with his brother, not so much over money, but because he had called his dearest girl a SMALL MINIATURE of himself.

On Sunday, December 10, he had a severe hemorrhage, and began to run a high fever. For eight nights, he could not sleep, with the feeling of suffocating in his chest; the more blood he lost the more blood the doctor took. Severn had found laudanum in Keats' things and had taken it away. Now Clark would give him none to ease his suffering. He just had to go on without food and blood, apparently. John Keats bitterly told Severn that he would not allow a dog to die in the agony he was passing through. He wanted the death to come, and his suffering to end. By February, he held her letters by him but would not read them. "I want them buried with me, unopened, and her lock of hair next to my heart," he said. He held the carnelian she had given him, and wore her ring. "Her energy is in them," he whispered. "Part of her is still with me."

Severn wrote that a shining brilliance was coming into his eyes. He heard that where he would be buried, in the Protestant cemetery, violets bloomed. "I would have found violets for her to carry when we were married," he said.

February 23 was on a Friday, and at four that afternoon he began the last valiant struggle of his life. By now his lungs were completely eaten away; how he had lived as long as he did, for even the last two months, the doctors later could not tell. "Severn, I am beginning to die. Lift me up - I shall die easy. Don't be frightened. Thank god, it has come."

He coughed up blood to breathe, by instinct to live, and almost on the midnight hour he drifted away. He was buried the next Monday. Only seven people attended his funeral, and they all put tufts of daisies upon his grave. Not one of them had known, or ever would know, the joy he would have had in seeing, and smelling the nearby violets.

Upon his tombstone was written what he had requested.

> Here lies a man whose name
> Was writ in water.

When she heard that her dearest Keats had died, she did what duty demanded, and what she wanted to do first. She wrote to his cherished sister, who had not been allowed to see him by the much-hated Abbey. "I know my Keats is happy, happier a thousand times than he could have been here, for you can never know how much he suffered. So much, that I do not believe were it in my power, I would bring him back. All that grieves me now is that I was not with him, and so near it as I was... and yet it was a great deal through his kindness for me, for he foresaw what would happen... it is now known that his recovery was impossible before he left us, and he might have died here with so many friends to sooth him, and me – ME with him. All we have to console ourselves with is the great joy he felt that all of his misfortunes were at an end. The truth is I cannot very well go on at present with this, another time will tell you more."

He was gone from her life, but she could not reconcile his departure. Bright daffodils began to bloom in stands of bright sunshine, and he would have stopped their walking on their country path, and he would have seen miracles in those daffodils no one else could.

And when warmth came with April, and when his favorite flower, the violet, bloomed, he would have brought them to her, as he always did, to match them he said with the color of her eyes. She thought she could not bear the coming of spring, a glorious, glorious spring, for in the tide of its energy and its magic she was in the agony of grief that would not abate. He did haunt her days and all of her dreaming nights.

She took their walk to Highgate hill, on their Milfield lane. Her mother insisted that Sammy go with her in her walks through the day's gloaming, and he did it willingly, too, because he would never hear the tale of Lancelot finished, or hear that musical laugh, or even see the lights in the eyes of John Keats, who knew everything in the world, and he would never see him look at his sister again, with such naked adoration. "Oh, here. *Here,*" his sister said, and Sammy went with her off the lane, where she walked to an ancient oak, and touched its gnarled bark, and there she wept, and leaned against the tree, as if she wanted to get as close to it as she could.

"Why do you keep touching this old tree?" Sammy asked, not unkindly, or even impatiently.

"Because he touched it, the last time we were here," she said.

"Do you think a part of him is with us?"

"Sammy, *all* of him is *always* here." She pointed to her heart.

Before darkness fell she looked out over the heath, over emerald green fields, and she watched the wind move through them - weaving the patterns of light and shadow he loved so much. "The *tide,*" she said softly.

"We aren't in water," Sammy contradicted kindly.

"There is another tide of energy - *his* tide, Sammy."

"Does it have anything to do with Sir Lancelot?"

"Maybe everything," she said. They walked on, the wind moving the leaves high in the trees. *There is a tide of energy, an invisible tide of wonder, he said. Oh, my dearest love, come to me again on that tide of the magic and the wonder you brought into my life! Never, never bid me an entire farewell!*

As they walked to Wentworth Place, the three city watchmen for their area were lighting their whale oil lamps. Sammy's sister went up to them. "I think you should know the young man I used to walk with -"

"Mr. Keats?" asked one.

"Yes. The poet, Mr. John Keats."

"You are *married!*" said the one with the oil, and he was smiling in companionship and joy.

"No," Sammy heard his sister reply softly, and he saw tears come to her eyes. "John Keats died February 23 in Italy - in Rome, where he had gone for his health."

The three men fell silent, and their faces were stricken as the young woman took her little brother's hand and walked away from them. Then, they saw her stop in her walking toward her house, and she led her brother right back to them. Her eyes seemed to catch the emotion they so often had seen in the eyes of John Keats. "He is dead," she said. "But his poetry is not and never will be."

The three stricken men had never read a poem, and never would read one, even written by their friend, but somehow, they knew that this beautiful tiny little woman was right.

She became ill with grief, and stayed in bed, and had decided to sleep her life away. Then May came, the shining jewel of the English year. She worked in the kitchen every May morning, and as she did, she imagined him in the garden again, sitting under the plum tree, listening to the same nightingale that was singing now, *in full throated ease*. She said his poem, as if it would bring him back - to take again the song of this nightingale and make it into deathless poetry.

*The magic casements were within him, from his mind into the truth and the beauty of his own soul. There lies the light, and the life wrought by light. Within the deepest dark, he told me, an angel saw lovers kiss, and then stars came to the sky, and the Evening Star is as constant as is my love for you.*

"Do you suppose she sees him out there, under the plum tree?" Sammy asked his mother.

"I do not know. But she has to get on with HER life," his mother replied, frowning worriedly.

By December, the month of their engagement, her hair had turned white. She was hardly into her twenty-first year.

Then - when once more the Christmas bells rang out from one snowy village to another, as carriages and their horses wore holiday bells, and the mail horns sounded with the joy of the season, and if the dark fell early the red-breasted robin still sang all of the way through it, BLACKWOOD'S launched another vicious attack upon John Keats.

It cut through her heart. She read it with her whole body shaking in rage, and she sat right down on the stairs, the pages trembling in her hands, so she could hardly read them.

"What is it?" her mother asked, looking up at her face, as white as her hair.

"I will read it to you," she said, and did.

"The present story is thus: A Mr. John Keats, a young man who had left a decent calling for the melancholy trade of Cockney poetry, has lately died of consumption, after having written two or three little books of verses, much neglected by the public. His vanity was probably wrung not less than his purse; for he had it upon the authority of the Cockney Homers and Virgils, that he might become a light to their region at a future time. The New School, however, will have it that he was slaughtered by a criticism of the QUARTERLY REVIEW. O flesh, how thou art falsified! ...We are not now to defend a publication so well able to defend itself. But the fact is, that the Quarterly finding before it a work at once silly and presumptuous, full of servile slang that Cockaigne dictates to its servitors, and vulgar indecorums which that Grub Street Empire rejoiceth to applaud, told the truth of the volume, and recommended a change of manners and masters to the scribbler. Keats wrote on; but he wrote INDECENTLY probably in the indulgence of his social propensities."

"This is because of Shelley's tribute to him in his *Adonais*," Fanny said to her mother." Now here is a vicious and sick parody on THAT." She read, and her voice was tremulous.

> "Weep for my tomcat! All ye Tabbies weep,
> For he is gone at last! Not dead alone,
> In flowery beauty sleepeth he no sleep;
> Like that bewitching youth Endymion!"

Frances Brawne threw the papers down the stairs, and down and down they went, beyond the startled faces of her mother, her sister, little Sammy, "I cannot bear this!" she wept. "He had no business dying and breaking my heart!"

"Fanny, *dearest* child," her mother said, but the winds of separation absorbed her sweet voice, the love of her family, and they took her away from them all, her mother, Sammy, Margaret, and around and around the pendant world she went, lost within viewless winds, for he was gone. He had chosen to go to a grave in Rome, where violets bloomed, and never again would he to pick another one for her.

*You said that God threw jewels of himself out into a night sky, and then created the light so they could shine, and live, and reflect back to him in ever growing light. You said we came here to this earth as light to be individualized and to expand in the light we bear - to return light ten fold to our creator.*

You lied. You lie. You drowned in your own blood and mine is all gone, seeping from this mattress to the floor, and our child is no more than death!

Did you leave so soon for no more reason than swallows suddenly taking to the sky?

"My god," she wept. "Where am I?"

"With me, my dearest girl," a male voice said huskily.

She opened her eyes and looked into the eyes of a complete stranger.

# Twenty-One

Behind the eyes, the handsome face of a man, she could see shafts of sunlight streaming into the room. It was no room she had ever seen before. It was a sterile white, but there were red roses in tall vases. She looked again at the man. "Where am I?" she repeated.

The man was exceedingly handsome. He had thick black hair and dark brown eyes, and the eyes were filled with relief and joy. "Where are you?" he repeated. "Awake, at last," he said, and ever so gently bent to her, and kissed her forehead.

"Is this a dream?" she asked.

"Yes," he said grimly. "It has been a real nightmare."

"Who are you?" She was straining after particles of light as he had done in medical school.

"I am your husband."

"I am not married. Not yet - that is much, much later -"

The handsome man looked stunned. "Well - what else would I expect?" he asked himself.

She studied him and she studied him, and he was still a stranger.

"We are married, very, very marvelously and wondrously married, and we just had a baby son and his birth was breech and it damned near killed you - as you had no help at all -"

"I went to a dance -"

"No. You damned near died. One of their happy helpers - put you into a room and forgot all about it - and our whiz of a doctor is fired and can now devote himself *exclusively* to golf -"

"We are married. I to you - and you to me?"

The lights of joy that had been in this man's eyes vanished. "Do you know who *you* are?"

"I am - I am - lost," she said.

And so she was. She was *educated* into this new life she was in, but she really could not enter into it.

She had technically died. Very technically, her brain had been deprived of oxygen. Doctor after doctor disagreed as to the result.

Is the damage permanent?

Will she harm the baby?

Will she fall in love with her husband again?

And the medical bills mounted.

Her husband - her "husband" seemed a gentle man. He made no demands on her. He left her alone in a beautiful master bedroom of a beautifully restored *charming* Victorian house.

They shared it with one man, who seemed a friend - named Hal. She remembered how to cook and the kitchen was a delight to work in.

Something will have to jolt your memory - to jumpstart it all up again, said a new doctor.

Michael, you *will* have to win her all over again," said another.

Is there something she really dreads? asked another. Dread - a real horror - that might dredge up *what was afraid* of the horror -

And the medical bills mounted.

She nursed the baby and became more and more attached to "their" child she immediately named Mickey.

Her quote husband unquote - was an interesting man, a lawyer and helping the liberal cause against the world's fascist pigs he said. He adored the baby. Hal told her he had made her into a goddess. You cannot imagine the love between you two, said Hal.

She tried to imagine it, and could not.

Then one night the midnight chiming below in the hall awakened her, and a voice spoke in a ghastly haunting way,

*Ring a ding ding, another Keats' thing, but hang on to your bed- for the tabby cat is dead!*

She screamed.

In seconds her husband was in her room. "Mary? What happened?"

"I heard a man talking to me - a grisly poem- like -"

"Oh, Aaron has broken through," he sighed in relief.

"Who is Aaron?"

"You have to remember that on your own."

"Why?"

"Then, I am told, you will remember me."

She did not want him to leave. There was a fire in the bedroom fireplace, and she wanted him to stay and she did not know the connection. "Michael, Could you stay with us awhile?"

The baby was asleep and contentedly so.

Michael sat down by the bed.

"You are a very handsome man. Surely, you must want to find another wife -"

"I already have a wife."

"But what if I don't remember - what if I am brain impaired."

"I know you are not."

"Tell me about - us."

"What do you want to know?"

"How did we meet - fall in love - we did do that, didn't we?"

"Very much so."

"Well?"

"I drove to your uncle's to bring you here to the University - for graduate work. And you had already decided that I was going to save you from your uncle's house you called a castle of death."

"I don't remember his house or him."

"I am sure you will. He made quite an impression upon you."

"Good- or bad?"

"He just made you scream. I would say the impression was generally very, very bad."

"Hmm."

"You gave him supernatural power - as if he is death itself - "

"*What?*"

"Yes. That is why his home at the end of his shitty, shitty road is a castle of death. Both of your parents were killed on that road."

"I remember *them.*"

"Just not me." His voice was bitter.

"Not you," she said sadly. "I am sorry. I feel I was in love with someone else - eternally committed to someone else."

"Someone alive?" he asked cautiously.

"Of course. We exchanged rings -"

They were silent, and the fire in the grate made comfortable crackling sounds. It was cold outside and the windows of even the skylight frosted up against it. "Tell me some more about us. When was the first time I saw you?"

He stirred the fire and put on more wood. "Well, that all depends-"

"What?"

"I would say that the first time was when I kept you from drowning on your uncle's sea stairs - but -" He stopped.

"What?"

"You were sure we had met before. Many, many years before."

"What? When?"

"I think it was in 1818 - maybe 1819 -"

"*What?* Why would anyone think *that?* That is absurd!"

He sighed and looked gloomily into the fire. "I don't know if I should tell you this - or if you are supposed to remember this on your own - my *god!*"

"Tell me what? Did I think I was the man in the moon?"

"You are getting close." He shuddered.

"Tell me. How I thought we met in 1818 or 1819."

"You were sure that you were Frances Brawne and I was John Keats."

She was stunned. "What are you talking about?"

"Reincarnation of lovers forever to be united and all of that."

Anger flashed through her being, her very soul. She felt the anger grow into rage as if John Keats had been maligned and she could not bear it. "I remember that John Keats is my favorite poet - are you *mocking* John Keats?"

"God forbid!"

They were silent, wary - one to one -

"Well, at least you remember John Keats."

"I remember how to cook."

"That, too."

"Did I have a brain injury before?"

"Yes. In the accident that killed your mother."

"Then I was also brain damaged - when we first met -"

"Well - I just had to convince you that I was *not* the reincarnation of John Keats."

"Did you?"

"You said it did not matter any more." His eyes became wet and his hands shook. "You said you loved me for what I am - now - and I was freed of the burden of John Keats. I had told you that if you did not let him die, I could not live."

"Well - in reincarnation - that would certainly be true."

"I don't believe in reincarnation at all."

"In my death experience - I went somewhere else."

"You said to a dance."

"Yes.   I remember the ornate ceiling and the candle lights that shone from it. And they were dancing around energy that gave them life so they were not just shadows against it."

He got up to leave.

"Was I *sexually* attracted to you?" she asked suddenly.

"I would say so."

"What makes you say that?"

"Well, when I dragged you up from the bottom of the ocean you had hardly opened your eyes than you covered my lips with kisses, and I mean *kisses*."

"Well, I was glad you saved my life."

"And that night you appeared in my bedroom - at your uncle's *castle of death* - and you took off your robe and your gown and - and -"

"*What?*"

"And got on me naked and *demanded* sex."

She looked genuinely horrified. "I didn't! I couldn't!"

"You could and you did."

"I do not believe you at all!"

"You had as a prelude for sex - some of his poetry - I know now it was from his poem - *The Eve of St. Agnes*."

She bit at her lip. "Did I get the sex?"

"After we were married."

She looked disappointed. "You must not have been very attracted."

He smiled grimly. "I was attracted - you had better believe it."

The phone rang. Michael answered it and looked at Mary. "It is

*211*

Meg. Do you remember her?"

"No."

"Mary still has not re - entered this life," Michael told Meg.

"Well," said Meg. "Aaron just left it."

Molly got on the line. "Michael - tell Mary that if she wants all of this money she must come here before the body is taken away -"

When he finished talking with Molly, Michael sat back down on the bed. "Your uncle just died. And if you want his vast, vast, *vast* fortune, you must return to his house and look upon him to be sure he is dead before the undertaker takes him away for burial."

"That seems like an easy enough thing to do. Especially if I didn't like him as you say I did not."

"That house - remember - you said was a *castle of death*. It has a hold on you – in fact - you told me the whole damned point around it - is *supernaturally* under his control."

"Well - he is dead, isn't he?"

"You were sure that he could get around that."

"Dead is dead."

"Not if you are Mr. Death himself."

"The symbol of death - you mean the *symbol.*"

"I think you were horrified of more than Aaron as a symbol."

"Then I *was* crazy -"

"I believe you were filled with fancy - your own unique kind -"

"Because of Aaron's power and this Keats' - thing."

"Yes. Only that. But you gave Keats up and fell in love with me instead, and I am not John Keats or never could have been John Keats."

"I know you need money, Michael. I know about the bills and the second mortgage - and the cost of your causes -"

"I am dropping them and will be way ahead of the bills - I can make a very good living at law-"

"That is not what you want to do."

"That is what I *must* do."

"I will go and look at this dead man, and we will be rich. You should be compensated for putting up with a wife - who isn't."

He built up the fire again, sighed unhappily, and left her alone.

The baby was awake and looked after him, a smile on his sweet little face.

# Twenty-Two

Molly and Meg had made themselves a pot of green tea and they were drinking it at the kitchen table, and since they had last talked to Michael there had been no words between them. The teakettle sang on the wood stove, but neither wanted to get up to move it. It was as if they should not move, that if they did, they would conjure up more fear than already possessed them both. "It is so *strange* since he died," said Meg.

The windows of the kitchen blinded over against the January cold outside, but both women felt no warmth in the room. "There is a new unleashed *malignancy* in this house," said Molly, huddling as close to the stove as she could get.

"How? Why?" asked Meg. "I feel the same. I feel Aaron here stronger than when he was alive!"

"Mary should *not* be coming back. He wants her here for an evil purpose! Why didn't we see him as evil before?"

"I can't believe we are afraid of him *now!*" said Meg. "He is dead! When he was alive we thought him a friend - we liked him - and now - there *is* this feeling of evil in the whole house - a menacing all around us. *It is - Aaron.*"

"Why are you speaking so softly?" asked Molly, speaking softly.

"It's as if he's right here - listening." The kettle had stopped its persistent singing, and was in danger of burning up, so Meg got up and took it off the stove. Neither had eaten since breakfast. Neither wanted food, for they were afraid to move about to fix it. They both felt as if they were *intruders.*

"The house is so quiet," whispered Molly. "I feel as if we are buried in it."

"Why are we afraid of Mr. Aronsby now? He did us no evil - if he did torture poor Mary."

"He is here. He should not be here! He should go where the dead go – to heaven or to hell."

"Is he here for Mary?"

"Is he here to trade his death for her life?" Molly put more wood in the stove and shivered all the time she was doing it.

"This awful cold! This damp *electrical* energy-" Meg could almost see Aaron through it as if it were a veil of fog that would soon dissipate. "I don't think I could see that smile again," she whispered.

"He is feeding on our fear," whispered Molly, who had not done much else but whisper all morning. "I believe *all* Mary said about him."

"Didn't she tell us he would never let us leave here - *alive?*"

Something suddenly became startlingly different. Something became even more ominous. "There is no sound from the clock in the hall!" said Molly, and she was not whispering.

They rushed into the hall. The grandfather clock had stopped. Its pendulum that had marked the time in the house for years was no longer doing it.

"I wound it last night," said Meg, winding it again.

The clock remained mute, its pendulum stilled.

Molly tried to wind it, but it was frozen from her touch. "It is as if *he* controls time."

"Time - *here*," said Meg, her face drained of color.

"Mary's *castle of death* - and now she does not remember anything about it. Nor Michael - nor us -" Molly led them back into the kitchen. "The birth has harmed her mind Michael said. She was like dead when they found her. What will she do here? Will she know what we now know about Aaron? If she does not know - how can she outwit him and get us all away from here?"

"You sound as if he is alive! What can the dead do?"

"Plenty," said Molly. "When they do not go on – and they are here for evil!"

Shivering, Meg put on a coat hanging by the kitchen door, and handed another to her mother. "Maybe he will leave with his body. Ghosts usually do this - ghosts - don't they stay with their bodies?"

"I think he is after Mary! I think he will enter her mind, for she is so vulnerable – and he will –"

"Will – what?"

"Kill her, as he did her father, her mother."

"He brings her back here to look upon his *dead* face –"

"So he won't be buried alive - have the blood drained away when he is alive – that was all a ruse."

"He is clearly dead. The dead don't walk – will – act."

"What is this cold – this damp smell of energy?"

"He is dead and upstairs."

"Do you want to go upstairs to see?"

"Will he kill us, too?"

Molly shuddered. "How did Mary say he kills?"

"He creates death though the power of illusion."

"Those red tail lights that led her mother off the road –"

"And fog that blinded her father. I saw that fog. It almost killed Mary when we got to the sea stairs with the tide coming in. If Michael had not been there she would have died."

"His malice would include Michael."

"And their baby," Meg shivered.

"All of us," said Molly. "We are all doomed."

Outside of the frosted-over windows a storm was building from the north. They only were aware of the increasing sound of the wind.

"We can defeat him," said Meg.

"How?"

"By Mary. She was always on to him."

"But Mary has this post partum depression - or something that makes her not Mary -" Molly looked toward the hall in which the clock now made no sound. "Mr. Aaronsby," she said. "We served you well. We loved you as a dear friend. Would you now harm us? Would you so strongly haunt us - with this feel - of such - *evil?*"

The stark silence of the house replied in its own voice, and the sky outside of its windows steadily darkened.

"I know why you are still here!" Molly suddenly exclaimed to the empty air. "You are here to feed off of us - my God! You possess - the weak - the vulnerable - *you are going to take Mary's baby away from her!*"

The newly filled tea- kettle suddenly shrieked and they both jumped. Molly took it from the stove and made them more tea. "I can't wait for them to get here, the body taken away and all of us away right after -"

"John Keats wrote that death lurks behind a baby's smile -"

"What does that mean?"

"I don't know."

"Then why did you say it?"

"I don't know."

Molly went to put more wood into the stove and found she had just filled it.

# Twenty-Three

Michael drove them almost to Aaron's land without a word to her. But before he drove on Aaron's private road, he stopped the car. "This is where you made me solemnly promise I would never let you return to that shitty road and to that damned old house. Do you remember?"

"No."

"Anything involving *me* - you do not remember!"

"Yes," she said, checking on the sleeping baby.

"Don't you think that is a little strange?"

"Yes," she agreed promptly.

"Who replaced me?"

"I don't know," she said unhappily. "You are an intelligent wonderful companion. You are a good and loving father. I enjoy your company very much."

"For tea and crumpets only."

She sighed, and looked at the sea cliff road ahead. Clouds were building in the sky. "I cannot even kiss you unless I have fallen in love with you. That is the way I am. I told you that I would understand if you wanted a divorce."

He looked at her, this handsome agreeable stranger she had made love with, and she wondered what it had been like. Since her return with the baby, they had not even held hands.

He studied her face. "Do you remember your terror of the road ahead of us?"

"Because it killed my parents?"

"No memory of sneaking away with me - lying on me naked the first night we met and saying lines from *The Eve of St. Agnes?*"

"I don't know *The Eve of St. Agnes.*"

"Have you forgotten the poetry of John Keats?"

"Did I know it?"

"So John Keats and I are *both* gone - to wither the wind blows-"

"If I thought I was Frances Brawne, I was indeed crazy. And I am sorry I pushed you into trying for the reincarnation of John Keats."

"It had its moments," he said dryly, remembering the power of those wild kisses right up from the sea bottom.

"How can I be two people?" she asked herself aloud. "Getting on you *naked* - a perfect stranger!"

"Because you *did* see yourself as two people is why you got on me *naked*."

"Frances Brawne - and I."

"Yes. And from every man's dream of beauty you came -" His voice deepened, and he looked at her with such adoration it took her breath away.

"But you resisted. I must not have charmed too much -"

"You were sacred to me - I was horrified that I could even think of kissing you then - and I dreamed every night of making love to you until we were married - when I could and I did."

"Hal says we were deeply and passionately in love."

"I say we were deeply and passionately in love." He gently touched her face, her lips with his hand, and then moved a wisp of a curl from her eyes.

"But here I was - naked - on you - and asking for sex! And what did you do? Did you succumb to the dream of beauty thing? No."

"No," he repeated.

"It does not say much for my power to allure - to *arouse* -"

"Would a man take beauty *beyond* purity - and sully it with even a kiss?"

"Evidently so. In the back seat we have this baby."

He smiled. "That is when a goddess came to *earth* to share it with me."

"And left heaven on its own."

"And all of the stars in the sky." He smiled and touched the wayward curl from her face again.

They then sat in silence, looking down on Aaron's road. "You want to do it? To drive on that road - to what *you* called *a castle of death?*"

"Yes."

He shuddered. "I have a terrible feeling about it."

"I want the money. You say there is a fortune for us, and all I have to do is look upon a dead old face."

"That might be a serious mistake. You have a real horror of him."

"I am said to have *had* a real horror of him - and now he is dead. What can the dead do?"

"Apparently - with you, Mary, a lot." He turned from her and as he started the car and drove onto Aaron's road, he had such a look of sadness and of defeat upon his face, she eerily felt as if they were in another place and another time, long, long ago, and he was putting a worn scarf at his throat to walk away and never see her again.

# Twenty-Four

As his car took them up the drive Michael looked anxiously at Mary. "Do you remember this house?"

"Yes, I do. But look - it has bars on the front windows now."

Michael was surprised to see that as true. "Why would Aaron have had that done?" he asked.

Meg and Molly came rushing out of the house to greet them.

"Mary, this is Molly - and her daughter Meg. "

"I know," smiled Mary, and got out of the car to hug them both. "You remember us, and not Michael?" asked Meg in surprise.

"I guess I just have to work my own way back into her life," said Michael, very unhappily.

Meg and Molly cooed over the baby, and the baby smiled for them. Molly suddenly saw Aaron's smile and she cringed. Had the smile left his face when he died? Yes. It had. She remembered that very clearly.

Inside of the house Mary knew every room downstairs. "Why did Aaron put those bars on the front drive windows and not on any of the sea view windows?" she asked Meg.

"He said no burglar could climb the house wall to get into the sea windows, but one could get in from the front windows. They would fall to their death if they tried the sea windows - obviously."

"Burglars way out here - on this shitty road?" asked Michael.

"He paid a fortune to have those bars done, but *everyone* hates to drive the road here," said Molly. "We both thought it quite irrational, too."

Mary noted the silence of the grandfather clock in the entrance hall. "It stopped this morning," said Molly.

"We have wound and wound it," said Meg, "but I guess his clock

*221*

stopped because he did."

Michael took over the clock resurrection and had no more luck than had Meg.

Molly had started a nice fire in the dining room and Mary and Michael sat with Mickey by the fire while Molly and Meg brought in their early supper.

Mary had begun to nurse the baby. "It is so weird - this silence in the house. That clock ticking was always an integral part here - how I hated it when it chimed the midnight hour!"

"You remember Aaron now?" asked Michael.

"I remember the horror he created when the clock struck midnight."

"The midnight grisly poetry?" asked Meg.

"I just remember the horror of the midnight chimes."

"Midnight - when that ghastly childbirth began," said Michael.

They were eating and the light of the darkening day was going into the early nightfall of January.

"Will you look upon his face tonight?" asked Molly.

"I will do that when the undertakers take him away," said Mary. "Where it will be signed and witnessed. Leave him alone upstairs -"

"But you and Michael will be sleeping down the hall from him, in your old room, Mary."

"Well, I will *not* look at him until he is being carried out of here."

"You must remember Aaron," said Meg. "His supernatural power was as real to you as the fact that you would be rescued from here by -" She stopped.

"By John Keats," said Mary evenly. "I know now that was crazy. My brain injury from the accident - I guess I lived in some kind of a fantasy world then."

Michael checked on the baby and put his jacket back on. "I have never felt this house so cold before - but it is winter."

"It is more than that," said Molly.

"It is much colder since he died," said Meg, putting more wood on the fire.

"What are you saying?" asked Michael. His skin suddenly crawled as if a clammy energy had come into the room.

"He is here now!" whispered Molly.

"Who?" asked Mary.

"The master!" whispered Meg.

"He is dead upstairs," Mary snapped.

"He is not dead, and he is not upstairs - he can travel all over this house now," said Molly, and Meg nodded her head in vigorous agreement.

"Are you two mad?" asked Mary, but she clearly and suddenly did feel an invisible presence in the room.

"I want us all to get out of here as soon as they take the body away," said Molly. "Everything is so *different* now - he is *not* that dead body! He is - in every room in this house - *wherever* he wants to be!"

"That is silly," said Mary.

"He is here to possess a new body!" said Molly suddenly. "He will try that!"

"Molly! You cannot believe in *possession!*" said Mary.

"Well, you used to believe in reincarnation, and what is that but possession?"

"It is different."

"How?" asked Michael.

"It just is," said Mary.

"How?" Michael repeated.

"Reincarnation is voluntary, and in the *myth* of possession, the weak and the vulnerable are cast into death, their bodies stolen - and it is *not* voluntary," said Mary.

"His spirit stays for a reason," insisted Molly. "And I think the baby is the reason!"

"What do you mean?" asked Mary

"If they can possess the weak, the vulnerable - what is more vulnerable than a wee baby?"

Mary went for the baby but Michael beat her to it. "Not that we believe you," said Michael, "but I don't like Mickey too close to the fire."

"Do I see Aaron's best brandy on the side table?" asked Mary. "The brandy he saved for only himself?"

"You remember *that*," said Michael, having memories of the

brandy and the problem his indecent had brought to him. No. It was the entrance of Mary that had brought forth the beast - the beast and the brandy - no - Mary and the beast - the beast was *all* Mary's fault - and right now, feeling a real menace of an uninvited, his longing for Mary – as she was before the baby - was almost unbearable.

"Yes, I remember Aaron's brandy -"

"But not me!" said Michael angrily.

"Well - not Aaron - just the *horror* of him -" She poured them all a generous amount of brandy and gave herself more. It made her warm and tingly, safe and distant from a presence she felt was sitting on the empty chair of Aaron's. "I *almost* see you, you old bastard," she said, raising her glass to the empty chair. Firelight flickered on it, making it seem to move. She glimpsed a man within the fire shadows, and then he was gone, but a baby- like smile lingered after him. "Did he smile a lot?" she asked.

"Like a tic," said Michael.

"You always said he had a baby's smile, and Keats said that is where death is, and you called Aaron death," said Meg.

"All of that?" asked Molly, tipsy herself, but Mary immediately made herself more so.

"Mary, you do not drink," said Michael.

"I am trying to *see* the old bastard," Mary replied, reeling toward the empty chair. "Why do you want me to see your dead face?" she asked it, as if the chair had a face and it could speak.

"Mary, you are about to fall down. Leave some brandy in the decanter."

She did not. She turned from her conversation with the empty chair and back to Michael. "Why did I think you are John Keats?"

"It was his eyes," said Meg promptly.

"Why wouldn't you be John Keats for me?" she asked, feeling sorry for herself with the brandy making her feel lonely, lost, and deserted.

"I couldn't be anything but what I am now."

"You could change time - make it go all away -" she mourned.

"You are teetering -"

Mary turned back to the empty chair, more alive with fire

shadows. "Aaron - go away - be useful - go outside now and *fertilize* something!"

"You are putting on a real horror show," Michael said to her.

"Who are *you* to talk to *me?* You didn't stop time! If you *had* loved me, you would at least do that!" She was choking on tears.

"Mary, you are maudlin drunk."

She went back to the empty chair, and leaned over it to address an unseen occupant. "Here is a poem for *you* –

> Hickory Dickory Dock,
> Aaron has stopped his clock,
> Over brook and knell
> He is running like hell
> Just going there."

She then passed right out, right onto the table and what was left on it, which was the dessert. Michael sighed in deep discontent, picked her up and put her over his shoulder. "I guess it is time for us to retire," he said.

# Twenty-Five

By morning the coming storm still threatened. "As soon as they come for him, we are out of here," Michael said.

"We are all packed," said Molly, and she and Meg loaded their things into Mary's new car. Michael had done the same except for the baby's bed, which he always rode in anyway. Michael looked anxiously out of the kitchen windows. "Those dark clouds just seem to sit there. I hope they sit until we are out of here. In the best of conditions the road out of here is Russian Roulette."

Molly and Meg had the kitchen all cleaned, the food they could not leave being packed in a box.

The front bell was ringing, and Michael went to let in the morticians. They looked like morticians. They wore black, and were corpse skinny, and he helped them carry Aaron in his casket down the stairs and to the double front doors. "My wife will be right down," Michael said. "You know she has to look at his face."

Molly joined them and looked silently at the closed casket. "I feel he is watching *us*," she said.

Michael did, too, but this was a nut house he had known from his first step into it. "Was he smiling?" he asked one of the morticians.

"Oh, no, of course *not*. You do not smile at death!"

"Where is your wife to look upon the face?" asked the other one. "There is a storm coming, and we want to clear his road before it hits."

"Here she is now," said Michael, and he saw Mary coming slowly down the stairs. She paused at the silent clock, and went up to the casket. "Open it," she said to the morticians.

"Don't look at him!" said Molly. "It will cast you *into his power!*"

The morticians paused, and looked from Molly to Michael. The whole thing was insane. Having to sign an affidavit that she looked upon the face of a dead man to see if he was dead! A man dead was a man dead. And that *damnable* road! Well this craziness was worth twenty thousand dollars - in advance.

"Don't open the casket!" said Molly.

"Open it," said Mary again.

And they did.

And Aaron was smiling.

And the horror of that smile, *of Aaron realized, seen again,* made Mary faint. She fainted into the arms of Michael, and he gently placed her limp body on the hall sofa. "You said he was not smiling," he said to the morticians.

"There was *no* smile on the face when we put it into the casket," said one mortician, and the other agreed.

"It is too late for that to come naturally -" said one, shaking his head in disbelief. *What is natural here, anyway?*

Michael snapped the casket closed. "Now sign these forms," he said, "and get the smiling bastard out of here!"

"It has to be rigor mortis," said one of the morticians as Michael helped them carry the casket to the hearse.

"That would have set in long ago," said the other.

"Goodbye," said Michael shortly. He waited on the front porch to watch the hearse drive out of sight. A strong wind was bitterly cold. The coming storm would surely bring iced rain. *We will leave right now* he thought.

He went back into the house to get the three women and his baby out of it. In the entrance, right where the casket had been, they faced him with terror about equally distributed upon their faces. Mary was holding the baby. "Mickey has a raging fever!" she said, her eyes filled with panic. "You have to go for the doctor. He needs some antibiotic right away! We can't take him out there in the cold wind - we couldn't get the car warm enough for him! Michael - please - go for the doctor! He has no phone. He is retired and has no phone. He lives at the end of the point - you can bring him back in no time! We can't let our baby die!"

"I can get your car warm - let's all take him to the doctor - right now!"

"No! I will *not* take him out into that cold-"

Michael took Mickey's temperature. His fever is so high it is a wonder he is alive, thought Michael. He rushed for his coat, and before he left for the car, he turned and looked at the panicked women, his child, and the stilled clock. Somehow, they seemed all connected. "Don't leave Mary and the baby alone," he said. "NOT FOR ONE MINUTE!"

"As if you have to tell us that!" said Molly, and Michael rushed out of the double doors, and drove out of the drive as fast as he could.

In the hall, the women looked at the motionless clock. It was silent but it screamed with life. "Where *can* we go to be safe?" whispered Molly.

"I will not take the baby back to my room," said Mary. "*His* room is right down the hall -"

"Not near where he died-" said Meg, her face gone as white as Molly's.

"Where?" asked Molly. "The kitchen is too small for us and the baby's bed -" And from the kitchen she could too clearly hear the rushing in of the tide as it came in to cover the sea stairs to the top rung.

"In my favorite room in the house - the library," said Mary. "Build a fire in its grate - and we can all wait for Michael and the doctor there."

The fire was started; the baby's bed was placed near it, and the three women huddled near the fireplace. The room gradually became warm and cozy. Mary saw the fire casting light on the books. *Books make me feel safe. Dearest - there are your poems and the story of your life - that brief, brief life of so much pain -*

"I remember Michael!" Mary said. "Gentle lover, tender and joyful companion - I *remember*," and she began to cry. "Aaron will kill him on that damnable road! Aaron will take him away from me again!"

Meg took her hands. "Aaron is here with us. He never left this house with that corpse. That was the reason for his last smile."

"That is right," said Molly. She shuddered and looked out at the blackening sky.

The baby began to cry, and Mary took him within her arms. "He has no fever," she said flatly.

Meg and Molly both found this to be true.

"Aaron's power of illusion," said Mary. "He will kill Michael on his road as he did my parents. He will take everything from me - everything!" She rocked the baby and began to nurse him, but she did not stop her weeping.

"He is not on that road to kill Michael," said Molly firmly. "He is *here* - to destroy *you*, Mary."

"You know him. You know his power of illusion and you lived through it, Mary. You did not die with your mother!" said Meg. "You have to be stronger than Aaron!"

"Aaron is death!"

"Then you must be stronger than death!"

Mary held her baby to her heart and rocked him to sleep. "How can I do that?" she asked herself and them, over and over. "How can I do that?"

"Didn't you bring John Keats back to you? Haven't you two already defeated death?" asked Meg.

"*Meg!*" said Molly, never buying into the Keats' story at all.

"Michael is John Keats. You are Frances Brawne. He will save you and your child!"

"Meg, stop this nonsense now!" said Molly.

"I don't know who I am, or who I was, Meg. That was all fancy - a way to save myself from the horror of Aaron -"

"Aaron is not death," said Molly. "No one can be death!"

"He was a symbol," corrected Mary.

"He is more than that now," muttered Molly. "That sky is so *black*."

It enfolded the house and it was as if the day had never dawned or that night had fallen before its time. Lightning came in great streaks across the sky with thunderclaps following, so close, the house shook with them.

"Michael - Michael -" said Mary, putting the baby into his bed near the fire. She paced in front of the dark windows. "I never said goodbye - I never said I love you, I love you, I love you!"

Iced rain began to drum against the glass. *When could I ever say*

229

*goodbye?*

"Mary, it will be all right," said Molly. "Michael will be safe on that road, for he loves you and his child so -"

"Believe in your fancy, Mary!" said Meg, putting more wood on the fire. "See this as a castle his poetry saved you from! Believe as you always did in the power of fancy, right through the casements of the soul into its light - you said - where there are no dark corners of the mind to declare fancy a false prophet assigned only to dreams!"

"We will be safe here," said Molly. "We will be warm and safe among the books you love so much -"

"*His* poetry," added Meg.

"Aaron used our worst fears to create the illusion of Mickey sick - my fear - Michael's fear - your fear for our child - he feeds on our worst fears - and he makes them seem *real.*"

"Mary, we will not let him fool us again," said Molly.

"We will stay together, and not leave this room," said Meg.

It was only the clock that remained silent. The wind shrieked, sent iced rain to drum against the windows, and the thunderclaps hurt their ears.

"I did not give him a last kiss," Mary said. "I wanted that last kiss, so!"

"He will be back with the doctor. I know it," said Molly.

They all looked to the driveway windows to see the lights of Michael's car. If one did not walk to the windows, another did. But the drive remained empty except for swirls of wind driven rain.

"I must fix us something to eat," said Molly.

"The food is in the car," said Meg.

"I can find something left here," said Molly. "I can put rice or beans to cooking - there is plenty of wood in the kitchen for the stove."

Mary was nursing the baby again.

Meg put more wood on the fire and watched Mary and the baby as if she were guarding them with her life.

Time passed as stealthily as ever. Meg looked at the growing dark corners of the room. "We have defeated you, Aaron," she said. "Do what Mary told you to do - go away - there is nothing for you here - for love is stronger than you are!"

"Meg, did you get that from me?" asked Mary.

"Yes," replied Meg.

"What did I say I meant by that?"

"Death is illusion and only absorbs itself."

Mary's heart was a stone in her breast. *Beloved, do not go into the tide of light before me again – so, so long before me again!*

"Molly should be here," said Meg. "I'll go see what she is doing."

Mary put the baby back into his bed and went to the front drive windows to see if Michael's car was in it. It was not. Something made her go to the sea windows and look down on the beach below.

She froze in horror. She could see Molly was down there, on the beach! And Molly had never once gone down the sea stairs! She had a horror of the incoming tide and even hated to watch it rushing up toward the house. She was calling Meg, as if Meg was down on the beach somewhere when she was not there at all!

"What are you doing down there?" Meg was screaming down at her. Molly did not even look up at her, and Meg rushed down the stairs as fast as she could move.

Mary ran to the kitchen, opened the door and screamed down at both of them. "Come up here! The tide is coming in!"

"Molly - Molly!" Meg was screaming. "Get up the stairs - get up the stairs!"

Molly did not hear. Meg reached her and led her back to the stairs. Mary started down after them when the tide swept in, and when it swept out again, she was on the stairs alone. She looked blankly at the roiling sea. They were both gone within it. It was as if they had never been. Mary reached the top stair and beyond it just in time, or she, too, would be gone. She stood convulsing in the freezing rain, not believing what she was seeing. Molly and Meg were gone. Some power of illusion had taken Molly to the beach - the place she dreaded since her first days here, and Meg had gone to save her - and she to save them both - and now - she was alone - *Mickey!*

Mary rushed into the kitchen and into the library. The baby was peacefully asleep, her precious baby, their precious baby they had wanted so much. She dried her hair by the fire, would not go upstairs for a dry robe, one of her mother's still in the closet - she would not leave Mickey. *You will not entice me away from my child, you sick grinning bastard!*

She sat close enough to the fire to dry her clothes - mostly, at least. She sat on the rocker so near to the stone hearth, and she rocked back and forth and she wept for Meg and Molly, for her parents, and for Michael she had sent to his death because of the power Aaron held over them all.

The dark corners of the room were growing and the firelight made their darkness even starker.

Night was falling and it would be long. She needed light. She took every lamp downstairs and lit it, making a halo around her and her baby. Meg had brought in enough wood for the fire to burn all night. They would stay warm if she kept the hall doors closed, which they had done from the beginning.

*I know you, you grinning son of a bitch! You will not harm me or my child - you tried to kill me twice and failed, didn't you?*

By her baby she rocked, ever vigilant. The fire was bright and the classics books of Aaron's library gleamed in its light. A full-blown gale pressed against the house. Its old timbers creaked under its onslaught, and she remembered how she always felt as if Aaron's house was secretly straining to the cliff to fall into the sea below.

*You will not control my mind, will you? Your smile is gone now, a grimace at its own decay to come?*

There was no doubt of her own terror. Meg and Molly were being swept away again and again and again, and again she saw her mother's eyes when life had left them, and she pictured Michael out in the gale, gone into that same tide of death, and she wept and could not stop.

It was just before midnight. *It was always before midnight - for that is when you died and took the Evening Star with you-*

*A thing of beauty is a joy forever.*

The baby stirred, went right back to sleep.

> *Old ocean rolls a lengthened wave to the shore*
> *Down whose green back the short-lived foam, all hoar,*
> *Bursts gradual with a wayward indolence.*

She felt comforted. She stopped weeping. The wind was shaking the house, shrilling high in all of its gables. The fire leaped crazily in a sudden wind draft, and settled back down to a cheery comfort. The lamps burned steadily on. They would last the night, all filled and trimmed. *You cannot touch me, or my baby, so get out of here and go off to the viewless winds yourself! Be a part of what the mad hear howling -*

She felt a reply. She did not *hear* a reply, but she *felt* it. *I am here,* said Aaron. *I am here and near -*

And then she *heard* the reply.

The clock was ticking!

The grandfather clock in the hall, right outside of the closed doors, was ticking the time to its midnight chiming.

Boldly, she went into the hall. The great clock there *was* ticking, its large pendulum moving back and forth in its own tick tock deliberation. Its hands *were* approaching the midnight hour.

Rage made her shake. Rage to *kill* consumed her. "You bastard," she snarled. "Whatever power you have, *I have more!*"

A new gust of wind pushed violently against the house. She went back into the library and tightly closed the sliding doors.

*Let the wind howl and send iced pellets against the windows - let the darkness be and the fire crazily dance in the grate - this is my kingdom now and here I am safe within a halo of light and within the soul light of these books - protected by my beloved's poetry - he lives within it - our child lives now, and you- you son of a bitch, cannot do a thing about it !*

She picked up the fire poker. *Show me your smiling face again - one more time, and I will smash it into a bloody pulp!*

The library doors were wide open. She had closed them and they were wide open, and the hall behind them was without any trace of light.

She was not afraid. She was all -powerful, for now, she would do what she always had wanted to do. Smash and smash away that smile, smash and smash away that hateful baby smile. "All right, Aaron," she panted. "Now - just you and me!"

"And baby makes three," he replied.

# Twenty-Six

Michael pounded so furiously on the doctor's door, the old man opened it with terror in his eyes. "Who in the hell are you?" he asked him.

"I am from Aaron's house," Michael replied, shivering in the rain and the wind.

"Well, I am no longer in practice," said the doctor.

"I am not here to argue that!" Michael shouted in hysteria. "My baby is at Aaron's house with a temperature of one hundred and SIX!"

"Then he is dead by now," said the doctor, getting out of the cold for the warmth of his house, with Michael right behind him. "Get your bag and your needles and drugs and go there with me right now!" yelled Michael.

"I told you, I am retired," said the doctor. "I don't want to ever see another patient, and I would never drive on that death road to Aaron's!"

"Well, I am driving and you are going to save my baby's life."

"I wouldn't even RIDE on that death road to Aaron's."

Michael picked up the doctor for better eye contact. "You are and NOW, OR I will make your family fatherless and your wife a widow."

"I have no family, and never had one," said the doctor struggling to breathe.

"Then you have a choice here," said Michael furiously, setting the doctor back down on his floor. "You will be paid one million dollars for going to my baby and curing him, or you can stay here, without your head, which I will have pulled off."

"*One million dollars?*" the doctor kept repeating as Michael drove him away from his house and on to the road to Aaron's. "Your wife has inherited *everything?*" he asked happily.

"Everything," Michael replied, hugging the land part of the cliff.

"You are driving too fast."

"I will get us there. Have no doubt about it in the world."

The doctor could not help but look over the edge of the road into the ocean below, and the road seemed to be crumbling toward it right under the car wheels.

"I will get us there," Michael repeated.

But there was an impediment. The wind had blown most of an oak tree by the road onto the road. "We can never get around this," said the doctor.

"Of course not," said Michael. "We will have to move it out of the way."

"How can two men move that tree out of the way?"

"There will be a way. I am thinking."

"Of twenty men?"

"I know how. We will let the car do it."

"It will still take all day and all night."

"Maybe most of the day, but we'll get to my baby," said Michael grimly, and got outside of the car. "Well?" he said to the doctor, still sitting in the car with his doctor bag.

"Well -" The doctor thought. "A *million dollars,*" he said cheerfully and got out of the car.

Mary sat down near the baby, and held the poker tighter. Mickey still slept, and she centered herself within the poetry of John Keats, just as she used to do to combat her terror of Aaron in all of the years she had been his prisoner here. But nothing about the beauty of *magic casements opening on the foam of perilous seas in faery lands forlorn* came. The truth of beauty did not come. Nor came the tranquil lines to autumn - of mists and mellow fruitfulness, a maturing sun - apples bending the moss'd cottage trees with fruit ripened to the core -

Lines came that she had always hated.

> When I have fears that I may cease to be
> Before my pen has glean'd my teeming brain..

When I behold upon the night's starr'd face,
Huge cloudy symbols of high romance,
And think I may never live to trace
Their shadows with the magic hand of chance...

And it got worse.

Who hath not loiter'd in a green church-yard,
And let his spirit, like a demon-mole,
Work through the clayey soil and gravel hard,
To see skull, coffin'd bones and funeral stole;
Pitying each form that hungry death hath marr'd
And filling it once more with human soul?

She cringed near her baby, clinging more tightly to the poker

This living hand, now warm and capable
Of earnest grasping, would, if it were cold
And in the icy silence of the tomb,
So haunt they days and chill thy dreaming nights
That thou wouldst wish thine own heart
            Dry of blood
So in my veins red life might stream again,
And thou be conscience calmed - See, here it is.
            *I hold it toward you.*

Were the library doors left open, or had he opened them again?
Had she closed them, or had she not?
See, here is my hand in death - I hold it toward you. I will take your blood - so in my veins red life might stream again, and thou, for being alive, be conscience calmed -
"Why did you write those lines to me?" she wailed. "Why?"
Only the wind replied, and the ticking of the clock.
She talked through all of the lost years, to *him.* Did I not grieve enough? Was my life not lonely enough? I had no lover to make love to me, to kiss me again - not even in goodbye - it was *you* who left *me!*

Suddenly, all the lamps in the room went out. It was as if she had never lit one.

The only thing she had left to see by was the light of the fire, and the only thing she had to smash Aaron into *nothingness* with was the fire poker.

"You will not kill our child," she panted. "Our baby lives and will prosper and grow into a man and even an old man, and you will not stop this!"

Aaron was with her. So clearly, so clearly, he was. She felt the coldness of him, the malignant power of him, the electrical energy of him, his *evil* of illusion. "Aaron, show yourself - if you dare!" She held the poker before her. "Show yourself!" she repeated.

Across the room I will race,

*To show again my smiling face!*

He had spoken to her right from the baby's bed!

With a cry of anguish she went to Mickey, but he was gone. She was about to pick him up, but Mickey was gone. The baby smiled up at her. It was not Mickey. This baby bore the face and the smile of Aaron.

She cringed before the horror of it. Her heart was in her throat for their precious baby was lost, hurled out into the viewless winds and into what the mad imagined howling.

She heard herself moaning, and she felt flung down into the ocean, swept away in it with Meg and Molly. In the body of Mickey, Aaron still smiled up at her. She came to her senses. She stopped moaning. She stopped grieving, for now she could have revenge against death itself. "So, Aaron, you have become a helpless little baby, have you?" she asked.

The baby smiled and cooed.

"Aaron, that was very, very dumb." She picked Aaron up and sat down on the rocking chair, but she certainly was not going to nurse *death.*

"That was very, very dumb," she repeated, and the baby foolishly snuggled against her warmth. "How will I kill you, Aaron? Shall I bash in your head with the poker here - or throw you against the rocks of the hearth?"

Aaron lost his smile and anxiously began to squirm.

"Hush. Hush. Hush, little baby. I will rock you to sleep first, so I don't have to look into your eyes before I kill you. For kill you I *will*."

Aaron began to squirm violently, its little eyes *knowing*.

"I told you taking a body of a baby was *dumb*," she said, and in her clear and lovely voice she rocked and sang,

> Rock a bye, baby
> On the tree top.
> When the wind blows,
> The cradle will rock.
> And when the bough breaks,
> The cradle will fall,
> And down will fall baby, cradle and all.

# Twenty-Seven

It was just after midnight when Michael and the doctor reached the front door of Aaron's house. The storm had passed, but a thick fog was rising from the ocean, and they could barely see through it. Michael rang and rang the doorbell, but no one came to open the doors to let him in.

"I am going into the barn for an ax," said Michael. He ran there and found no ax, not a thing that would allow the breaking of those thick solid oak doors. "I can't imagine where they are," he said. "Even this old fashioned door bell wakes up the whole house!" Then he noticed a faint light showing from the library windows. He rushed to look through their bars, and inside of the room he could clearly see Mary rocking the baby. All of the lamps in the room had been allowed to burn themselves out, and the fire in the grate was sinking into its last embers. The window bars kept him from pounding on the glass, but he yelled her name outside of it as loudly as he could. She should have heard, but she gave no sign of doing so.

"Is she deaf?" asked Woelner, the doctor.

"Of course not!" said Michael. He should have felt better, for the baby had to be alive for her to be rocking him like that, and Meg and Molly might have left her alone, although they promised they would not.

"The baby must be all right," said Woelner. "She wouldn't be rocking him if he had died."

Michael did not feel assuaged by what he had seen. In fact, such a terror came over him, it all but stopped his breathing. "It is *not* all right," he said. "I have to get into there!"

"Not through these windows," said the doctor.

"They're no bars on the sea windows," said Michael, and ran to them.

The doctor followed, and through the fog he could see enough of them to shake his head again. "Not through these windows, either," he said. "You would fall a hundred feet below. Michael, you have to wait for her to see you or hear you and let you into the house."

Michael looked at the doctor, and even in the fog, Woelner could see the panic on the young man's face. A lamp was burning in a window above them. "I have to get into that kitchen window; something ghastly is about to happen, and I have to stop it!"

The doctor looked at the window with the dimly showing lamp and shook his head again. "How can you climb the back side of this house into there? Ring the bell again! The cook and her daughter -"

"There is no time!" the young man all but wept. He walked over to the house wall he was going to climb. "See, there are bricks. The whole thing is covered with bricks, and I can move from one to another - they do stick out enough for a grip -"

"The hell they do. And this fog is blinding -"

"I have no choice. I have to get into that house!"

"You will kill yourself and not save your wife and child who are safe and warm inside. Wait until she does hear you!"

"She won't!" said Michael. God, he knew, she would not hear him. He knew something had gone terribly, terribly wrong with her mind - the whole damned house - Aaron's *mad* house.

"Don't try to climb that wall!" the doctor pleaded. "One slip and *you* are dead!"

"I'll do it because I have to," said Michel grimly. He began the tortuous climb. The fog pressed against him, as if hands were gently pressing a blinding veil over his eyes. *Let the bricks hold! God, give me the strength! Let me find my way to the light - help me see it!*

Inch by inch he moved, more blinded by deepening fog. *I am living an old nightmare - climbing toward light in a window - and if I do not reach it - we are all dead -* How had that nightmare ended? He recalled no ending, and he strained body and soul toward the dimming light.

Immediately, Michael disappeared from the doctor's sight. He had never seen such thick fog on the point before, and he had lived on it many years. The fog was moving with an energy of its own, as if it had a life of its own. *The poor devil*, he thought, shivering in the iced cold. He probably did not need me at all. The baby will live or die, as if I had not come. "Michael?" he yelled. There was no reply. Below him the ocean was thundering against the cliff, but the fog kept it invisible.

*I will do this, I will do this, I will do this,* Michael commanded himself. *I will find the casement into that light.* But he didn't. He couldn't. He was weaker and weaker, his hands aching to stop their tenuous hold upon a wall that simply meant life. He inched and he crawled on and on. He could not see what progress he was making, if any at all. Blindness engulfed him as it hid the ocean he could hear so far below. He became more and more light headed, and he felt as one whose life blood was drowning him within the last breath of his life.

*Then it is goodbye, my beautiful girl. With lips and their kisses unmet, with no warmth of my body for yours, and no more violets to pick to match the color of your eyes.*

Tears were ice upon his face.

He had to tell her one more thing. From the depths of his soul, he had to tell her one more thing.

Thou art my Heaven, and I thine eremite.

The night changed. The fog gently withdrew as if by magic, or as if it was made of magic all the time. The dark became clear light as a full moon bathed both land and sea in a soft and silvered radiance. He felt the benevolence of pure enchantment, its center, in a heaven of perfect love and all of its expressions. He saw the lamp, the light within the casements to light, and he thought - *those words are not new to me. I have been through these casements before.*

He smashed the glass with his hands and entered the house.

On the shredded glass he had cut both wrists. He found the towels to stop the bleeding of his arterial blood, and he rushed to open the front doors for the doctor, and then he ran into the library.

The night, so changed now with new light, was no longer centered in a heaven of love and all of its expressions. He lost all of that, if he had ever been there in the first place. What was left was Mary.

She was rocking by the fire's embers, but she held no baby. She looked at Michael as if she were hardly with him, or hardly in the room. "The baby does not need a doctor any more," she said.

The doctor quickly began to stitch Michael's mangled wrists. As the doctor worked, Michael looked, but could see no sign of the baby. "Where is Mickey?" he asked.

She looked up at him and her eyes filled with tears. "Mickey is dead," she said. "Aaron killed him, just as he killed Meg and Molly."

Michael recoiled, and was speechless.

"And he will kill all of us, too," she went on, her grief stricken eyes becoming wild with emotion. *"If we don't kill him first!"*

"I thought you said, Michael, that her uncle was dead," said the doctor, looking at Mary.

"That is my recollection," said Michael, and he rushed to the baby's bed placed on the other side of the library. Mickey was wide-awake and cooing up at him. "Mary," said Michael, "the baby is fine."

The doctor touched the baby's face. "His fever is gone," he said. "His temperature is normal."

Mary had not even been presented to the doctor, but she looked at him suspiciously. "But *he* isn't," she said.

"Mary," said Michael. "What are you talking about?"

"That is not our baby," she replied.

*"What?"* asked Michael.

"Because he is Aaron." She said it so calmly, she might as well have been telling them the time. "It is a matter of *possession.* Aaron uses his power to possess the - the weak. The vulnerable. The sick."

Michael put his two bandaged hands to his head. "My God - Mary - how can you say such a thing? Our baby - *Aaron?"*

"I was going to kill him when he fell asleep, but he just stayed awake," she said. "That is how clever Aaron is. But he cannot stay awake *all* of the time, can he?"

The doctor saw tears rush into Michael's eyes. The poor devil, he thought. His wife is as mad as a hatter.

"I'm getting my family out of here," said Michael.

"He won't let us go. He caused Meg and Molly to *drown themselves.* He has cast Mickey out into the winds that go around and around to nowhere!" She sobbed, and both her husband and the doctor looked at her in disbelief.

"We're leaving *now*," Michael said.

"He'll never let us leave alive. We will never get off this point," said Mary, her voice flat with despair. "He *won't* go to sleep so I can kill him!"

Michael picked up the baby, and more tears flooded his eyes as they walked toward the car. "Mary -" he said and stopped.

"Do not get that monster near me!" she said.

"Doctor," said Michael. "You will have to drive. I cannot, and my wife - can't either," he said lamely. "We'll get into the back seat."

The doctor prepared to drive, and Michael sat in the back seat, separating his wife from his son "I am still going to get my million dollars?" asked the doctor, driving toward the sea road.

"Yes," said Michael. "I told him he could have one million of your zillions for coming on this damned road to save Mickey," Michael said to Mary.

She indifferently shrugged.

Michael kept seeing the doctor looking at them in the rear view mirror. It made him uncomfortable, and the doctor's face was not the same. It seemed to be slowly changing, and Michael did not know how.

They reached the cliff road. "I think you should not look at me in the mirror," said Michael. "I think you should look at nothing but the road ahead."

"I don't want to drive off the damned thing any more than you do," said the doctor.

"Mary," said Michael. "Look at the baby. How could you think our beautiful child to be *Aaron?*"

"I won't look at the monster, and I won't nurse him -"

"Just one look - look at him again!"

Mary looked, and the baby was her own!

"*Mickey!*" she breathed happily. "Aaron is gone!" She took the baby within her arms and covered his face with kisses. "Aaron is gone! Thank God - the monster is gone from me at last!"

"Doctor -" began Michael. "Are you feeling all right?"

"I don't know," the doctor said in surprise. "Something - is different -"

"It is your *face!*" gasped Michael, and in the mirror he saw the

243

smiling face of Aaron. In seconds he had his wife and child out of the car and leaped out after them.

The car was going slowly on, and in it the doctor was slumped over the wheel, dead.

"Michael -"

"He is dead. He is already dead."

The car continued to roll off the road, and it plunged off the ocean cliff, down and down to be lost in a brief spraying of foam and then into the entirety of the ocean itself.

Michael looked after it, all trace gone.

"How did you know to save us?" asked Mary.

"I saw him as Aaron. His face changed to *Aaron's*."

"Possession," she said. "He left Mickey to kill us all through the doctor. Death – he was always death to me. Death takes the weak, the vulnerable – Molly said it- but you saved us from Aaron –"

"I would not be discussing this with the general population."

"Never."

"I had other strange things manifest - our soul never sleeps -"

"You do not believe in them."

"Our soul is never silent," he finished. "Our soul never sleeps, and our soul is never silent," he repeated solemnly.

"Michael you always said dead is dead, that there is no soul to live beyond our mind."

"You remember what I said?" he asked joyously. "You remember - *me?*"

"I do," she said with a catch in her voice. "I remember now what I knew all the time. And I want that last kiss."

"I thought I could not have one until you knew you were in love with me."

"I am *still* in love with you."

"Then I will take the kiss, my dearest girl, and it will not be the last one."

They kissed. And then they kissed again. And again.

They walked toward the freeway, and for both, they were walking in Paradise.

He carried their baby and he held her hand, and he had been transformed. The soul never sleeps, he thought again. The soul is never silent. He saw stone angels with wings folded over their breasts, and they became alive and their wings were golden with summer, summer sun, summer golden wine, and the golden poppies that opened their hearts to the sun, and to the soft drowsing of the bees.

This was 20 January, the Eve of St. Agnes. It was death that counted his beads and died in the ashes cold. The lovers had escaped. "Mary, if you were - could *possibly* have been - Frances Brawne, what would you have wished for?"

"To live another life with him," she said promptly. "Michael, if you were - or could *possibly* have been - John Keats, what would *you* have wished for?"

"To keep us together in a poem that will not die," he said as promptly.

They were at the end of Aaron's road. They paused and looked back on all of Aaron's land. Wisps of fog still clung to it, and in some places it would be blinding to a person still there.

"Death consumes death, Aaron," she whispered, and then they were gone from the sight of all of Aaron's land. Above them the full moon of that night was setting, but the evening star continued to shine in the sky. Holding hands they watched it as a kind of sacred benediction beyond time, and they watched it until all of its light was absorbed into the light of a new day.


THE END

# ODE TO A NIGHTINGALE

My heart aches, and a drowsy numbness pains
My sense, as though of hemlock I had drunk,
Or emptied some dull opiate to the drains
One minute past, and Lethe-wards had sunk;
'Tis not through envy of thy happy Lot,
That thou, light wing'd Dryad of the trees,
In some melodious plot
Of beechen green, and shadows numberless,
Singest of summer in full-throated ease.

O, for a draught of vintage! that hath been
cool'd a long age in the deep-delved earth,
Tasting of Flora and the country green,
Dance, Provencal song, and sunburnt mirth!
O, for a beaker of the warm South,
Full of the true, the blushful Hippocrene,
With beaded bubbles winking at the brim,
And purple-stained mouth;
That I might drink, and leave the world unseen,
And with thee fade away into the forest dim:

Fade far away, dissolve, and quite forget
What thou amongst the leaves hast never known,
The weariness, the fever, and the fret
Here, where men sit and hear each other groan;
Where palsy shakes a few, sad, last gray hairs,
Where youth grows pale, and spectre-thin, and dies,
Where but to think is to be full of sorrow
And leaden-eyed despairs,
Where beauty cannot keep her lustrous eyes,
Or new Love pine at them beyond tomorrow.

Away! Away! for I will fly to thee,
Not charioted by Bacchus and his pards,
But on the viewless wings of Poesy,
Though the dull brain perplexes and retards:
Already with thee! tender is the night,
And haply the Queen-Moon is on her throne,
Cluster'd round by all her starry Fays:
But here there is no light Save what from heaven is
        with the breezes blown
Through verduous glooms and winding mossy ways.

I cannot see what flowers are at my feet,
Nor what soft incense hangs upon the boughs,
But in embalmed darkness, guess each sweet
Wherewith the seasonable month endows
The grass, the thicket, and the fruit-tree wild:
White hawthorn, and the pastoral eglantine;
Fast fading violets cover'd up in leaves;
And mid-May's eldest child,
The coming musk-rose, full of dewy wine,
The murmurous haunt of flies on summer eves.

Darkling I listen; and for many a time
I have been in love with easeful Death,
Call'd him soft names in many a mused rhyme,
To take into the air my quiet breath;
Now more than ever it seems rich to die,
To cease upon this midnight with no pain,
While thou art pouring forth thy soul abroad
        In such an ecstasy!
Still wouldst thou sing, and I have ears in vain
To thy high requiem become a sod.

Thou wast not born for death Immortal bird!
No hungry generations tread thee down:
The voice I hear this passing night was heard
In ancient days by emperor and clown:
Perhaps the self-same song that found a path
Through the sad heart of Ruth, when sick for home,
She stood in tears amid the alien corn;
The same that oft-times hath
Charmed magic casements, opening on the foam
Of perilous seas, in faery lands forlorn.

Forlorn! the very word is like a bell
To toll me back from thee to my soul self!
Adieu! the fancy cannot cheat so well
As she is famed to do, deceiving elf.
Adieu! Adieu! thy plaintive anthem fades
Past the near meadows, over the still stream,
Up the hill-side; and now 'tis buried deep
In the next valley glades:
Was it a vision, or a waking dream?
Fled is that music:—Do I wake or sleep?

# Biography of Gayle Rogers

Gayle Rogers was born on May 17, 1923 in Watsonville, California. U.C.L.A. graduate, with graduate work completed at U.C.L.A., Northridge University and California Lutheran University. Schoolteacher for twenty eight years. Author of The Second Kiss, Nakoa's Woman, Gladyce with a C, and Dark Corners. A death experience at age seven left author psychic and open to the power of the soul, its core of divinity, its eternal seeking of growth and the power of human love to inspire that growth. The window opened into the soul through the death experience expanded further and expands with each book written and is considered by the author to be the jewel of her life.

## Other Books by Gayle Rogers:

The Second Kiss
Nakoa's Woman
Gladyce With a C